I0691999

SAGA OF A NEUROSURGEON SERIES, BOOK TWO

Anything Goes

Garven Wilsonhulme takes on all comers
in the jungle of modern competition

CARL DOUGLASS

Neurosurgeon Turned Author Writes with Gripping Realism

PO Box 221974 Anchorage, Alaska 99522-1974
books@publicationconsultants.com—www.publicationconsultants.com

ISBN 978-1-59433-358-2
eBook ISBN 978-1-59433-329-3
Library of Congress Catalog Card Number: 2012949577

Manufactured in the United States of America.

Disclaimer

This is a story, a fiction, where all but a very few names have been changed to protect the people deserving of great respect and are, in all cases, cast in a deservedly positive light. They are minor characters in the book and its story. Other characters and the part they play in the *Saga* are loosely based on real people, including the author, whose names are changed; the places they work in the book are fictitious or different from where they were actually encountered by the present author. Some of the experiences described and the characters depicted are amalgamations of persons, places, and actions, and some diluted and altered autobiographical remembrances. There are healthy dollops of whimsy running throughout even the autobiographical hints.

The world of Garven Wilsonhulme is indeed fiction, but while not exactly real, it is faithful to an era of neurosurgical training and experience that is almost entirely a thing of the past. The independence and cowboy experience of being trained in a blood and guts trauma hospital in that era is not an exaggeration. There are some of those old men (and women) out there who will smile as they read and remember. If nothing else, the experiences of those semi-pioneers are the stuff of legend, humor, and pathos that invite endlessly fascinating yarns by all those consummate raconteurs.

The world of medicine and surgery is far more sophisticated and genteel now, far more of a closely controlled corporate money and legalistically driven environment. No longer can residents work 120 hours a week by federal and state law. It is all but unthinkable for a trainee to act with cavalier unsupervised independence in the closely monitored environment of the programs of the twenty-first century. A Garven Wilsonhulme would never make it into or through the training or the vicissitudes of neurosurgical practice in today's world without a very considerable amount of refinement and bowing to the ethical, moral, legal, and scientific standards of the present day. But then, neurosurgeons are eminently tough and adaptable. Maybe even Garven could make his way in the new paradigm as he did in the era of forty and fifty years ago, when this *Saga* took place. The author would like to think he could.

Dedication

The series of books is dedicated to those giants upon whose shoulders I stood, including Harvey Birsner, MD, my partner and friend; Shelly Chou, MD, PhD, my great mentor; Kemp Clark, MD, The Chief; Stephen David Durrant, PhD, professor of biology/evolution/comparative anatomy, a curmudgeon, humorist, inspiration, and friend; Lyle A. French, MD, PhD; the grandmaster at Minnesota; William Wallace Newby, PhD, professor of biology/embryology, my greatest friend and help; Lito Porto, MD, The Indian; J. Charles Rich, MD, my worthy opponent in premed, and the consummate neurosurgeon and contributor to the neurosurgical community; Theodore Roberts, MD, my start; Duke Samson, MD, the great builder of neurosurgery and foremost of brain vascular surgeon; Charles Sternbergh, MD, the rock of integrity; and Clark C. Watts, MD, JD, my friend and support during the lean years.

Acknowledgments

The author acknowledges with appreciation the direct contributions to the books of Harvey Birsner, MD; Keith Hooker, MD; Kim Oliver, MD; Brent Pratley, MD; Charles Stewart, MD; all of the general surgery and neurosurgery interns, residents, and professors in California, Utah, Minnesota, Texas, and Virginia; and the men and women of the navy, who served with me.

" I am sure you see Ahab as more than just a whaling boat captain out to catch a whale for the market. Ahab represents mankind in a sense. He sought to capture the great white whale to assert his own, and therefore, man's, supremacy over evil, or as Ahab termed it, the monomaniac incarnation of a superior, oppressive and evil power. Ahab spent forty years on a great quest, one taken for all mankind, to subdue the evil of the universe, a desire possessed by us all. Here is how Ahab describes it:

"'I see in him outrageous strength, with an inscrutable malice sinewing it. That inscrutable thing is chiefly what I hate; and be the white whale agent, or be the white whale principal, I will wreak that hate upon him. Talk not to me of blasphemy, man; I'd strike the sun if it insulted me.'"

—Herman Melville, *Moby Dick*

Garven identified himself fully with Ahab's sentiment.

"School is learning things you don't want to know, surrounded by people you wish you didn't know, while working toward a future you don't know will ever come."

—Dave Kellett

CHAPTER
One

The first Pacific Coast Athletic Conference wrestling meet was scheduled for the third week in October. Garven had made a valuable discovery, had made a very sensible choice, and was, by his observation, getting into pretty decent condition for the match. His discovery was that while he could not hope to beat out Hector Trujillo for the 136-pound weight class, nor could he starve himself down to the 130-pound division without risking collapse. There was a free opening at the next higher weight level, 144 pounds. His sensible choice had been to enter his name on the roster at that weight and to take his chances against the expected larger opponents. He had followed Hector and Derek's advice and had started to jog five miles almost every day—every day he could. And thus far, he was jogging and walking, if the truth were known. Still, he was getting a lot better wind and stamina. He was chronically tired, though, because of the merciless schedule of late-night studying, early morning running, classes all day, and hard workouts before supper. The true saving grace for Garven was the miracle of his youth.

The first meet of the 1949-50 wrestling season was a three-way dual between Stanford, U.C. San Diego, and Cal Poly at Pomona. None of the schools were wrestling powers, not even in the California system, which was weak by Midwestern competitive standards, certainly. The meet was held all the way down in LA County, in the new California Polytechnic College sports auditorium. They had a new mat and sharp-appearing matching workout uniforms, including the new wrestling outfits that had undershirt-type tops. Stanford's uniforms were motley in comparison. The originally crimson red tights were in varying ages of fading, and the colors were a continuum from pink to a dull blood red. They wore white shorts over the tights that varied not so much in color but in style since each wrestler was obliged to procure his own pair after the original matching shorts had finally worn themselves into ill-fitting droopiness. Their shoes varied from Hector's professional high-top black wrestling shoes to Derek's white low-cut tennis shoes to Pete Barnhienel's bare feet. He said he preferred the traction he got and the purchase on the mat, but Garven presumed it was an economy measure. By past performances (four years' worth), the Stanford wrestling team was not considered any more of an athletic threat than it was a sartorial challenge.

Pomona is a long ways from Stanford, and Garven brought his books and papers along on the team bus, so he would not get behind in his competition with the other premed students while he was away for three days. He was subject to a plethora of good-natured abuse from his teammates for his excessive devotion to his books. None of them were in premed, so he disregarded the source of their opinions and smiled indulgently.

"Are they using books in the poly-sci program yet?" he would ask Derek in comradely retort.

"The word things require stuff called writing," he would say sarcastically to Pete, who was in engineering. "And that requires books that we regular students have to study. You numbers people can get by with your pencils and slide rules. No need to study, right?" He felt like he gave as good as he got, but still, he was insecure enough to feel as if he needed to work at being one of the guys.

Pete Barnhienel won his match on points. Hector Trujillo pinned his opponent in the first three-minute wrestling period; otherwise, everyone else on the Stanford team had been pinned in the weights below Garven. It was now Garven's turn to walk alone to the mat and shake hands with his opponent, a muscular oaf from Cal Poly. At the weighing-in preliminaries, the wrestlers had urinated, defecated, and even stuck their fingers down their throats to get down to weight. They all looked like they had some debilitating blood disease before the morning was over. On the other hand, Garven had purposely left all his street clothes on and had carried two towels when he had weighed in, just to rub in the fact that he had absolutely no trouble making the cutoff weight. His opponent had taken Ex Lax and had spent the whole morning in a sweat closet to get down to 144 pounds. His eyes were sunken with dehydration and his complexion was sallow. He barely made the weight. Garven presumed he had an advantage because he felt fit as could be when he bounced out to shake with his tired-looking opponent. That advantage seemed important because, as Garven looked at the Cal Poly senior, the guy looked half again bigger than himself.

The ref faced off the two wrestlers, raised his arm between them, and made sure the timer was on zero. It had been on the fritz occasionally during the morning. He dropped his hand, and Garven charged in with a flurry of movement. He ducked in after his man's legs, he spun around to get behind him, he dodged, and he swerved. The Cal Poly wrestler seemed to lumber around, lackadaisically deflecting Garven's attacks. Garven was frustrated by the useless standing clenches his rival combatant enveloped Garven in, wasting match time. Garven could not take the brute down, and the Cal Poly contestant did not seem to be making any great effort to get the first take-down himself. Garven was starting to sweat and to puff.

The three-minute whistle blew, and the wrestlers and the ref met in the center of the mat. Garven lost the coin toss, and his competitor chose to take the underneath position. The ref's hand slapped the mat, and Garven's long hours of work with Hector paid off. The Cal Poly wrestler tried to sit-out, to drag-roll Garven to an inside sit-out, to front roll out from below the wiry Stanford fighter, all unsuccessfully. He spent most of his effort repeatedly attempting to spread out his strong legs and to force his way to a standing position so he could break away from Garven for a single point. Garven was not sure if his opponent had even broken a sweat, but he was panting and struggling for full breaths and pouring sweat himself.

The second period ended without a point being scored. Garven stood up and felt a little light-headed, as if he had gotten up too fast. His mouth was as dry as the inside of an old boot. He could feel his heart pitty-patting like a machine gun, too fast. He was tired into his bone marrow.

It was Garven's turn on the bottom. He tried to remember what Hector had taught him, but his mind seemed fuzzy, and he found himself concentrating more on his overwhelming desire to lie down and rest than on any strategy. The Cal Poly guy gave Garven a real case of insecurity by doing a series of jumping jacks before he knelt over Garven. It seemed to Garven that he was doing all he could do to kneel there without trembling.

The ref slapped the mat, and Garven felt a powerful arm forcing itself into a half Nelson on his right side. The other wrestler kept his weight situated in such a way that Garven had to support it all the time while trying to fend off the attempted pinning holds. The Cal Poly brute came a hair away from turning Garven over on his back. At best, that would have given him a two-point advantage over Garven. Garven summoned up some unknown reserve of strength and screamed at himself inwardly that he was not going to let anyone pin him. How could three minutes be so long?

Sensing his competitor's impending exhaustion, the Cal Poly senior over-balanced himself, trying to push Garven onto his back. This came on the tail of his great effort to pin Garven twenty seconds earlier. Garven could feel the awkwardness of his rival's body position and knew it was now or never. He leaped to his feet, carrying the off-balance opponent clinging to him. He struggled and twisted until he was loose and completely free from the other wrestler's grasp.

"*One point! All that for one lousy point. Better Garven C. than the Cal Poly brute,*" Garven thought briefly. He was shaking with exhaustion. How much more time was there?

There was more than a minute. Cal Poly unceremoniously dumped Stanford onto his back in the next ten-second interval and tried to hold Garven down by enveloping his whole body with his sweat-glistening arms. Garven could smell his armpits. He did a frantic neck bridge and succeeded in getting off his back at least. Three points for Cal Poly—two for the takedown and one for the predicament (full control of the opponent with endangerment of a possible pin). Garven simply had no more to give. His goal changed from winning the match, to avoiding being pinned, to somehow lasting out the final seconds of the match. Mercifully, the whistle blew, and it was over. Garven did not know how he got up, and could not have cared less when the ref raised his competitor's hand in victory.

Garven had tunnel vision; the periphery of his vision was closing in on him, and he was afraid he would black out. He knew he was supposed to go back to the benches his team had staked out to accept their camaraderie, but he was afraid he would humiliate himself by fainting like some girl, for cripes sake. He felt an overwhelming nausea. He was going to have diarrhea. Wouldn't that be great, to crap his pants? Garven moved as fast as he could to the men's dressing room. He felt like he was swimming through molasses but moving right along. In fact, he was shuffling like a zombie. Sweat was streaming off him. It was awful.

He made it to the toilet, then to the sink to puke, then slithered to the floor, unable even to stand up any longer. He did not know that it was possible for a human being to be that tired. This was real exhaustion. His heartbeat felt faint and stringy. He was actually unconscious for a few seconds. Sweat pooled in rivulets around the impression of his body left on the tile by his perspiration. He was quivering. He hoped desperately that no one else would come in. It was a vain hope; he heard footsteps and recognized Hector's voice coming from the void. It was calling his name. It was laughing.

"You okay, Garven? Yoo-hoo, Garven. Anybody home?" Hector was saying.

Garven mumbled incoherently. Something was wrong with his tongue. It felt so dry. He could not choke out clear words.

"Hey, don't worry. It happens to us all in our first matches. This wrestling stuff is tough, no, amigo?"

"You can say that again," Garven managed. He was ghostly pale, almost blue.

Hector laughed gently, a little mockingly. "I did the same thing. I browned up my tights even. Worst day of my life, you know."

"I'm grateful for small favors," Garven said and felt enough like himself to achieve a wan smile. "At least I skipped that."

"You will get over it, my friend. But I hope you learn the lesson. We all have to. You have to run. You have to run," he repeated. "You can't wrestle if you don't get in decent shape, and the only way to do that is to run—not jog, run! At *least* five miles every day. The lesson really is that you don't ever want to feel like this again."

"Boy, is that ever the truth. I hereby swear and affirm that I will run every day for the rest of my life. I am not ever going to go through anything this bad ever again. Nosiree," panted out Garven in his little, weak voice.

Hector got him over to one of the benches, and Garven stayed there for the rest of the morning. He felt good enough to stagger to his feet to get lunch with his teammates. He was still shaky and as weak as an old lady when he had to go out for his next match. He got pinned in the second period. Garven thought it was something of a miracle that he lasted five minutes.

He felt "lower than a snake's belly in a wagon track," he said to Hector when they boarded the bus the next day.

"Don't let it get you down. There's a bunch more matches. You just got to work. I know you can be a great wrestler. You got heart. You just got to work."

Garven could hardly wait.

The weekly chem quizzes were simple. All Garven had to do was to pay scrupulous attention to the quiz section instructor, Greg Allen, who tried his best to get the chemistry principles of the week across. The students in Section "I" were reasonably decent, not like the jocks in "P" through "Z." Garven had to wonder where the denizens of "Z" had come from, or more precisely, how they had gotten into Stanford in the first place—probably football players. To his surprise, the chemistry math, that is, the balancing of chemical equations, was clear to him, and, once clear, served as a good basis for understanding everything that followed. He not only got a good grade on all three quizzes, but he got one hundred percent on every one of the tests. Greg Allen was tickled because it raised the average of his section. He did everything he could do to help Garven. Garven felt easy enough with the balding grad student to ask him what could have been an affronting question.

"Look," he said during the first quiz section meeting of the fourth week of the quarter. "I don't want you to take this the wrong way or anything, but, well, you know, I've got a really important question."

"Why don't you just get it out, Garven?" Mr. Allen asked.

Garven shuffled a little. "Anyway, Mr. Allen, is it true that all of the A's are given out in the first three sections?"

"You know, Garven, much as I hate to admit it, that's about the truth. It's sort of the secret that everybody around here knows. It's not my doing, not even Terwilliger's; it's just the system. Always has been." He gave a small shrug of resignation.

Garven could not afford to resign himself to the fates decreed by the god, Tradition. "I'm in premed. I have to get an A," he said. "Terwilliger, uh, Mr. Terwilliger, himself, told me he would let me in Quiz Section A if I did well on the first few quizzes. How about you putting in a good word for me?"

"I'm pretty busy, Mr. Wilsonhulme. You may not realize it, but I've got a couple of other responsibilities."

Garven leveled a frank gaze at the graduate student, who was not so much older than himself. "Would it really be so much to just talk to the man? It would keep me from going down the drain. I don't want to beg; I just want the chance to show that I'm a good enough student... Please."

"Why not? I'll just add it to my impossible list. It isn't really any skin off me. I'll do it. Just get off my back, okay?" Greg Allen smiled at the eagerness, at the intensity of the freshman. *This kid will get whatever he wants. He has the will. I don't know if he really has the brains, that doesn't even matter; his willpower will make up for any deficiencies,* he thought.

On the weekend, Garven's floor at Madera House had an exchange with one of the Branner Hall, girls' dorm, floors. It was a yard-and-a-half party that required each freshman boy to pair up with a girl in advance. The potential awkwardness of the pairings was eliminated, or nearly so, by the simple expedient of assigning dates by alphabetical order. Garven and Stephanie

Anne Wilson were thereby fated to be the participants in Garven's first date of his college career—the first date in his life.

The premise of the party's theme was that each boy was to buy a yard and a half of material for his date. She was required to make her party outfit from the material, and could not supplement it with more or different material. As spice, prizes were offered for the girl who produced the best outfit, for the most interesting costume, and for the costume with the most cloth left over. Garven remembered to call Stephanie in advance and even had the presence of mind to find out what kind of material would suit her tastes. In his copious free time between wrestling practice on Friday and a frantic study session with his German class friend, he dashed over to Palo Alto, to a cloth store, and bought exactly one and one-half yards of green brocade satin. It cost him major portions of an arm and a leg, and a campus cop gave him a speeding ticket. He hoped Stephanie was worth it.

Garven had to call Stephanie to find out what she thought he should wear.

"Something casual, silly. Cool, but casual. I have my reputation to uphold. Remember that, okay?" she said.

There was a hint of self-deprecating laughter in her voice that Garven appreciated.

When he met the girl in the main lobby of Branner Hall, she was among a throng of laughing young women, all in a party mood, and all covered with ankle-length winter coats despite the mellowness of the autumn day. Stephanie had striking blond hair, was not fat, but the coat effectively covered all of the most important characteristics. She had a dimpled face with an omnipresent smile that showed expensive, perfect, white teeth. Her face was long, aquiline in its sharply cut and angulated features. Her nose was prominent and had the hook of an eagle's beak. Her eyes were set too closely together and had no particularly engaging feature otherwise. She had pimples that she had scrubbed, patted, and covered with makeup. After seeing her face, Garven quietly hoped all the more that she had a good set of knockers.

"You must be Garven," she bubbled with genuine and engaging enthusiasm.

"How did you know?" he asked. He had not had a chance to introduce himself or even to speak to her.

"I have my spies. A self-respecting girl has to," she answered, leaving an air of mystery in her reply.

"I guess you didn't get the material, so you had to wear this full-length coat instead," Garven commented with a flat expression.

She laughed and showed more of her teeth in her response. "I'm chicken, just like everybody else," she said and pointed with a panoramic movement of her long, pianist's forefinger. "We're all chickens and, if you must know… overly modest young maidens."

"The costumes must be worth a blush. I can hardly wait to get to the party to have a look," Garven said with a theatrical Oil Can Harry leer, twisting his invisible mustache.

She gave him a broad smile in response, and he was sure he was doing all right despite his initial uneasiness over his social aptitude. The fact that she stood more than a head taller than him had not helped.

The party was held in the open hall on the third floor of Branner Hall. The girls had spent an inordinate amount of time decorating the spare old room in a Greek motif for some reason incongruous with the concept of Dogpatch and Sadie Hawkins. In part, the choice was inspired by the yard-and-a-half apparel requirement that lent itself best to a toga costume, and in part to the secret yearnings of the girls to be accepted in the Greek system that would begin its life and death level decision-making process the following week. Garven was by nature nothing of a joiner, and by his own interest and public proclamation, a GDI (Greek: G-D Independent).

The young man was not unique enough to be quite *sui generis*, but he was more different from than similar to his Stanford compatriots, a set of dissimilarities that would only increase with time. He was therefore bored with the elaborate decorations, and disappointed with the costumes, although he never hinted to anyone that that was the case. He did not see a single really skimpy outfit, no décolletage, no serious display of attractive legs. The Stanford girls were, after all, at heart, conservative; the institution was a bastion of the Republican Party, with a student body that gave only the merest lip service to progressive or liberal aspirations. Garven and the other testosterone-driven freshmen had hoped for more excitement, but had not really expected much more than they found at Peebles Hall.

Garven was short and rather slight of build, but reasonably handsome, an acceptable male in appearance. Without her coat, Stephanie was, to use the most careful euphemism, very slender. The most accurate euphemism would be angular, and in truth, the most accurate term would have been bony. Garven wished the girl could put her coat back on but knew that it would be impolitic to suggest any such thing. She was the skinniest girl he had ever seen. Her busts were like olives. When he danced with her, and he was expected to dance most of the night with the girl, he kept hearing his father's raucous rendition of "It ain't no sin to take off your skin and dance around in your bones" echoing from out of his dim memory bank.

He was glad when Stephanie suggested that they sit the next one out because she had something she wanted to talk to him about. She looked so businesslike in that party atmosphere that he had to comment, "Ooh, this seems pretty serious. Did I do something unmentionable?"

"Don't be silly. You're fine. I just want you to be a part of my scientific survey," she soothed.

"Is that all the hush-hush whispering I have been seeing tonight, Steph?"

"I prefer Stephanie, okay?"

"Excuse me, no harm intended."

"And none done."

"So, what's the big secret survey?" Garven asked, his curiosity mildly piqued. He knew better than to expect anything very titillating or profound, but he was so bored with the rest of the evening that he could not help but feel a rise in expectations.

Stephanie retrieved a small Script notebook from her purse, fumbled her way to the desired page, and put on her reading glasses. The horn-rim glasses were too large for her face and too masculine by several degrees. She thought she looked scholarly in them and put them on more to effect that facsimile than for any real visual need. Garven thought it made her look even skinnier, if that were possible.

"Are you a virgin, Garven?" Her face was altogether serious.

Garven was a little surprised, a little more embarrassed, and after a moment of reflection, a lot amused by the question. He worked at suppressing his grin. "Who wants to know?" he asked, friendly but with a clear communication that he intended to be evasive, as he had decided a man of the world ought to be.

"If you are offended by references to sexuality in 1949, then I will have to respect your…conservatism. It was not my intent to embarrass you. Many virgins are reluctant to admit it, thinking that they will appear inexperienced or even backward to the interviewer," Stephanie said, fingering her glasses as she had seen her psychology professor doing when she interviewed.

"I'm not embarrassed. It's not a subject I've discussed before, especially with a nice-looking classmate."

"Thank you, Garven," Stephanie said primly.

There was a pause.

"Well?" she asked after a moment.

"Are *you?*" Garven asked defensively.

"What?" Stephanie replied with her own question.

The conversation was not going too well for Stephanie. It never seemed to, even though the *College Woman* magazine article had assured her that it was a great icebreaker and was a successful way of conveying one's sophistication.

"A virgin?" asked Garven, feeling like he was repeating himself.

"The interviewer must stand aloof, Garven. Don't send up a smoke screen. It is immaterial to the poll whether I am or not. Are you going to participate, or should I just mark you as one of the non-participators?"

Garven thought hard and quickly about how to answer. He was caught between telling the truth and being considered an inexperienced drip, or lying and being regarded either as a bon vivant or as some kind of slathering predator. Her face did not reveal her inclinations. He decided. "I have to confess," he lied.

"Then, am I to mark you as a nonvirgin?" she asked, growing a little impatient with the effort of burrowing for this nugget. At this rate, her clever little survey would take all night.

"You may," Garven said in a definitive prevarication. He watched her face. She was so impassive that he felt the need to embellish. "I have had lots of girls, if you must know. Girls of different races, like Indians and Mexicans, women of several different ages. Why, once—"

"I don't need the details," Stephanie said, seeing that the conversation was getting out of her control. He was probably just trying to impress her, so he could get to her, she thought. She even thought he might be making the whole thing up. He was probably just a virgin after all, and a lot of talk, like most boys.

"What about the rest of the people you've talked to? I should say, interviewed?" he asked with an unduly ironic emphasis on the "interviewed."

She did not like that. "You may be surprised to learn, Mr. Wilsonhulme, that no more than twenty percent of the men and two percent of the women have lost their virginity."

"I am surprised. How about you?" he asked, as a dig.

She did not like his tone and attitude. She was beginning to think that she did not much like Garven Wilsonhulme. "Well, I think that's enough scientific survey. Shall we dance another before we call it a night?" she inquired with an excess of politeness.

Garven had had enough of the phony politeness and interview, the dippy dance, and this gawky girl. He decided that he did not like her well enough to tough it out any longer. "Naw. Let's quit. I'm tired. I have to get up early tomorrow to workout. I've had enough of this phony party. I'll walk you back to your room."

"I don't think this is a phony party at all. I thought it was fun. I was on the decorating committee, and I don't think you appreciate how much went into making the evening a success. I think an apology is in order!"

Things had really deteriorated. Garven was getting intensely bored. Who cared about the stupid decorations and the stupid dance anyway? He could not wait to get out of there. "I am very sorry, Ma'am. I did not mean to cast the slightest aspersion on your fine affair," he said with a voice heavy with sarcasm.

"That was completely insincere, Mr. Garven Wilsonhulme. I don't need to sit here and be insulted. And I don't need you to see me home, either. We will say good night now, thank you very much!" Her eyes glittered with ire, then to her chagrin and his dismay, tears began to well up in them. She stood up and made for the ladies' room.

"Nice job, Aloysius," Garven said aloud.

CHAPTER
Two

Stanford University had, for some time, tried to diminish the influence and activities of the Greek letter sororities and fraternities with conspicuous success with the former and little headway with the latter. Two years previously, the sorority system had been so weakened by scandals, including pregnancies, voluntary participation in panty raids, and the decline in grade point average among the Greeks compared to the independents that enrollment fell to an all-time low. Parents exercised their rights of control and kept their daughters out of the sisterhood in ever-increasing numbers. The women of Stanford themselves came to regard membership as déclassé. There was no widespread lamentation when the university announced in 1947 that sororities would no longer be welcome, or even permitted, on campus. The few remaining houses were obliged to relocate off campus or disband if they lacked the resources for the expensive transition.

Male fraternities possessed a more persevering popularity and exercised considerably more influence than their feminine counterparts. Greek introductory week in the first week of November saw no fewer houses participating in 1949 than ever previously and no diminution in supplicants. Devon Upshire had dreamed of being a frat man since childhood, when his father, then his uncle, then his brother recounted the adventures and extolled the superlatives of the Greek life, each in his turn. Devon was the picture of stimulation for the week preceding the Greek open houses. He became a nuisance to Frosty and Garven, pestering them unmercifully to follow his lead and to join up. They did not know what they were missing. They would regret it for the rest of their lives if they did not avail themselves of the only opportunity they would ever have, he told them with the repetitiousness of a stuck phonograph record.

"Nobody's a GDI anymore. Except queers and nerds, and they don't count," Devon told Garven every time Garven repeated his intention to remain affiliated with the unaffiliated. "Even Jews have their house. I don't know how you can be a Greek Jew, but you can," he would argue. "Frosty, you come on with me, then you can talk sense into this little desert peckerhead."

"Not interested," was Frosty's infuriating stuck-record reply.

Devon threw up his hands in despair and rolled back his eyes at the cretinous arguments of his friends. He was going to convince them if it took the rest of the year. Finally, his persistence paid off, at least in a small measure. Garven relented and agreed to a compromise. Devon would shut up, and Garven would visit four houses. Garven had to promise not to make any more disparaging remarks about the fraternity system until he had done at least that. Devon could not get Frosty to budge.

"Waste of time," Garven's roommate insisted to the last.

Garven and Devon went to Alpha Sigma together first because it was the only fraternity in the world for Devon. His whole family had been Alpha Sigs, and Devon was going to be an Alpha Sig. He dressed in the coolest threads for the first impression—gold button blazer with pocket insignia, red and white striped Sea Island cotton shirt, white cotton twill pants, and white buck shoes. He carried letters from his male progenitors in his inside coat pocket that all but ordered the actives on campus to honor the tradition of family preference when selecting this year's pledge class. Garven felt out of place and melded into the woodwork as soon as Devon was brought into the fold of jolly camaraderie. He met Pete Barnhienel at the Epsilon Delta Xi house the same day and had to admit that there were some good guys in frats after all. As far as he could tell, though, Pete was the only non-phony in the whole system. The chitchat visits were a matter of agitated boredom for Garven, but he kept his part of the bargain and visited exactly four frats.

The Lambda Delts a new frat, enfranchised only in 1946, invited him to a very fancy dinner at the Sutton mansion in San Francisco for the upcoming Saturday. He decided to go, partly because he was flattered by their sincere attentions (and he always seemed to go for the underdogs) and partly because Devon responded with such disdain at the very suggestion that he, Garven, would evince a serious interest in such an upstart frat.

"Nobody, but nobody, joins the Lamby Delts," Devon derisively insisted.

It was only slightly better than being a GDI.

So, Garven decided to go even though he had to wire Dr. Wilsonhulme for more money to be able to rent a tuxedo for the affair. He had never been to a black tie dinner and was curious, and a bit invigorated by the opportunity to breathe the rarefied air of the upper-upper crusts like the Suttons. If, in Boston, the Cabots speak only to the Astors, and the Astors speak only to God, in San Francisco, the first family hierarchies held that the Suttons spoke only to the Sutters, and the Sutters had the lonely opportunity to limit their conversations to deity.

The Suttons were hosting the elegant affair because the Lamba Delta fraternity had been the only one who would take their son, Eric. Ordinarily, his wealth and position would have guaranteed his place in any snob-centered fraternity of his choice. However, in Eric's case, they were all willing to make an exception. He was rumored to be a queer, which was not true, and an opium addict, which was true. He also enjoyed the dubious reputation of having set the Omega house on fire during one night of debauchery the previous pledge season. He became persona non grata everywhere even though his father, Landers, had practically built the Omegas a new house. The hasty withdrawal of actives by their alarmed fathers, along with their handsome contributions, threatened to reach epidemic proportions before the Greek council took the unprecedented step of sending a soothing letter, letting every Greek parent know that there would be no possibility of extending an invitation to the disruptive element, as became Eric Sutton's euphemistic sobriquet.

Garven knew the story, of course, and far from turning away any incipient enthusiasm he was developing, it caused him to become mildly fascinated. He had had little exposure to the decadent rich, and he felt a perverse need to expand his repertoire of experience. There had been rich boys at Burton-Cagle, some of the richest, but, so far as Garven knew, no serious or entertaining decadence. He was fascinated by a family that could plink down that kind of money for an errant son, and since he had every intention of having that level of wealth one day, he reasoned that he might just as well begin learning how they lived.

He had met Eric at the introductory afternoon tea in the Lambda Delt's new fraternity house, and he had wrangled himself a ride to the Sutton mansion in the Sutton limousine with the Sutton son. While he was not yet any great shakes with the women, he had to admit, in all frankness, that he did seem to be developing a winning way with influential men, which appeared to the freshman to be of considerably greater long-term value. In the limousine, Eric seemed even more dreamy than ever, languid and unconcerned. Garven felt a shiver of excitement just being in the elegant vehicle.

"You like Stanford, Eric?" Garven asked, making frat small talk.

"It's okay," Eric responded, acting startled as if he had been disturbed in a reverie.

"Is the frat stuff all it's cracked up to be? I mean, do you really enjoy it? Do you make all those great connections you're supposed to?"

"Um hum, I guess you do. Yeah, you really do. My best friends are frats, not just ours, either. And besides, it's the only way to get girls."

"They can't even be in sororities, Eric. I can't believe all of the good-looking girls are going with frat guys and nobody else."

"Hum?" Eric asked, waking up again.

"About girls?"

"Oh yeah, they're attached to the frats. The brothers get the pick of the litter." He smiled pleasantly, apparently having brought an agreeable memory near the surface.

"Is that really true? I mean, there's got to be good-looking GDI girls, right?"

"Um um," Eric said in his slowed, musing, speech pattern and shook his head; His breath had a peculiar sweet odor that Garven could not place. "That's wrong. At least, you never see a worthwhile girl at any non-Greek function. They know better. You ever see any decent pieces at a freshman do?"

Garven had to admit, and for the first time, realized, that what Eric was saying was true. He had assumed that the old saw that nine out of every ten girls in the U.S. were beautiful and the other one goes to Stanford was operative. He had not considered the idea that there was a definite influence acting on the women's choices.

Eric seemed so peaceful in his own special space, wherever that was, that Garven left him alone for the rest of the ride. The party was elegant with exotic canapés, liveried servants, tuxedoed men, and evening dressed women, whom Garven knew for a fact could not have been Stanford students. For one thing, they wore low-necked dresses, and did so with success and nonchalance having the proper accouterments. Garven had not seen that much well-positioned adipose tissue in his life to date, and he enjoyed each view as much as he did the marvelous food.

Dinner was rack of lamb with a minty plum sauce, braised carrots, twice baked Idaho potatoes, a garden salad with a princely array of fresh vegetables even though it was nearly winter, a platter of gorgeous fruit, and for desert, cherries jubilee. Garven felt like a real spiff as he sipped the three wines, one with each course. He did not like the taste of any of them; they seemed sour, kind of vinegary, to him, but he acted as if it were the usual thing for him. He even made a pretense of puffing on the huge Havana cigar he was given after desert. It was a nauseating experience that recalled his first experience at smoking homemade cedar bark cigs back in Cipher a hundred years ago, when he was a kid. He knew he had better leave well enough alone.

Despite all of the elegance and perhaps partly because of it, Garven found his interest in joining in the fraternity declining rather than increasing as the evening wore on. He envisioned the cost of maintaining the fraternity life-style, probably exaggerated by what he saw. He was also bored to distraction by the contrived non-conversations he had with the actives, the prospective pledges, and even with the decorative women at the party. The discussions were brainless and pointless, just as Frosty had told him they would be. He found himself wishing the evening was over. He reaffirmed his decision to remain a GDI somewhere during the aperitif course and the limo ride back to campus that night.

The flirtation with fraternities did not end with his personal withdrawal from the frenetic competition. Although he failed to induce Garven or Frosty to enter a pledge class with any fraternity, Devon Upshire did involve the pair in a time-honored rite of passage in the Stanford University Greek system. Ten days after the formal wooing process started, the form of the pledge class for each fraternity was finalized and the serious business of fraternity life could begin. Garven and Frosty were invited to participate, but in an unofficial capacity.

"Doing anything tomorrow night?" Devon asked the roommates innocently enough.

"We thought you had to limit yourself to frat activities and people, and to forsake all others," Frosty said, and looked up from his geology textbook at the visitor as he spoke that Thursday evening.

"It's true. Almost true. However, I have a proposition to involve you GDI types in a fraternity activity even though you have been dumb enough to miss your golden opportunity to be an integral part of the hallowed system," Devon said with mock sententiousness.

"I know you have something wicked in mind, Devon. Let's hear it," chimed in Garven, bored with his German vocabulary list.

"Ah, to the heart of the matter, then," Devon said now that he had their attention. "We probationary Alpha Sigs are planning a little commando raid on the actives before everything has to settle down with pledge week. You guys want in?"

"Knowing you, Upshire, this can only mean pain and trouble, conflict with individuals in a position of authority, and potential disgrace that any sane person would reject out of hand. Of course, we want in," said Garven with a straight face.

"Frosty?" asked Devon.

"Why not?" replied Frosty with a bemusedly resigned expression.

"That was tough," said Devon. "You guys don't even know what the gig is."

"Doesn't matter. You're our bud," said Frosty. "Even if you have gone over to the Philistines."

"My fraternity stuff isn't going to change that, either. You ready for the plan?"

"Shoot."

Devon outlined his ridiculously precise and complete plan to perpetrate an outrage on the Alpha Sigma house and its paying occupants. The three boys agreed to meet in front of Mem Chu at two o'clock Saturday night—technically, Sunday morning.

At the appointed hour and place, Garven and Frosty, clad all in black, met a small band of similarly dressed commandos led by Devon. Devon handed the GDIs a jar of black grease paint to camouflage their faces. Garven had to admit that the young men were almost invisible when they stood in the shadows. Devon carried a long rope coiled over one shoulder that was attached to a three-pronged grappling hook.

"Where in the world did you get that?" Frosty whispered, since everyone else was whispering.

"My brother brought it down to me last week. His pledge class used it against their actives when he was here. He figured it would come in handy."

"Yeah, you never can tell when a need for a grappling hook will come up," laughed Frosty.

"Have you put any thought into how we can get into that frat house, team members?" Devon asked, directing his question at Garven and Frosty.

The two GDIs confessed that they had not.

"I am sure you are aware that the actives put their houses under siege precautions, with guards posted twenty-four hours a day during this week. It is a sacred tradition and responsibility of the pledge class to execute a coup against them that warrants historical remembrance. The unspoken rule is that the outrage has to come from inside the house, not outside. Like we can't burn the place down or demolish it with a tank or anything."

"So, do you think maybe they might've locked the doors and windows?" asked Garven.

"You betcha. The actives gave us pledgies a complete tour to see the bolts, locks, and bars. The place is a fort. They are convinced that it is impregnable."

"But you know better, I suppose?" asked Frosty, knowing this had to be the direction of this conversation.

"Another legacy from my brother. There is an attic window that can't be locked and no one has ever given it a thought because it is only approachable from the roof," Devon bragged.

"Hence, the grappling hook," Garven said.

"Hence, the grappling hook," Devon repeated.

"Do you think all of us can climb that rope three stories, Devon?" asked Frosty doubtfully.

"Most of us," Devon admitted.

"That's a serious fall," someone commented in a voice filling with doubt.

Devon shrugged. That was answer enough for the eight young men, who knew that they could do anything they set their minds to and that they would live forever.

CHAPTER
Three

It took three throws to get the grappling hooks to fix on the third-floor rain gutter. The noise seemed deafening out there in the still night, but no lights came on, and there was no other apparent activity from inside the Alpha Sigma fraternity house. Of the group of pledges and the two GDIs, only Devon and Mark Euliss (known by everyone as "Useless"), Shephard Packer, Garven, and Frosty made it to the top. Nobody fell, fortunately.

After they stopped coughing blood and the heaving in their tortured lungs settled down, Devon said, "Lets lower the ropes back down; so, we don't take any chance of an active looking out and seeing them."

"Like burning your bridges behind you?" Shephard Packer asked with a small grimace.

"*Alea jacta est* (The die is cast)," said Devon. "That's how Julius Caesar put it when he marched his army across the Rubicon River in defiance of an order of the Roman senate. That's another advantage, all right." Devon grinned. He was really into this commando stuff. He watched too many war movies.

As promised, the window opened without undue difficulty, and the five boys crept into the house. Garven was afraid he would drop into a black clothes chute or something, but the floor was only three feet from the window ledge. So far so good.

There were supposed to be two actives on guard duty. Since it was the weekend of the UCSF game, the rest of the brothers were up in the city, having a great and degenerate time. And the two actives who had drawn the short straws were none too thrilled to be left behind. Lacking enthusiasm, they had drifted into fitful slumber in their chairs at about midnight, secure in the knowledge that the house was so well locked up that it was well-nigh impregnable. They were in for a nasty surprise.

From his bag of tricks, Devon pulled a bottle of chloroform he had filched from the biology lab and two white hankies. Garven just shook his head.

The pledge boys crept silently across the old Persian rugs then jumped two at a time on the slumbering guards. Frosty was afraid they were going to smother the guy he and Devon jumped, but Devon seemed to know what he was doing. After a very brief and feeble struggle, the fraternity brother was breathing calmly, and he was hors de combat. Garven had to help wrestle the other victim down in a brief struggle before all five of the intruders could keep the chloroform-soaked cloth on the frantic young man's face long enough to do its job. The pledges rested a moment, then Devon sprang into action.

He raced to the front hall and unbolted, unlocked, and debarred the pair of large doors. He gave a low whistle into the outside darkness that brought six laughing boys in from the blackness. Garven next heard the rumble of a truck motor and went downstairs to see the action. A mid-sized van backed up the frat house driveway and parked a short distance from the front doors. The truck's occupants clambered out, laughing too hard to be effective. Devon flung open the van's twin doors.

"Get a move on," he hissed at his confederates.

Frosty and Garven were the only ones not in the know, apparently.

The pledge class swept into their frat house and efficiently began to carry the furniture into the open yaw of the van, with Devon directing every action.

"Who died and left him in charge?" grumbled one sweating pledge good-naturedly.

But they all seemed willing to acknowledge Devon's command status.

"Hey, you lazy bums, go upstairs and tie up those actives, all right? Can't have someone setting off an alarm now, can we?" Devon instructed Garven and Frosty.

The two GDIs were as obedient as the pledges. Devon was something of a natural leader, largely because of his boundless enthusiasm.

Most of the first floor furniture, including the rugs, fit into the van. It took two hearties to force the doors closed, then the van rumbled and coughed away from the house.

"Going to the furniture mart up in 'Frisco," Devon told Frosty and Garven.

"What for?" asked Garven, thinking it was probably a dumb question.

"What'd you think for? To sell these fine antiques, of course." He laughed uproariously at the magnitude of his coup and his joke. This would be one for the Greek history books.

In the days following the coup, Devon had a hard time keeping from boasting—a minor character flaw of his. He let other pledge groups know of his exploits and of his GDI friends' participation. In all, three other groups enlisted the aid of Garven and Frosty, who, flushed with their early and easy success, were finding the raids more fun than anything they had done since high school.

In one fraternity house, the pledges spray painted the entire inside chartreuse. At the Tri-Lambdas, Garven and Frosty participated in an abortive attempt to board up the doors and windows from the inside to lock out the actives, and pledges. It was an ill thought out caper, and they were surprised by a prepared contingent of actives, who foiled their efforts that had taken up so much study time. Garven and Frosty chalked it up to the can't-win them-all column.

The most outlandish prank, and one that brought down the wrath of the university on the fraternity system, was executed against the hapless Sigma Epsilon Omegas (the SEOs). They usually called themselves the Sigma Epsilon Xis (the SEXs) and were known by their preferred acronym largely owing to the sparsity of available material for humorists on the Stanford scene. In a nighttime raid, planned and executed very much like Devon's, and, in fact, Devon had had a hand in the planning stage, the pledges, with Frosty and Garven's help in execution, crept into the darkened SEX house on Monday night. There was one guard because the rest of the frat brothers were off campus, attending a beer bust with one of the three remaining sororities. He was awake, but offered no resistance as the pledge class intruders broke in. He was not about to get hurt for a silly and expensive tradition. There was nothing he could do about whatever prank the pledges had in mind. Besides, he knew that the actives would retaliate in the next week or two, according to tradition.

The studious, rather pasty-faced, active made no struggle or protest as he was bound, gagged, blindfolded, and handcuffed. He, like Garven and Frosty, waited expectantly to find out what the pledge leaders had in mind. The furniture sale and painting gambits had already been done, and it would not have been much of an achievement to repeat them.

A wooden crate was carried into the dark foyer of the frat house, and its lid was removed. Garven and Frosty looked at each other questioningly.

"What's up?" Frosty asked the ringleader.

"Just a little mail service. Watch and you'll see."

The pledges then lifted the active over their heads and carried him outstretched in the supine position, like pallbearers, to the open coffin-like box. Four pledges got into the box, and the bound active brother was hoisted over the top of the box and laid gently on its wood floor. The pledges stuck their fingers in the previously drilled air holes to make sure of their patency, then the box top was replaced and the lid was overly securely nailed. The boys could hear the muffled fearful cries and banging of bound feet against the side walls and floor of the container. Garven and Frosty looked at each other with growing concern this time.

The natural leader and chief jokester produced a lading poster and tacked it on top of the wood box. The address read "Harlem, Montana."

"Where is Harlem, Montana?" Garven inquired, getting kind of nervous. "Is there such a place?"

"Don't really know," came the answer from the chief jokester. "But it has a train stop and a population of twenty-three."

He laughed, full of self-appreciation for the cleverness of his practical joke on the fraternity.

Garven and Frosty looked at each other with a hint of alarm.

The *Stanford Chronicle* carried an article by the president of the university himself the following Friday. The article decried the practice of playing expensive, vandalistic, and sometimes dangerous pranks on the fraternity houses and their actives. The author's emphasis was on the dangerous aspect of the silly prank tradition, and stated without equivocation that this year, the practice had gone too far. He briefly chronicled the terrible experiences of one poor and innocent active fraternity member, who had been mailed to some mail cul-de-sac in Harlem, New York. The promising Stanford student had suffered near starvation, frost bite, and serious psychological injury when the prank went awry.

According to the *Chrony* article's authoritative author, "The offenders had presumed that the box would arrive in Montana for some inexplicable reason and be opened in two day's time. Unfortunately, the letter they had sent to the railroad stop in Harlem had been addressed to the mayor, instructing him to open the box promptly, and there was no mayor. No one in the whistle-stop in Montana had known what to do with the letter, nor much cared, since there was no accompanying box. The box was sent to the main post office center in New York. The poor frat brother spent a full four days freezing and starving before his feeble kicking on the box walls attracted enough attention to get him freed in the middle of the Negro section of the nation's largest city."

The young man's parents were understandably irate, the president's article went on to say, and the resources of the university were pledged to the discovery and prosecution of the individuals involved.

"Anyone involved in the prank, even peripherally, will be summarily expelled, and the leaders would be prosecuted to the full extent allowed by the law," President Cheevers declared.

Frosty and Garven, alone in their room, read the *Chrony* article, looked at each other in frank dismay, and pledged to keep their mouths shut on the subject forever. Stanford University clamped down on the internecine strife between pledges and actives so effectively that the practice of the pledge-generated prank all but disappeared for a few years. The retaliatory hazing of pledges required another firm hand, and coincidentally, 1949 was the year to bring down the most substantial wrath of the powers-that-be on the actives in fraternities as it had on the pledges.

Garven witnessed a typical example of the pledge hazing that came to be vilified by the administration. He, Frosty, Useless, and Devon Upshire were minding their own business, walking from the music building, Dinkelspiel Auditorium, across White Plaza to the Old Union building on a clear, cold mid-November afternoon, having been to a jazz concert from the student performer series. From the milling crowd of students, a group of about ten young men set upon Devon from behind, wrestling him to the ground. The other three boys were about to intervene when it was explained with some emphasis that it was none of their business, and the ten guys were in no mood to let them help the jerk who had cost them a small fortune by selling off all their furniture. It seems they had had to buy all of the junk back at a tidy profit for the retailer in San Francisco. If Garven, Frosty, and Useless wanted some of the same payback, they could try to help. The three prudently decided to be bystanders.

The actives dragged the shrieking, yelling, kicking, and struggling Devon off the plaza and onto a small, grassy area beneath two leafless maples. He was bound by wrapping his entire body mummy style with ace wraps, and his mouth was taped shut. A good two dozen spectators stood by, figuratively holding the participants' coats, but there was no one to help or even protest. The whole scene took on a circus or party atmosphere.

One of the larger men produced a set of sheep shearing hand clippers and carved out a rough cross through the luxurious black curls over the vertex of

Devon's scalp. Another active shook up a can of Bryl Creme shaving lather and smeared it in the cross. He and a third brother then shaved the clipped area slick as a cue ball producing a rather striking white cross on the top of Upshire's head, where no sunlight had touched since infancy. He was powerless to struggle. The coup de grace came when still another tormentor produced a small can of red paint and very carefully painted the skin cross a brilliant vermilion. He was careful to make the lines sharp and clear. He did a very nice job, everyone thought.

"Big deal," Garven said in an aside to one of the actives holding the crowd at bay. "He'll get that paint job off with a few washings. He still got you guys better than you got him."

"Wanna bet?" said the active smugly. He handed Garven the paint can and indicated the lettering on the label.

"Sheep brand vital dye," it read. Garven turned the can around, not really knowing anything about the chemical contents described in small print. The opposite side bore the phrase in bold letters, "Guaranteed indelible life-long, or your money back."

Poor Devon.

A multiplicity of such incidents brought the force of the administration down on fraternities, which began to fear for their continuing existence in a hostile environment. It was deemed the better part of valor not to protest any too vociferously on the hazing issue, and the Greek system at Stanford capitulated quickly. Hazing was a pretty tame affair for years afterward.

The SEO pledge ringleader became the scapegoat for the whole set of pledge criminals. The heat over the kidnapping and near disaster was so intense that the university was threatening to use the incident as a pretext to drive the entire group of fraternity houses off campus. Pledges and actives alike from all of the houses screwed the pressure down on the ringleader, who had been self-destructive enough to boast of his part in the fiasco. Everyone involved seemed to know his name. He was man enough not to implicate anyone else, much to Garven's eternal relief, and manfully accepted the ignominy of expulsion. The injured young man was persuaded by his fraternity brothers not to press criminal charges over his parents' protests, and eventually, as finals and the Christmas season approached, the campus settled down. Garven actively sought a low profile.

Garven had one more thing to learn about the university fraternity system, and with that education came some cause to question his firm determination to remain an independent in the social structure. Mary Ellen Strangbul,

Garven's physics lab partner, was the physical opposite of his chemistry partner, Gwendolyn. She was petit, vivacious, and cute without being a cheerleader-type phony. Her face was attractive and smiling, although it could not be accurately described as beautiful or anything like that. She was as bright as Gwendolyn, but not withdrawn and careful. Mary Ellen had become Garven's confidant, as much as anyone except Frosty. She was a good listener, and a good talker. Garven liked the mix and felt more at ease with her than any other girl he had met. It was natural for him to want to expand the relationship; so he asked her for a date. The fraternity hullabaloo had quieted down, and they were between midterms and finals so that he had some time to concentrate on her.

The conversation, when he did get around to proposing the date, had a disturbingly familiar ring.

"Thanks for covering for me last Friday," he had started, as obliquely as possible.

"*Pas du tout*," she replied with a slight nod of her head. She was practicing her oral French, as she often did.

"We're all caught up today, again thanks to you," Garven complimented, finding it difficult to get to the meat of his intended purpose. For one thing, he was a little gun-shy, afraid of another rejection.

"You're full of compliments today, lab mate," she said, looking at him perceptively. "Do I detect something going on?"

"Nothing subtle about you, Mary Ellen. I was trying not to blunder in, to be sensitive and sincere, a real forties man as you women's movement people prefer."

"Some women's movement," she snorted. "It will always be a man's world, but thanks for throwing a crumb our way."

Garven took his little reassuring breath and asked directly, "Mary Ellen, are you free tomorrow night, I mean Saturday night?"

"Oh, Garven, I'm afraid not. I have another date, sorry."

"How about the next Saturday?"

She made an effort to appear to be giving her answer analytical thought. "Oh, dear. I'm booked up then, too."

Garven did not like the echoes of déjà vu. He had heard this very patter before. "Mary Ellen," he said, looking directly into her eyes and not letting her look away. "I just want to know if you will go out with me. I like you, and I think you like me. Please don't give me that stuff about being busy this night and that night. Are you busy for the rest of your life or what? I just want you to tell me 'yes' or 'no.' If it is no, I will shut up and won't bother you about it again." He wondered if he were some kind of a leper.

"Garven, there are things you don't understand. It's hard for a girl here. The system is rigid. Nobody talks about it, but that's the truth. If a Stanford girl wants to have any fun, you know, get invited to any parties or to a frat activity, she has to be committed to one of the fraternities. You see?"

He did not see, and stubbornly shook his head.

"Don't be dense. I like you, but you are not in a fraternity. If I go out with you, I will be cut off. I sort of signed up—not sort of; I signed up with the Tri-Sigs. I can't go out with non-Greeks, or even Greeks the Tri-Sigs don't approve of. Now do you get it? I'm really sorry, but I can't help it."She was getting flustered.

Garven wished he had not brought up the whole subject, but he could hardly believe what he was hearing. He spoke without thinking, a fault he would vow to correct after this. "That makes you like a…" and here he stammered and blushed. He had almost committed an unforgivable mistake. He had not meant to insult his friend. She was more important to him as a confidant than as a date, he realized.

"A what, Garven? Careful now."She was flushed. It hurt to hear an open suggestion of what she was feeling about herself in the rotten situation. She could not let him get away with saying that awful word without asserting herself. She had her pride.

"Never mind. I'm sorry, Mary Ellen. Let's just drop it. I understand."

"A what, Mr. Wilsonhulme?"She sounded snappish now.

"Oh, brother. A kind of slave, an indentured servant. I can't see why a pretty and bright girl like you has to be a toady for the fraternity boys, is all."

Her face was angry.

"Don't be mad. I didn't mean anything. I just like you, is that so terrible?"

Mary Ellen took time to think and realized that it was not his fault, and that he had not intentionally put her down.

"Toady?! Huh?" I'm not mad, Garven. I wish it could work out differently. You could still join a frat, you know. You're a popular guy."

"Thanks again for everything, Mary Ellen, for the conversation and all. I guess I'll see you on Wednesday. We'd better drop the rest of it. Still friends?"

"Sure," she said.

She felt a little sad.

"Nice job, again, Aloysius, my friend and alter ego," Garven said to himself as he left her.

Garven was more successful in his classes than he was in the various aspects of his social life. He was a definite strikeout in the dating department, and it was only by the grace of God that he had escaped being kicked out of the university or worse for his other involvements. He was thankful for small favors like an A in his German conversation class. Herr Roldorf said his accent was improving all the time, and Garven himself could tell that he was getting the vocabulary and syntax down because the flow of his German was now pretty easy. He even managed to include a few colloquial idioms successfully in his speech. He had become friends, in a limited sort of way, with the young German grad student as the result of a silly mistake he had made in one of the classroom conversations.

Garven had been selected to pose as a patron in a German restaurant, with Herr Roldorf acting the part of the waiter. Garven had read that all German waiters liked to be addressed as headwaiter; so, in an effort to show his new-found bit of knowledge of German, Garven had signaled Herr Roldorf with what should have been, "*Herr Ober*" (Head Waiter), but instead, for some reason he would never know, it came out as, "*Herr Obst*" (Fruit).

Roldorf looked at him with a careful scrutiny to see if he had been intentionally insulted. When it was apparent that the slip was innocent, the handsome blond German broke into a broad smile. "*Ein Obst? Ein Obst!? Mein herr? Entschuldig Sie mich!* (A fruit? A fruit, sir? Excuse me!)," he said with mock serious indignation. He laughed until tears ran down his cheeks when Garven blushed a scarlet hue and tried to hide his face in his hands. The class loved having an object of ridicule just as does the world at large, and Garven, by a strange inversion, became Herr Obst. By natural and near immediate means of communication, the nickname spread and stuck throughout his limited circle, even to people with whom he was barely acquainted.

Like every premed student in history, Garven worried and fretted about his upcoming finals. Everything he wanted was riding on those test scores. He was doing fine in class despite the time he took out for wrestling, but that did little to mitigate his apprehension. The week before finals was officially designated by Stanford University as Dead Week. Nothing happened during that week; it was as somber as Lent. There were no parties, no labs, no athletic workouts or contests. Nothing. It wound every red-blooded Stanford student up as a tight spring, awaiting the Mardi Gras of the two days after finals, when the quarter officially ended for the holidays.

German finals were a nightmare. The test was contrived to include everything from the most advanced university level high German scientific and romantic communications to the simplest set of greetings and conjugations. There was a very considerable portion of the examination that was completely above Garven's head; and he felt like he had not only flunked, but as if he had been dragged through a knothole sideways by the time it was over. He knew he had done well, admit it, even great, on the conversation class final. He got an A, to his surprise, in both segments of the class because the written exam was prorated according to the level at which the student was enrolled. He thought there had to be a less painful way, but who was he to complain about an A?

He had been informed correctly about the grading system in chemistry. Greg Allen had gotten him into Quiz Section A, and Mr. Terwilliger had tutored Garven and his fellow section members to a corner on the high-grade market. With a sort of inside trader's advantage, the final had not been particularly difficult. He got his coveted A in chemistry and refused to think about what would have happened if he had sat docilely by and stayed with the knuckle-draggers in Section P.

Professor Nicholson gave Garven an A minus in English and suggested that it should only have been a B plus. He smiled when he said it, and strongly recommended that Garven follow up with the advanced expository writing course, or at least the chairman of the department's creative writing course. Garven knew he had his plate full just to get the minimum core humanities requirements past him so he could get into med school in three years. He had to take two more basic English classes—American literature and British literature—as it was. He would have to take those standard freshman classes during his sophomore year because his advisor had gotten him into such an upside-down schedule. He was not about to complicate his life further by adding to his humanities burden. He could not tell Nicholson that, however. He thanked the professor for the grade and for all his help.

"I'll be in the expository writing course as soon as I can work it in," he lied, feeling good about how he had finessed his way through the course and over its stumbling blocks.

With his friend Mary Ellen's help, he got an A in both the lab and the lecture portions of the physics course. He did not understand a thing, but by memorizing the lectures virtually verbatim and disgorging them by rote in the tests whenever a cue word appeared in a question, he shined through with a "Good Work!" inscribed in red pencil on his blue book when it was returned after the final. He had a straight A run for his first quarter. He was feeling very well indeed when the dam-break festivities of After Finals Days burst onto the campus.

"Hey, Herr Obst," Devon called up to Garven's room from the grassy field behind Madera House.

Garven was lying about in a post-finals stupor. "What do you want?" he yelled out the window.

"Bring your roomie, and come out and play," Devon called. His red cross was especially vivid from this perspective.

"Is this the Red Cross calling?" Garven taunted.

Frosty joined his roommate at the window and waved at their friend below.

"C'mon, we've got a game of touch going. You need to get out, get some air. You need to wake up for a while so you can sleep well this afternoon; no sleeping tonight, you know." Devon waited on the grass while Garven and Frosty put on their football grubbies. Useless joined him, carrying the official Wilbur Hall football that looked like one of Knut Rockne's originals.

"Hey, Red Cross, you coming or not?"

The nickname had stuck because, for a long time, it did not look like Devon's hair was going to grow back in at all.

"Just a minute. Obst and Frosty are coming down."

"Where can we play?"

"It's pretty crowded here by Wilbur; lets drive over to the field behind Roble and Lagunita dorms, by the lake."

"Okay with me. I'll get the pledges and meet you guys there. Don't take all day; it's nearly noon now."

It was a delightfully warm day, with a bright December sun in a cloudless day. The freshmen took on a mixed group of sophomores and juniors and did reasonably well against them before they all stretched out in the fragrant clover grass, sweaty and relaxed. Garven felt a little strange before he slipped into a restful nap. It was nothing he could clearly identify, just a little strange.

He began to feel seasick. In his deep sleep, he felt as if he were rolling on the ocean. He sensed that he should be nauseated, but as his head cleared, he realized that he was not sick to his stomach. He still had the sensation of rolling on the ground, as if on waves, as he became fully alert. He looked towards the back of Roble Hall, and shook his head to rid himself of the hallucination that the ground was rolling and buckling. It was a most disconcerting feeling. Garven was sure something was very wrong with himself. The other boys were all awake now, some sitting, some leaning on an elbow; all looked perplexed.

"Frosty, are you okay? Something's wrong. I have something wrong with me. I feel terrible," Garven said to his friend, definitely worried now.

"Relax, I think it's just an earthquake," Frosty said, not sounding relaxed, either.

"That's all it is; take it easy," said Devon, being cool.

"Just an earthquake, huh?" Garven said. "It feels like the Big One."

"'California splits off into the ocean!' says the headline," contributed Useless.

"Thanks for cheering us up, Useless," said Frosty and Garven.

The rolling ground suddenly became completely still. Birds clutched their tree branches and were silent. None of the boys spoke for a minute.

"So, that's an earthquake," said Garven.

"I guess so. Feels creepy, doesn't it?" said Useless.

All the boys nodded.

"I've had enough outdoorsiness for one day," said Garven. "Who wants to ride back to Wilbur with me?"

Everybody did.

There was a little chatter about the earthquake, but soon the excitement was extinguished. There had been no damage so far as anyone could tell, and there were no aftershocks.

That evening, as soon as it was dark, the next in a series of strange Stanford traditions began to take place. From every window and doorway in every residence hall on the campus, bottles and glasses, mirrors and ashtrays began to fly out onto the brick courtyards, eventually covering the spaces with an inch-deep pile of glass shards. When the glassware supply petered out, odds and ends of furniture, notebooks, sofa cushions, pencils, briefcases, and old boxes were added to the litter. The campus looked as if there had been a grenade war in the courtyard of every residence.

There was a cacophony of screaming and yelling, cursing and singing that polluted the air for miles around. Every dram of booze that had been smuggled in all quarter and not already drunk on the sly was now consumed. Some drunk, evidently a returned vet on the GI bill, sang the 101st Airborne Screaming Eagles' song, *Blood on the Risers*, accompanied by a bugler and a guitarist from adjoining dorm rooms. The tune was *Glory, Glory, Hallelujah*:

He was just a rookie trooper,
And he surely shook with fright,
As he checked all his equipment,
And made sure his pack was tight.

"Is everybody happy?" cried the sergeant looking up.
Our hero meekly answered, "Yes," and then they stood him up.
He leaped right out into the blast; his static line unhooked.
HE AIN'T GONNA JUMP NO MORE!

Chorus
Gory, Gory, what a helluva way to die!
Gory, Gory, what a helluva way to die!
He ain't gonna jump no more!
Gory, Gory, what a helluva way to die!

He counted long, he counted hard, he waited for the shock.
He felt the wind, he felt the clouds, he felt the awful drop.
He jerked the cord, the silk spilled out, and wrapped around his legs.
AND HE AIN'T GONNA JUMP NO MORE!

Chorus

The risers wrapped around his neck, connectors cracked his dome.
The lines were snarled and tied in knots around his skinny bones.
The canopy became his shroud. He hurtled to the ground.
AND HE AIN'T GONNA JUMP NO MORE!

Chorus

The days he's lived and loved and laughed kept running through his mind
He thought about the girl back home, the one he'd left behind.
He thought about the medics and wondered what they'd find.
AND HE AIN'T GONNA JUMP NO MORE!

Chorus

The ambulance was on the spot; the jeeps were running wild.
The medics jumped and screamed with glee; they rolled their sleeves and smiled.
For it had been a week or more since last a 'chute had failed.
AND HE AIN'T GONNA JUMP NO MORE!

Chorus

He hit the ground; the sound was "splat!" his blood went spurting high.
His comrades then were heard to say, "A helluva way to die!"
He lay there rolling 'round in the welter of his gore.
AND HE AIN'T GONNA JUMP NO MORE!

Chorus

There was blood upon the risers; there were brains upon the 'chute.
Intestines were a'dangling from his paratrooper's boots.
They picked him up, still in his 'chute, and poured him from his boots.
AND HE AIN'T GONNA JUMP NO MORE!

Chorus

The song was not altogether inappropriate under the circumstances. Morons ran up and down the halls and stairwells; idiots ran out across the glass-shard strewn courtyards in flip-flop sandals, incurring a hundred cuts. Drunken adventurers fell out of second-story windows, and punched-out windows. The dispensary recorded their busiest night ever, treating young invincibles.

Despite his previous vows to lead a trouble-free life, Garven was caught up in the horde of liberated men from both Wilbur Hall, the freshman dorm, and from Stern Hall, the upper class dorm, who poured into the street and laid siege to Branner Hall across the street. The girls of Branner Hall obliged the spirit of bacchanal, throwing down clouds of panties and brassieres and other filmy things. The campus cops called in the Palo Alto police when some of the drunker boys began to batter at Branner Hall's locked doors. It was a night for records; this was the biggest panty raid in Stanford's history.

Garven made it away from all the cops and dodged the debris flying out of the dorm windows, so he could get back to his room. Alan Crowder and Martin Bolechein, caught up in the spirit of frenzied good fellowship, brought over a couple of bottles of Cutty Sark, and the three of them proceeded to get stinking drunk, all past differences extinguished out in the camaraderie of alcohol fumes. None of them knew where Frosty was.

It was the first real drink Garven had ever had. He hated the taste, but after his fourth or fifth shot (glass full), it did not seem so bad. It was his first drunk—his first commode-hugging, gut-emptying drunk. He figured he must have had a great time. He could not remember a thing about the night before when the morning after dawned. When his eyes first opened the next day, he was afraid he was going to die. When he became fully awake, he was afraid he was going to live.

CHAPTER
Four

Devon Upshire, with the light fuzz just beginning to cover the conspicuous and enduring red cross on his scalp, drove back across the Great American Desert to Arizona with Garven. His parents were in Europe, taking the Grand Tour for their twenty-fifth wedding anniversary, and he had no particular reason to return to his home in Florida to rattle around in the large seashore villa alone. Garven had been glad for the company for the drive across the Mojave when Devon had suggested it.

The returning college freshmen spent most of the Christmas holiday vacation in Emmett with Dr. Wilsonhulme, which was boring to Devon. Garven was somehow reluctant to drive up to Cipher; he acted a little embarrassed when the doctor and Devon both pressed him to go home. Garven stalled, or so it seemed, by taking a side trip to Phoenix. He enjoyed the city more than Devon.

"C'mon, Garven, we only have three days left before we have to drive back to the salt mines. You know you have to go see your mother. I'd like to meet her, too. I'd really like to meet the wild Indians and the hillbillies and cowboys you tell all of us about, c'mon," Devon coaxed.

"It's desert rats and cowboys."

"Right, whatever. I want to see the local aborigines, whatever they're called."

The following day, the two boys drove the three hours to Cipher. The main road into town was still not paved. The December Arizona morning was as hot as a Florida summer afternoon, but without the debilitating humidity, when they finally stopped in front of Rachel Carmichael's little house.

"This where you grew up?" Devon asked.

The glance he received from Garven suggested that he may be prying. "Not really. I lived mostly in Phoenix. We just moved to this little dust spot a couple of years ago, when my mom took the job as the town school teacher. She thought it would be an adventure to help the underprivileged. We could have stayed in Phoenix," Garven said.

It seemed like a lot of unnecessary explanation to Devon. Garven had a look of discomfiture bordering on pain as he explained. Devon thought it prudent to drop the subject. "Do we get to meet your Apache friend, and the giant?"

Devon's reference was to the description Garven had given the freshmen back at Madera House of the wild and woolly friends from his past. "I'll find out if they're in town," Garven said, showing more inclination to enthusiasm.

Rachel Carmichael approached the car.

"Hi, Mom," Garven greeted Rachel as she ran the last few steps to her son.

"Oh, Garven, I've missed you. I have been waiting so long," she said with only a hint of her pain at his having never written from California, and because of his choice to stay most of the vacation in Emmett instead of with her in Cipher. She realized that he was no more or less than the typical college boy, egocentric, even selfish. She had cautioned herself not to expect more.

Devon, who was more sensitive to others' moods and feelings, and more attuned to their unspoken communications than Garven, squirmed with minor discomfort when Garven and his mother greeted each other and embraced. Garven seemed stiff and un-giving; his mother, disappointed.

"Oh, Mom, this is my friend from school. Rachel Carmichael, may I present Devon Upshire from Florida?" Garven said and gestured appropriately.

Devon wondered briefly about the discrepancy between the surnames of the mother and son.

"Devon, this is my mother. She teaches school."

Again, the sense of Garven being ill at ease in his hometown and with his mother's position.

"How do you do, Mrs....uh, Carmichael?" Devon said, hoping he had gotten her name right.

"It's my pleasure. I am tickled to meet a friend of Garven's from school. Come on in, you'll roast out here. I have some iced tea made up. Want some?"

"You bet," both boys chimed.

They were dehydrated from the dusty trip across the spectacular wild desert.

Garven phoned Lyle Durche after passing the obligatory period of small talk with his mother. Devon was a more animated conversationalist and seemed more at ease than her own son, Rachel observed.

"Hey, Lyle, do you know who this is?"

"Don't be dumb, big college boy. Sure I do."

It was good to hear the big fellow's voice again. Garven guessed that he did miss some things about this dump of a town. "I brought a friend from school. I want you to meet him. You busy this afternoon? Wanna do something?"

It was Saturday morning.

"Well, I'll check with the secretary and see if I can fit in one more appointment," Lyle answered, as if there could be anything to do in Cipher, Arizona, on a Saturday afternoon except drink beer. He was not one of the active Mormons for whom even that small diversion was denied. "What should we do? Drag main?"

Garven laughed at the old expression of small-town boredom. "Is the wild Indian still around?" he asked. "I don't suppose they have telephones out there yet," he said, referring to the Apache reservation.

"He's still out there. Probably at his auntie's house, drunk as usual. He hasn't killed himself falling off a horse yet, so far as I've heard. Wanna go out and get together with him, Garven?" Lyle asked.

"Sure. How about one o'clock? I have to eat lunch with my mom," Garven replied, oblivious to the small hurt he had inflicted on his mother by suggesting that being with her was a burden.

"Wear your old Levis and kickers. Can your fancy friend from school ride a horse?" Lyle inquired with the slightly derisive tone Westerners reserve for soft Easterners.

"Probably not," said Garven. "We can find some old spavined mare for him, I guess."

"Will he be needin' a side saddle?"

"He's just an Easterner, not a queer. Don't be a jerk, giant."

"See you at one," Lyle said and laughed.

Garven drove the Chevy down the block to where Rachel had told him Lyle was living now that he had moved out of his parents' home. It was one of the dilapidated old places on the Kanesville side of town. Like most Western towns, no matter how tiny, there was an upscale or uptown side of the city, and a less desirable downtown side, the equivalent of the wrong side of the tracks. That side of town in Cipher was generally and politely known as Kanesville because of the several down-at-the-heel jack Mormon Kanes that clustered there. Lyle's having chosen a life of independence and dissolution, his dad kicked him out, and he now roomed in the most degenerated segment of Kanesville with two other professional reprobates from Garven's old class.

The inside of Lyle's apartment was a study in clutter. Where the university dorm rooms Garven and Devon were accustomed to were untidy, even messy, they were not actually dirty because Wilbur Hall employed housekeepers to make the halls and rooms presentable on a weekly basis. Stanford knew better than to leave the option of cleaning entirely to the discretion of a bunch of spoiled seventeen- and eighteen-year-old boys. Lyle's place, on the other hand, was stacked with old magazines, beer bottles, and assorted junk. There was no place to sit. After shoveling a pile aside from the seat of a chair so his guests could sit down, Lyle took note of the real extent of the dirt and spillage, and thought better of his invitation. They remained standing.

"Maid's day off," Lyle mumbled.

"Let's go," said Garven. "I want to see if you can still stay on a horse. You putting on weight with your life of leisure?" He cocked an eyebrow.

Lyle ignored him, and extended his big, callused hand to Devon, "Lyle," he said. "Devon," the pale college student said by way of his own introduction. He had heard that these country folk did not talk much. He took the large, muscular paw in his soft hand and winced as he and Lyle shook hands.

"Don't pay no attention to this shrimp, Devon. He wouldn't know a good day's work if it bit him on the butt," Lyle commented, now cocking his own eyebrow in Garven's direction.

Devon laughed. He liked the big, crude fellow. He guessed that this was what desert rats were like.

He was unprepared for contact with a real desert rat. Edward Sespootch bounded out of his auntie's house as soon as the Chevy negotiated the last few ruts to stop in a cloud of dust. He must have known they were coming for five miles by the plume of red dust that the vehicle kicked up. Edward practically tore the driver's side door off to get at Garven.

"Yahoo!" he yelled in his version of what an Indian war whoop should sound like and half pulled Garven out of the Chev.

"That's what Indians are like, huh?" commented Devon to Lyle.

"Yep."

Edward's hair was in a ponytail that hung down to his waist. His hair was dirty and had an obvious collection of burrs in it. The ponytail was more or less held in place by a thick rubber band. He wore a greasy and food-stained tee shirt with a pack of Camels folded up in the sleeve on his shoulder. His pants were faded and soiled Levis, and the fly was two buttons undone. He did not wear underclothing. His feet were covered with unkempt old cowboy boots that still had the spurs on. He was only a little drunk, but then, it was only two o'clock in the afternoon.

"Hey, Garven. Did they soften you up too much or can you still break a nag?" Edward asked once the initial amenities were past.

"It's only been three months, Edward. I haven't lost the knack yet. Guess my butt is softer though. I take it you have some of your work for me to do."

"Like always," Edward replied and laughed, and threw his arm affectionately over the smaller boy's shoulders. His scarred face was happy and relaxed now that his best town friends were there.

"This here's Garven's friend, Devon. Devon, this criminal here is Ed Sespootch, the nicest Indian as ever cut a throat or scalped a woman," Lyle said.

Edward gave Devon a broad grin, pleased with the comradeship of defamatory introduction. "I like to be called Edward, not 'Ed,' like the giant here always does. The drink has made his memory bad." He was a big man, six feet tall and approaching 190 pounds. Even at nineteen, he was developing a paunch. The ravages of his dissolute life were not yet seriously marking his body, but signs were available if one looked at all carefully. Lyle was six inches taller and fifty-five pounds heavier, the nearest thing to a giant that Cipher had to offer, and the largest man Devon had seen outside of a circus.

"*They must feed that one Gro-pup,*" he thought to himself.

Edward walked over to a wild-eyed, nervous roan gelding in the smallest of his auntie's three corrals. The medium-sized horse had hobbles on all four legs. The gelding snorted at Edward, who, with no hesitation, socked the fool horse on the end of its nose with his heavy fist. The horse reared back its head, and Edward gave it a powerful shove; so it toppled helplessly over on its side, emitting a huge gasp of air. The horse struggled for air but otherwise laid quietly.

"Never give a horse an even break," Edward said and proceeded to put on a bridle with a heavy and sharp tongue depressing bit.

Edward, Lyle, and Garven got a saddle on the bronc and heaved on it until the brute was again standing.

"Real nice horse," Garven said.

"Just the right mount for you, California boy," Edward replied to Garven with a teasing smile, handing him the reins. "Want me to blindfold him?"

"I do," said Garven. "Looks like he needs a muzzle, too."

"Don't worry. He don't bite. Leastwise, he don't bite me. He knows I'll just slug him. You got to get his attention, ya know."

"Does he fall on his back?"

"Nah. He'll give you a pretty hairy ride, but he's not nuts. I think he's gonna be all right," Edward said, speaking professionally.

"Is that an Arabian, Edward?" Devon asked, seeking not to be left out or to be treated as a puny Eastern outsider.

Edward and Lyle gave the college boy an incredulous look.

"Arabian?! Arabians are stupid and little. They are for dudes, Californians, and Easterners...and girls. This here's a real horse, a true Western quarter horse. Quarter horses is the only ones smart enough to cut cattle, dodge snakes, and do what you tell 'em. They're the only horseflesh tough enough to last out in the heat without having to drink every other minute or to hunker down against the cold in the mountains without dyin' because there ain't no barn," Edward expostulated, giving a longer speech than either Garven or Lyle could remember.

He was very opinionated on the subject of horses.

"How about thoroughbreds?" Devon asked Edward, who was flattered by the scholarly looking college boy's genuine interest.

"Too spindly and high strung."

"Appaloosas?"

"Okay. They're really just another kind of quarter horse."

"Peruvians and any of the soft-gaited horses?"

"I seen some in a parade once. They look great! They're big and strong and smart. They do what their rider wants like a good dog. I would love to just get on one to feel its gait. Wouldn't you? I would give my left nut to have one. You gotta be a rich Spaniard or Peruvian or something to own one. I hear they don't even sell them to gringos or other Americans."

"My family has a set of four silver-gray Peruvian high-steppers," Devon said quietly and modestly.

Edward Sespootch looked at Devon with a mixture of awe, longing, and newfound respect. There was no more inclination to joke about soft Easterners, or side saddles, or queers.

"Well, let's get done with this nag's daily ride, Garven, then we can all take a trip up to the red-rock specters," he said, referring to the apparition-shaped rock formations in the nearby hills of the Apache reservation that were once revered as hallowed ancestral ground and were now exploited by Indian and white picnickers.

Garven got on the roan, which stood docilely as he mounted. The hobbles and blindfold had a kind of tranquilizing effect.

Edward slipped the hobbles first, carefully avoiding being kicked, and warned, "Ready? I'm gonna take off his blindfold. He turns into a wild honyock soon's I do."

Garven nodded his head.

Edward softly untied the loose knot on the handkerchief then let it slip, off restoring the beast's vision. It paused for a second like the last sputter of a fuse before the firecracker ignites. The untamed horse then wrenched back its head, reared backwards (taking its forefeet off the ground), and tossed forward as hard as it could, throwing its hind legs into an oblique line, reaching for some distant point in the cloudless azure sky. Garven held on with both hands. None of that rodeo etiquette one-handed grip for him. The horse bolted and bucked, squirmed, reared, and jumped off all four feet. He ran about the small enclosure with a vengeance, trying to scrape Garven and the saddle off. Garven clung like a monkey on a tiger.

"Open the gate," he yelled when the horse began to show some signs of losing steam. "I want to bring this critter back ready for a parade ride."

Edward unlatched the corral wire and swung open the gate. The horse galloped out, his head down, and his ears back, spewing frothy saliva in his excitement. Garven and the horse disappeared over the first hillock behind the Apache hogan, where Edward stayed with his auntie, Fern. The other three boys laughed.

"Let's saddle up our horses; he'll be gone a while. We can put tack on the little black for Garven when he gets back. That rotten horse he's on now will be in no shape to go on a mountain ride."

Each boy saddled his own horse. Edward and Lyle watched out of the corner of their eyes to see if Devon needed any help. He did not. He mounted up and cantered about as if he were part of his horse's flowing musculature, never bumping in and out of his saddle seat. The two locals nodded in acceptance.

Garven returned at two forty-five with a sweat-drenched, slowly ambling horse from whose eyes all of the fire was gone. The horse looked as if he would stagger and fall, but he aimed for the security of his pen with a dogged determination. He leaned against the rail when his saddle, blanket, and bridle were removed. The boys hosed him off.

"Bet you can saddle him and take a ride tomorrow, and in a week, kids can ride him," bragged Garven.

"From the looks of that critter now, I won't take your bet. Good job, partner," said Edward with an appreciative smile.

Garven tipped his hat.

The mountain ride brought back pleasant memories, and cleared the college students' minds of the impediments of stress and the modern world. Lyle and Edward just enjoyed being there and having the satisfaction of knowing that their old friend was not too much of a big shot to get dirty with them still.

It was well after dark when Garven and Devon pulled back into the front of Mrs. Carmichael's house. She had dinner ready, somehow with the accurate timing of a mother's intuition.

"You look filthy and pooped," she said, wrinkling her nose in mock disgust at the young men. "Must have had a good time."

"It was great, Mrs. Carmichael. You should have seen your boy ride. He's something else," enthused Devon.

"Devon comes from a horse family, did you know that, Mom?"

She shook her head.

"He can ride us desert rats into the ground. He's okay."

"You must know that's high praise, Devon. You're in like Flynn, I'd say," Mrs. Carmichael observed.

Devon gave her a satisfied smile. She was a great mom, he thought. Garven was lucky to have so many people who cared about him so much. Devon did not mind coming from a truly rich family, but there were times like this when he would almost have traded the wealth for the affection he saw. Almost.

Garven stayed up after Devon had gone to bed to talk with his mother. She had asked him to, and it had taken more persuasion than she had wished.

"Garven, I've missed talking to you. You were gone for so long at the prep school, now at Stanford. I feel like I'm losing you, that I'm too small town for you, your own mother," she said with a kind of weary sadness.

"I'm not much of a writer or telephoner, sorry, Mom," Garven replied. "I love you, but it's tough fitting into the world where people like Devon live, competing at Stanford, being one of the successful people, you know. Sometimes I just forget; I get too involved."

"Don't get too big for your britches, Garven Aloysius Carmichael Wilsonhulme."

He winced.

"Remember that I know all about you. You will always be my kid, no matter how fancy you get."

"Maybe so, Mom, but I can't always be the kid from Cipher, Arizona. Can you imagine telling some swell that you're from a place named 'Nothing'? I have to break out, or I am never going to be anything. I am going to be a great doctor if I have to kill myself or somebody else in the trying. And I cannot forever be a desert rat. I have to forget this place, or no one important is going to pay attention to me!"

"There are good people here, son," Rachel said softly. "With a lot of good values. You'd do well not to forget them or what they stand for. You will get into trouble if you do."

"You have to be tough nowadays, Mom. Good doesn't always cut it. You have to do what you have to do to compete. Nothing…Nothing is going to stop me!"

His eyes were burning, intense. It was evident that anything and anyone who got in the way of that boy would rue the day, his mother thought.

Garven and Devon drove back to Stanford, leaving Cipher in the wee hours of the morning on Sunday. It was brilliantly sunny but cool from the Mojave to Stanford. The boys were zombies when they finally alighted from Garven's Chevy and fell into their beds still dressed. Registration was more perfunctory since it was required that the students pre-register for the Winter term in advance. Most of Garven's classes were in a series that took the full three-quarters of the academic year and, therefore, the only time-consuming aspect of the process was the obligatory quarterly interview with the premed advisor, Dr. Carter. Garven ignored his titular counselor, Dr. von Tauben, and found that his life was much the better for doing so.

Grantland Kurze from Fort Worth, Texas—"twelve miles and a century away from Dallas," as he described with a laugh—was the richest young man on Garven's floor. Over the Christmas holidays, he had remained busy at Stanford. He was no more active in academics then than he had been during the previous quarter, when school was in session, but rather, he had been employing his abundant talents and more abundant resources to a major endeavor. He installed a broadcast radio station in his room. Fortunately, the homesick New York boy in 12-B had dropped out, which provided Grantland's roommate, Harley Prince, a place to bunk when Grantland took over Harley's half of their room.

This was not some citizen's band receiver and transmitter, nor even merely a ham outfit. Grantland had brought in the paraphernalia of a well-equipped, if modest scale, broadcast radio station, complete with amplifiers, antennae, microphones, boosters, and all the whatnot that, for some reason, he had taken the time to learn about. Garven and the rest of the dorm floor-mates knew next to nothing about the technicalities, but were in awe of the accomplishment.

On Tuesday evening, at the end of the second day of classes, Grantland had scheduled the inaugural broadcast and had sworn each of his friends to absolute secrecy about the exact frequency over which he would broadcast. He had no license, of course. It had never occurred to him to try and get one. They probably would not give him one in the first place, and the application process would require tedium and time consumption that were completely alien to Grantland's personality. He did not let administrative necessities, schoolwork, family obligations, or similar peripherals interfere with his current singleness of purpose.

The broadcast followed a simple format: Grantland talked (mostly sharing his gargantuan fund of obscene jokes and anecdotes), he sang (entirely Texas cowboy ballads), he philosophized (the Texas perspective), and he interviewed (with long, convoluted monologue questions approaching soliloquies, intermingled with brief and to-the-point answers from his nervous dorm fellows).

It was fascinating and exhilarating that first Tuesday night, tinged as it was with the hint of the clandestine underground broadcast. Over the following few days, it became less exciting and, finally, repetitive and stilted as even the prodigious young Texan exhausted his repertoire and began to rehash old material. Grantland became touchy when he encountered Garven or Frosty or one of the other residents of the third floor of Madera House of Wilbur Hall, and they had not been keeping up with his media genius. For his part, Garven took to avoiding Grantland as much as possible since he could not afford the luxury of considering studying and the books, and "that crap"— Grantland's expression—as impediments to his education. Garven was still in premed, the most ferociously competitive arena in existence; and he dared not let down for half an hour, no matter how persuasive Grantland tried to be.

Garven did feel more at home and at ease in his college role. He was more or less accepted by his fellow students, as much as anyone else could be in the intensely egocentric environment. As long as he kept up, his classes became routine and were none too stressful, day to day and week for week. The dating situation was status quo; he was frozen out of the pattern with the presentable Stanford women due to their self-imposed indenturement to the Greek system. He was left with the options of acquiescing to the unpalatable remaining "nice" or "interesting" women, as his mother would diplomatically have described them, or to giving in and accepting the adulations of the star-struck Palo Alto and Menlo Park High School girls. He eschewed the former choice, reasoning correctly that his reputation with his male peers would suffer, and quietly pursued the latter. It did not constitute an inspiring or satisfying social life, and his interest remained pallid. Hormonally, it was satisfactory. He was, therefore, able to concentrate more of his intensity and personal interest on wrestling and found a real measure of satisfaction in the comradeship of his teammates and with his minor accomplishments.

Winter quarter wrestling was all a prelude to the Pacific Coast Conference finals, the championships. Although Garven worked out every afternoon with Hector Trujillo and was regularly beaten, he was competing for the laurels in a higher weight division. He could learn Hector's championship secrets with a little pain to his ego, and without interference to his own pathway. He had taken Hector's advice, and had gotten into aerobic shape with a grueling schedule of running (no longer just jogging, and long past the early days of combined jogging and walking) and skipping rope. Derek had suggested weight training for Garven because the Iowa and Minnesota teams were advocating that kind of buildup strongly. He did not mention to Garven that it might improve his youthful thinness.

Garven gradually became a good wrestler, nothing like Hector, and not as good as Derek or Pete, but a serious and accepted member of the varsity team. Whereas he lost every match during fall quarter and the first two matches in winter quarter, he had met significant opponents and had learned important lessons each time he walked off the mat. He won the next two matches with Oregon and Washington. Hector and Pete had let him know that the Washington 144 pounder was known as the one to beat in his weight division and that the win was a real feather in his cap.

Thus buoyed up, Garven walked out for his first match of the last tournament of the season at the UCLA auditorium. Stanford, UC Berkeley, USC, and College of the Pacific were involved with a sufficiently large number of contestants that each wrestler could accumulate enough wins in this one tournament to qualify for the conference championships. It was Garven's only chance, given his meager record thus far. He had trained fiercely and had given rapt attention to every nuance of advice from Hector. Garven felt ready. This was his moment of athletic truth.

Eugene Eyre from USC strode onto the mat with a decided air of hauteur, accompanied by the practiced yells of an organized cheering section. USC's yellow and muddy maroon colors were everywhere in evidence, and the rich private school was the only one represented by cheerleaders. It was exhilarating to Garven, like big-time athletic events. Too bad the cheering was not for him.

The referee checked their fingernails, making sure they had been trimmed short, gave each wrestler a quick patting down to make sure he had not been greased, then raised and dropped his hand to start the contest. In ancient Greece, wrestlers were the premier athletes, recipients of magnificent prizes, even lifelong wealth, for winning Olympic contests for their cities. In modern America, wrestling, like all individual sports, had become a little-heralded sport, watched by a meager few aficionados and a sprinkling of uninformed girlfriends. For Garven and the other wrestlers, however, a wrestling contest was no less personally momentous than if it had been the finals in the arena at Olympus in 1,000 BC.

Garven assumed a coiled-spring defensive crouch and watched warily as his USC opponent strutted about, probing for an opening. Eugene extended his arms to lock Garven in a standing struggle for the first takedown. As he did so, Garven made a sudden strong upsweep of his own arms. Eugene responded reflexively, bringing his own arms sharply up to grapple with the oncoming limbs. Too late, he realized, that Garven's movement had been a fake, a feint. Garven moved as fast as a mongoose and tackled Eugene, the bigger man, around both knees. Eugene fell backwards onto the mat, with Garven following into a position of advantage on the USC rival.

"Two points, takedown!" the referee shouted to the scorekeeper.

Eugene managed to crawl off the wrestling mat. The ref returned them to the center of the mat. Garven hunched down well behind his opponent in an awkward position for Eugene, who was in the mandatory kneeling position under the Stanford wrestler. Slap! went the ref's hand on the mat in front of them. Eugene burst forward to catch the man above him off guard, spreading his muscular legs to initiate a rise to the standing position. That move was exactly what Garven had been waiting for. He dropped back and enveloped the USC wrestler's legs, and used his own momentum to turn him onto his back. Like an irrepressible bulldog, Garven inched his way up Eugene's body from the thighs to the abdomen, to the chest, to the neck as Eugene flailed and bucked beneath him to prevent being held on his back and then, even more violently, to prevent being pinned. Garven kept his forehead pressed into the taller opponent's upper chest and put a figure-four leg lock around the long thighs. The more Eugene fought, the more he became entangled in the relentless onslaught of arms and legs of his wiry rival.

Eugene, in desperation, reached obliquely over Garven's back to force his own body to turn into the prone position. Garven felt the straining shift beneath him and took advantage of the other contestant's momentarily off-balance and vulnerable position. He threw his left arm backwards over Eugene's neck and forced it behind the USC athlete. It was like being enwrapped in the coils of a boa constrictor. The more Eugene writhed, the more he allowed Garven's coils to become fixed around him. He knew he was pinned unless the time ran out. He was able to see the wall clock on one of his moves—forty-two seconds remaining.

The USC wrestler began squirming and scooting for all he was worth to move himself off the mat to cause a mandatory return to the wrestler's position in the middle of the mat. He would get three points against him for being in a near pin, but at least he could keep going in the match and could hopefully catch up. He felt as if the whole school were watching, alumni and all. Thirty seconds.

Garven hung on, pressing his strong and slippery opponent down into the mat. Eugene concentrated all his courage, strength, energy into one last effort to bring himself into a neck bridge and to force himself and Garven off the edge of the mat. He was succeeding. But he forgot a fundamental. As he pushed and strained, he neglected to think about what his shoulders were doing. They were molded flat onto the mat.

The referee counted the standard, "one, two," to himself, with Eugene still concentrating on the edge of the mat. Nine seconds to go in the match. "Three," the ref's lips moved, and the flat of his palm slapped the mat with the crack of a whip. It was like a grenade going off in Eugene's ear. He was pinned, pinned! He had never been pinned. The ignominy of that realization washed over him. The skinny nobody from Stanford had pinned him.

Garven was oblivious to the cheers and hoots. He had won his first critical match. Eugene was mortified and could hear every voice individually. He could not raise his eyes when the ref lifted Garven's arm in the victory sign.

In the third period of his second match, Garven's opponent from Cal Pacific forced his forehead down onto the back of Garven's head as Garven reared back to avoid a half-Nelson In a miscalculation of the force, speed, and angulation of the Stanford student's occiput, the Cal Pacific wrestler's lower lip was where his forehead should have been. The lip centered between the back rushing bony skull and the knife-edges of his lower teeth. The lip split like an orange peel, tearing two small arteries apart. An astonishing amount of blood erupted from the cut and onto Garven's back. With his own vigorous movements, the blood from Garven's opponent spattered in wide arcs around the mat. It happened so rapidly that there was no pain. Garven thought the sticky warmness was just sweat. Both young men were astonished when the referee stopped the match abruptly. Garven won the match by default. They had been tied on points up until the injury.

He won his third match on points, a grueling and debilitating contest. Garven, Pete, Derek, and Hector were all going to be in the finals for the tournament that night. Hector's season record already guaranteed him a spot in the conference finals, and Pete would probably make it as well even if he lost on points. A win by Garven and Derek would put the four men in the all-important finals and would be the first time that Stanford would make a serious showing. Even with all four of them succeeding, they would not constitute a large enough team to garner the team championship honors, but still, they would be a power to reckon with. It was a heady feeling.

Pete won his match and took the 128-pound title in a down-to the-last-second high point contest. He showed no pretense of modesty and whooped his success in an unseemly fashion that brought censorious looks and comments from the judges. He did not really care, but restrained himself to avoid some sort of reaction that would jeopardize himself or his team. Hector won the 136-pound class handily by a pin in the third period and became not only the champion in his class, but the tournament's grand champion by unanimous vote of the judges.

It was Garven's turn to defend the honor of the Stanford Indians. His mouth was dry, and he felt light-headed from a combination of tiredness and over-excitement as he walked onto his corner of the mat for the championship contest. The worse he could do was to get second place, but he really did not want to think of that. Going to the all-conference finals in his first year would be great. It would give him status. He could use some of that.

Slade Thompson, a junior from UC Berkeley, was to the 144-pound class of the PCAC what Hector Trujillo of Stanford was to the 136-pound class—two time all-conference champion and likely to do it a third time. Garven tried not to think of that. What he thought of most was how big Slade was. This was ridiculous. That guy could not be just 144 pounds. He was taller, bulkier, and bigger. Garven neglected the detail that he, at 137 pounds, should have been wrestling in the division below where he was matched at the moment. He told himself that he was just nervous and was exaggerating the size of his opponent. He felt cold even though he had warmed up for ten minutes.

Slade smiled at him when the ref had them shake hands. Why did he do that? It had not been a condescending smile, or a mocking smile, or a smug smile. It had been friendly. Garven thought that he hated him.

"Good luck, Garven," Slade said as they separated.

Now Garven really hated him. What did he mean by that?

Garven watched intently as the ref's hand went up. He tensed every muscle in his entire body, and when the ref's hand dropped, he sprang like a predator cat straight at Slade Thompson's legs. Slade had been in a match or two before, and he threw his legs out behind himself; so Garven ended up with his arms fully extended and his hands ineffectually clasping Slade's waist. Slade was stretched out over Garven's exposed back. His wrestler's kinesthetic sense told Garven that this was not good, not good at all. In the next second, Garven found Slade behind him and lifting his body off the floor. It is difficult to push or defend when your feet are not on the floor. In the next second, Garven was kneeling on the mat with Slade looming over him, holding him in the wrestler's standard floor position. Garven was beginning to feel tired even though the two men were only five seconds into the match. Two points, takedown.

Slade's next three points came from a predicament; he got Garven in a completely controlled position but was not able to convert that into a pinning threat before the ref called them back to the middle of the mat. Five to nothing with less than thirty seconds elapsed in the contest. Garven was not feeling good.

Slade got one more point for riding time before the end of the first period, because he was on top and in control of Garven through the whole period. The only bright spot in the dismal first period came when the referee chided Slade for stalling, and even that was offset by a similar criticism directed at Garven with ten seconds left. Six to nothing. Garven felt like he might as well have not even come for all the effectiveness he was demonstrating. This UC Berkeley junior was very good. Reminiscent of Hector. Too reminiscent.

Garven took the down position in the second period when he won the coin toss. He really did not feel like doing that. He very much wanted to be on top for a change, but every wrestling dictum started with the admonition to start on the bottom when it was your choice. *What did they know?* thought Garven churlishly as he struggled, sweated, and strained under the indefatigable and relentless Slade Thompson.

Garven was too busy to hate the guy, but was fully determined to catch up on his rancor when things quieted down.

The ref got after Slade for not trying to pin his opponent, for stalling. Slade had been killing himself to pin the skinny little snake from Stanford. He rolled his eyes back in his head involuntarily, indicating what he thought of the man's criticism and admonition.

"One point," snapped the ref.

Slade controlled himself from protesting.

Six to one with twenty-eight seconds to go in the second period. Garven, smashed down there under the sweaty and chafing abrasiveness of the wrestler controlling him, took scant pleasure in the little score. The ref probably took pity on him. At least he was not going to be skunked; that was something.

The third and final three-minute period started with a little calisthenics dance by the chipper Slade Thompson, demonstrating his disgustingly superb fitness. Garven hoped he did not look as ashen as he felt. It was all he could do to remain conscious. How on earth could Slade jump around like that after all the work he had done up there on top of Garven trying to pin him and all? Garven hated the guy.

The ref slapped the mat, and Slade, who was on the bottom this time, tried a front tumbling roll-out to get a two-point break out. For once, he miscalculated. Hector had done that to Garven a dozen times in practice, and Garven had grown vigilant. To his chagrin, Slade rolled only one-quarter of the way forward before he felt himself being gathered into an uncomfortable ball by Garven. Worse, his shoulders were on the mat. Garven gave every ounce of energy and strength he had to take advantage of this fortunate circumstance. He held on for dear life, but it was a pretty clumsy hold. It was not enough to get the pin because Slade wiggled and thrashed until one shoulder was off the mat; then he finally twisted until he got himself back down on the mat in the safe and supine position. Three-point near pin. Score six to four in UC Berkeley's favor. Time remaining: one minute and forty-two seconds.

Garven struggled to get a half-Nelson to force Slade forward into a roll again, to get a figure four and double arm bar, and to turn Slade over to get a full-body press. He was pleased that the ref did not think he was stalling for not trying to work for a pin, but he was making no progress towards getting the vital additional points that would at least tie up the match. Thirty-one seconds to go. One point for riding time! Score: six to five. Bless the ref's little timepiece.

At this point, it occurred to Garven that the worst thing that could happen was for them to be tied at the end of this period and to have to go into overtime. He did not think he could stand to see Slade—the jerk—jump up and down and demonstrate how great he felt again. He decided to go all out. He pushed, pulled, strained. He let his weight ease off a little to invite Slade to make a rash move. Slade had been there before, Garven realized. He did not make rash moves. Garven guessed it had to be his turn to make a rash move. Well, at least to do something to get a couple of points. Twelve seconds left.

Garven suddenly let go of his grip on Slade's shoulders and upper back. He threw his weight down to Slade's center and drove into the Berkeley wrestler's hips and buttocks to flip him over. To Garven's delight, Slade flipped over. To his horror, Slade flipped again, away from Garven's grasp and was on his feet with Garven clawing at the departing thighs, then the legs, then the feet, then the air. One point getaway. Seven to five, favor Berkeley. Seven seconds remaining.

Garven leaped to a crouch then hurled himself like a spear at Slade, presuming to bowl him over by shear brute force. It took more than Garven had. He was so completely worn out that he was undoubtedly slower than usual. Slade was as fast as usual and was not there when Garven speared at his waist. He deftly stepped away and stayed away for the remaining two seconds. Berkeley seven, Stanford five. Thompson in the conference finals; Wilsonhulme out of them. Thompson jubilant but gracious. Wilsonhulme exhausted and malevolent, feeling very ungracious.

The referee held up Slade's arm, and Slade, in a gesture of magnanimity, held up Garven's arm as well, and said perfectly genuinely, "Great match, Garven! You are a superb wrestler! Good luck next year!"

Garven smiled in what he presumed appeared more like a snarl, said nothing, sure that he did not have breath enough left to speak right out loud, and thought, "Jeez, what a jerk. I hate this guy."

Garven's season was over.

CHAPTER
Five

Despite the setback to his climbing self-esteem afforded by the wrestling tournament, and once he had a few days to get the brooding out of his system, Garven took inventory of his activities, and found himself generally on the positive side. Foremost, he was at the top of all of his classes, not just getting the essential A that would put him in medical school. He had even been approached by the biology professor to tutor one of the seniors who was struggling desperately to maintain a passing grade while he starred on the first winning basketball team in Stanford's history. He was having a few decent dates with some good-looking cheerleaders from Palo Alto High, occasioned by his varsity jock status. There was even a bit more hormonal relief. His friendships with Devon and Frosty were firm and assuring. He was on a reasonably cordial basis with his old roommate, Alan Crowder, who had agreed, after their commode-hugging drunk together at the end of fall quarter, to let bygones be bygones.

Billy Jones, the basketball player, had selected Garven for his tutor because he was a freshman and would be unlikely to give a senior any lip, and because he was a fellow jock who would understand the situation. He sat close enough to Garven in biology to see how well the skinny white kid did. Billy held two very important distinctions that made his success at Stanford of paramount importance to the administration and therefore to the faculty. He was their star basketball player—their first star—and would undoubtedly lead them to the Pacific Coast Conference championship they had coveted ever since Leland Stanford had founded his school. He was a Negro. Billy Jones was the first Negro in Stanford's history to excel on a major sports team, and the school was proud to demonstrate their progressiveness by not only having the young man be on their team, but to be given every aid to his succeeding. The university was on the cutting edge in that regard. There were, in fact, very few Negro seniors in any of the top universities of the country. Only after the end of World War II, when the troops came back from overseas, with their grateful government's educational compensation papers—the GI Bill—in hand, were the nation and the nation's universities' collective consciences pricked enough to admit the men who had given so much to the nation, irrespective of their color. That feeling was nowhere near universal. No Southern university admitted a Negro to sit alongside a Caucasian. They were firmly entrenched in the new fiction of separate but equal to replace the old publicly hallowed inequities—the Jim Crow laws.

Considerable exceptions had been made in accepting Billy Jones to Stanford. His SAT scores were forty points below the lowest entrant in his class, and his grades had been abysmal at his high school in Watts, California, the rotten core of racist ghettoism in Los Angeles County. The prospect of bringing a fine young man (he was all of that) out of the endless cycle of poverty, ignorance, and violence was exciting and invigorating to the intellectual liberals at Stanford, who were before their time in their enthusiasm to help the courteous and promising student. It did not hurt that he was the greatest basketball player Los Angeles had ever produced. Players of Billy's race had been playing on LA high school varsity teams for three years now.

Billy had struggled with his academics, and his professors with their consciences to keep the young man in the necessary C's to keep him on the team for the full four seasons. He had attempted to fill his biology requirements twice before, and the NCAA was now insisting that athletes, including Billy Jones, got out of the underwater basket-weaving majors and into honest courses. He had to get through biology.

Garven agreed to tutor him. How hard could it be to get the guy a C? he reasoned. Billy was unfailingly polite, reasonable, and diligent after a fashion. That was the fashion of big-time athletes, not the standards of leave-no-wounded that permeated the thinking of the premed students when it came to academic competition. Billy could not get biology, however. Garven was afraid he would go nuts. Billy could sit and listen to a recitation of the contents of the mammalian cell, or the classification of the invertebrates for two hours straight, and when asked to repeat what Garven had told him, to remember even one thing, he would smile and shrug, and confess that he could not. He was neither stupid nor lazy, but he was as nearly totally disinterested as a human being could be in the subject. No one had convinced him that this had any bearing on his only goal—to be one of the first Negro players in the National Basketball Association.

"Billy," Garven said more than once, "I have been told by the high kahunas of the athletic department and the biology department and by Coach Kinderson that you cannot get into the NBA if you don't graduate from college. You won't graduate unless you pass biology. You won't pass biology unless you pass this midterm. You won't pass this midterm unless you learn this stuff right here. Ergo, you have to learn this biology stuff."

"Okay," Billy said more than once. "Let's get to work."

Garven told the coach and the biology professor that they were not going to make it. Billy would not be able to pass the test with any amount of tutelage.

The coach looked very thoughtful about this revelation and said, "Garven, we appreciate your efforts. Billy and you have become friends, and he likes you a lot. Hold on there, and I'll see if I can't get a little something extra for you two."

The little something extra was provided in a subtle way, in sort of the mysterious way God works His wonders to perform. Billy was at Stanford on a stipend known as "working scholarship," which operated on the NCAA requirement that the student athlete was to earn his or her upkeep by having a job on campus. All of the jocks on scholarship worked as custodians at the student union building, making sure that the brass doorknobs and casings were the best polished metal on the planet. To their credit, the seventy-five or so thus employed maintained the doorknobs at a sheen and luster to compete with the platinum-iridium length standard bar at the Bureau of Standards in Washington DC. Shortly after Garven's conversation, some of the athletes were reassigned, and the doorknobs at the biology building began to take on a similar polish. In order to accomplish their tasks, the athletes had to have a set of master keys to the offices. Naturally.

Garven did not question how, but one day during the week prior to the biology midterm, Billy Jones presented himself at their regular evening study session with a facsimile of the upcoming test. Not an old test to review, but the new test to learn. It was to be Garven's test as well, so he did not create any squawk. Out went the books, and the lectures, and the outlines. The two earnest young athletes grilled endlessly on the questions and on the answers. The problem of the answers was simplified by the fact that the test was in the new multiple guess form. All they had to master was a memory of A, B, C, or D.

Billy got a decent C on the midterm. And on the final, for that matter. Garven got an A on both and a small stipend for being the tutor. He figured it was the best job he had ever had.

Billy told Garven, "Thanks. White guys have not treated me all that great, to tell you the truth, Garven," he said. "But you and I are friends. I don't even think of you as a white guy."

Garven said, "Billy, you're the first black guy I ever knew. You're okay. Even when you get to be a rich and famous pro, I hope you will remember your old bud back at Stanford."

"Sure, Garven. But I have to tell you something. I hope you don't take this the wrong way. My people don't like to be called blacks. That's kind of demeaning, you know, from the old slave days and the reconstruction period. It's like African, or African-American. We're not fond of any of those terms, which suggest that we're second-class citizens, or inferior, or not quite Americans. I'm a Negro and proud of it, but if I could be what I wanted, I'd just be an American. That make sense to you?"

"Partly," observed Garven. "You call us whites, and it doesn't seem like a dirty word. I guess I don't quite get why 'black' is so bad. Nobody with a brain has to be told why those other words are bad. They're just like someone was spitting on you.

"'Black' and 'African-American' are like that, only more subtle. 'Negro' has dignity. It's a proud word for a proud people."

"If I have to describe you, it'll be what you want. 'Friend' ought to be enough," Garven said.

"For me, too. Now, you little honkey, I've got to get to practice."

Both young men laughed as Garven headed out the door for his room.

Grantland Kurze's radio station, which he dubbed WSEX, operated for two months, almost to the day. Garven was in Grantland's room, sharing a bag of French fries with the boisterous Texan, when they heard the thud of footsteps coming down the wood-floored hallway. There were several men at least, and they sounded as if they were marching. The footfalls became progressively louder until it was apparent that the men were either in front of Grantland's door or at one door on either side of his. Grantland gestured to Garven to see what was going on, and Garven unrolled himself from his easy chair and took two steps towards the door.

The door then burst open. Garven wondered if the men had bothered to use the knob; they certainly had not knocked like gentlemen.

"FCC!" the foremost of the three men in near-identical three-piece blue suits said so loudly that Garven wondered if the man thought he and Grantland were deaf. He spoke more quietly, deciding apparently that it was not necessary to demonstrate full enthusiasm at this point. "You are under arrest!" he said.

"What's FCC?" asked Garven of no one in particular.

"Who's under arrest?" asked Grantland.

"You two," one of the suits said flatly.

"What for?" asked Grantland with genuine puzzlement.

"Me?" asked Garven.

"This your broadcasting equipment, Sir?" asked the first agent. "We are federal agents."

Garven did not like the sound of *that*.

"It's mine," said Grantland. "What's the problem?"

"I didn't make myself clear. We are agents of the Federal Communications Commission, and we are here investigating complaints filed against you, Sir."

"What kind of complaints?" asked Grantland, not looking quite as ingenuous as before.

"We'll ask the questions. Could you produce your FCC broadcasters license, please, Sir?"

"License? What do I need a license for? I'm just a kid horsing around with a little equipment here in my dorm room. What am I hurting? For that matter, I don't get any money for this. Why should I need a license?"

From his practice of secrecy throughout the two months of operation of his home-grown radio station, Garven suspected that Grantland was not nearly as naive as he was letting on. He kept his mouth shut, however, and made himself as inconspicuous as possible in the small room.

"Look, kid. We can do without the ignorant hick routine, okay? Anybody who can come up with this setup and broadcast falls out of that category automatically; so, we took two months to triangulate your position and to monitor the content of your transmissions. You're not all that dumb. I think you know perfectly well that you need an FCC license to operate a station. The local radio stations are screaming their heads off."

"Oh," said Grantland, chastened. "I'm really sorry, officer. I mean, I certainly didn't mean to do anybody any harm."

"You can cut that crap, too. Save it for somebody who cares. We have sixty hours of eight-track tapes of your foul mouth."

"What are you going to do to me?"

"I'll tell you what, kid. It's your lucky day since you didn't get any gain from this operation. The other stations, the real ones, are willing not to press charges if you cease and desist today. Not another word, understand?"

"Okay, all right, whatever you say, officer," Grantland said in his most exaggeratedly cooperative manner.

Garven was very near the door.

"This stuff goes now, right now. Get rid of it tonight. Get the shrimp to help you. I'll be back first thing tomorrow to check on you."

Shrimp?! Garven took offense. Silently. He wisely figured it was better to be obscure where the feds were concerned, even at the expense of his ego. He had learned from his dad and from the other fathers at Burton-Cagle that that was a good principle for life in the United States.

Grantland got the boys on the floor to help pack the stuff and to get it into a U-Haul he rented the first thing the following morning. He hired a bonded teamster from up in San Jose to drive the equipment to Texas. That alone must have cost a small fortune. There were no more hassles from the FCC agents once they saw the evidence of Grantland's good-faith efforts. Garven and the rest of the dorm-mates kept out of the whole affair. Garven made a mental note to keep up with Grantland Kurze during college and after. It couldn't hurt to have a friend with that kind of bucks.

During winter quarter, Garven wrote Lyle and Edward twice each and called each of them twice. He called Dr. Wilsonhulme four times. He wrote his mother once. It was a very busy time, difficult to keep up with everything, he reckoned. He got straight A's again. The only minor difficulty he had with his class work at all occurred in biology lab, when the assignment was to dissect out the nervous system of an earthworm. It was frustrating business because the structures were ill-defined and primitive, hardly recognizable as anything but a few irregular strings. Garven must have been tired and feeling cranky when he told the lab instructor that he could not find the nervous system because there was all of this "crap" in the way. She was a true enthusiast for her chosen career in invertebrate biology and did not take the reference kindly.

"That *is* the nervous system," she had said icily.

It took weeks to warm her back up.

Garven, Frosty, Derek van Leventhal, and David Applegate got jobs between quarters in San Francisco as furniture movers in Moose Larimer's dad's moving company. It was good money, and Garven liked having his own earned funds; so, he did not have to make so many requests of his dad in Arizona. Although Garven was small, his pound for pound strength was enough to ensure that he could carry his part of the load, and he had the respect of the other laborers on the job despite their built-in prejudice over his college-boy status. Moose, although far bigger and stronger than any of his friends, was being groomed as an executive of the company, and rarely ever turned his hand at labor work. He joined his friends at lunch on the job on the days they worked in the warehouse.

Garven became fast friends with the young men of the Stanford crew in that interim break. He was becoming more and more convinced of the value of the social connections he was making, a valuable future asset he was sure, just like Dr. Wilsonhulme had said when he was extolling the virtues of a Stanford education. Garven was actually looking forward to spring quarter when March 20 arrived.

CHAPTER
Six

Freshman spring quarter was little different from winter quarter for Garven, except that he no longer had wrestling to occupy him. That made the academic grind all that easier, and his grades remained all A's, keeping him in a fully competitive position for his goal of getting into medical school. He was on track for possible acceptance in three years instead of four. He wrote once again to his mother, explaining to Rachel that he was going to work on a large fishing trawler between Seattle and Ketchikan, Alaska, with a couple of his friends. He was going with Frosty McTavish and Peter Barnhienel. He had tried to get Lyle and Edward to go along, too, but they were reluctant to leave the old hometown, he explained.

When he got back to the Stanford campus in time to register to begin his second year of premed, Garven was tanned, work-hardened, and felt independent, with a $2,000 nest egg in his bank savings account earning three percent. He was bored to distraction and ready to get his mind back to work. Garven had his year and his work cut out for him with all series classes to fill in the premed requirements. He had the premed math series—college algebra, spherical geometry, and trigonometry; the second-year chemistry series—organic, quantitative, and biochemistry; the American and English literature course; and the core liberal arts classes—psychology, philosophy, art history, and his second-year German language series. Sixteen or eighteen hours a quarter. The only saving grace was that he could finish his requirements in three instead of four years at this pace and would be able to get accepted into med school and skip the useless senior year. Garven thought he would like to come back to school another time when he did not have to get grades, so he could actually learn something.

But for now, he had to get grades. He felt like a monkey at a typewriter when it came to math. He could barely manage to use his slide rule. Garven knew he had to concentrate the hardest on math—to waste his time on a subject that he would never use in med school or as a doctor. All of the guys in school and all of the doctors he knew had told him so. Still, he had to get all the circles on his ticket punched; so he could get accepted to a med school someplace. He made up his mind to hunker down and to do what was necessary.

College algebra was the personification of boredom. The numbers and symbols meant next to nothing to Garven. His only satisfaction was that he would not have to take calculus. If the symbols—the Xs and Ys of algebra—seemed foreign to a young man who would have been content to settle for simple Arabic numerals, and the simpler the better, the symbols of calculus were more like Martian than anything. Garven was grateful for the small favor that he did not have to wreck his GPA by getting into the advanced math. For him, advanced math consisted of any number more than nine.

On the first day in college algebra class, the professor (graduate student) explained, "In this course, we shall consider algebra in the narrow sense of the mathematics of ordinary complex numbers, or real numbers, of rational numbers and integers. Don't get lost in the broader definitions of algebra as a general mathematical discipline or of the pseudo-math of logic, quaternions, relations, or of groups."

Garven was already lost, and he had not been in the class for five minutes. The only thing he had understood so far was the teacher's name, because the lady had had the foresight to write it on the blackboard.

"So, first, we will consider the properties of assemblages—groups with members. This is a more difficult subject than meets the eye on first glance."

Garven was sure it would be.

"There are paradoxes about assemblages—take, for example, the assemblage of groups that do not have any members, like pigs that fly, or the assemblage of groups that have only one member, like a particular Raphaelean statue. In the first case, we can select a symbol like Z to represent all members of the group, and the group is $g\,Z$, and X can represent our statue in the second example. Our group of statues, of which we only have one, can be designated as gX in the symbolism of A. Is that clear thus far?"

"*So this is college algebra,*" thought Garven in a state of depression.

"Every two classes determine one or more groups. Say we have pigs that can fly made into statues by Raphael. In certain select instances, we would then have gZX, don't you see?"

Garven took the information down in his notes. "*You could never tell what would come in handy from a college education,*" he moaned to himself. "*Pigs that fly being made into statues by Raphael certainly seemed like something worth committing to memory.*"

He looked at his watch: fifty-five more minutes left in the class.

"Now, for the more pragmatic concept of similarity. In a properly equipped high school, every student has a ballpoint pen. Let us consider the circumstance wherein all production at the pen factory ceases at the point in the manufacturing process, which leaves every student with exactly one pen. It is clear, therefore, that the class of pens, and the class of students, stand in a special, intimate, mutual relation that can be considered one or one correspondence or similarity. We could express that fact as there are as many pens as there are students."

That seemed pretty clear to Garven. He did not care a whit, but it was clear.

"Observe that this identity in number can be defined prior to and entirely independently of number itself. We can call this assemblage B for clarity's sake."

That was less clear. There were fifty-two class-time minutes left. Garven shook his watch to be sure it was still functioning. Garven knocked the heel of his palm against his forehead to jump-start the neurons.

"Hereafter, we shall represent cardinal numbers by the letters of the Greek alphabet, a, b, c, d, e, f, g, h, and so forth."

That seemed like the right choice of alphabets to Garven, all right.

"And the cardinal number of our assemblage B then is represented by the symbol NcB. It is easily shown that our ordinary 0 is gX; 1 is $NcgX$, and so forth."

Garven took notes so he could memorize. He knew he had no chance of understanding. Forty-eight minutes. Garven shook his watch again, sure it had stopped. The second hand was still circumnavigating with glacial celerity.

The instructor checked her notes, then continued. "Zermelos's axiom affords proof that all assemblages are either similar to one of their own parts or finite in the ordinary sense of having one of the natural numbers as their cardinal numbers."

Garven let his mind wander enough to think this stuff was more mysterious than Catholicism's Nicene Creed. He knew that it was fatal to let his mind go afield; he might miss a tidbit for a test. He hung on through the remainder of the lecture on the theory of numbers, and was not heartened by the closing statement by the graduate student that there would be more on the theory in the days to come.

Garven wondered what more there could be since they had covered all the really interesting stuff like "the concept of greater and less among cardinal numbers (a > b if a is the cardinal number of some class C, which contains a part k, of which b is the cardinal number, and if the converse relation does not exist), addition (apples plus oranges equals oranges plus apples, or in other words, that the operation of addition, when performed on any two cardinal numbers, finite or infinite, is commutative, and in fact, is associative, as well), natural numbers (those numbers that are amenable to the method of mathematics according to the definition of Alfred North Whitehead and Bertrand Russell—the validity of the method of mathematical induction as applied to the natural numbers rests neither on an axiom nor on a theorem, but on the definition of the natural numbers), multiplication (if there are c apple fruits and d orange fruits in basket, then there are c X d fruits in the complete basket, i.e., the product cd is the number of couples of c and d formed by selecting a term from class c and then selecting a member of class d), involution, integers with sign, and extension of the number concept, with the graduate student emphasizing that regular algebra would soon be seen to be a desideratum."

That was all one sentence! Garven wrote it all down, knowing that he would have to get something of a transliteration some time to be able even to memorize the junk he had just heard. Like, what was a desideratum? And who cared? It made his head hurt.

Algebra was his last class of the day, and he was full of repressed energy when he dressed for wrestling that afternoon. It made no difference that his first match was two months away; Garven was the very model of enthusiasm that day, and every Monday, Wednesday, and Friday—the days on which his math classes were scheduled throughout autumn and winter quarters. At nineteen, he was a little bigger and stronger, and had matured in his sport with the experience of one year behind him. He now weighed 142 pounds, still able to make the weight in his class without dieting. What had seemed like pain and work the previous year was more routine and even pleasurable in his sophomore year in the sport. Garven could feel the tensions and confusions of the day disappearing as he ran his five miles, skipped rope for ten minutes, lifted weights, and wrestled for an hour. His muscles ached and felt heavy; he was weary. He felt great. It would be forty-eight hours before he had to endure another math day.

Day two of quarter one of year two at Stanford started at seven forty-five in the morning, with his psychology lecture course. There was also to be a lab, but that was only once a week on Thursdays. For the life of him, Garven could not imagine what there could be in a lab. He determined to have a positive attitude, however, consoling himself that everyone applying to medical school had to go through it.

"Psychology is the scientific study of mind and behavior," Garven was told by Johnathon Paternost Simpkins, professor and chairman of the Department of Psychology of Stanford University, "an *endowed* chair," the professor emphasized. "While it is concerned with the mental or behavioral characteristics of groups, this introductory course will be limited to the underlying causes of descriptions of the behavior of individuals," Professor Simpkins intoned.

The professor was a most distinguished and imperious man, unapproachable, urbane, erudite, a leading authority—he let slip—and professorial.

"*As full of crap as a Christmas goose,*" thought Garven.

Professor Simpkins was firmly rooted in psychoanalysis and had an especially keen interest in hypnosis for its use in clinical psychology. His laboratory interest was in hypnosis, and he was known to be ever on the lookout for students to be subjects of his experiments. "The assignment for today, and for every day, for that matter, will be to learn the precise meaning of the psychological vocabulary. If we do not, as scientists, use the same terms and use them with precision, we cannot communicate our findings, our patient data, nor can we effectively influence our patients. You will be tested on exact definitions, and here, I mean word for word from the textbook I authored. Your list today deals with the subject matter of modern psychology: sensation perception, striving faculties, emotion, innate patterns, learning, thinking, memory, personality, and behavioral pathology, although the latter subject will be dealt with in depth only by those selected to continue into the upperclass level. The information contained in that study is too sensitive for the general student."

Garven knew he had to get into that upper-level set of classes; all the premeds did. He would have to act enthusiastic, which would be a considerable stretch.

"On Mount Parnassus in Greece, Phoebus Apollo built the famous Temple of Delphi. On one of its walls is inscribed the underlying precept of psychology, 'Know Thyself,'" Professor Simpkins continued. He was reading from his notes, from the notes he had perfected for his opening lecture over an eighteen-year career of lecturing. He took pains to hide the fact that he was reading. "We are engaged, not in philosophy, which became outmoded with the advent of the experimental method, but in a science that makes great and steady advances firmly founded in fact, not fancy, in order that we may, indeed, 'know' ourselves. To a limited extent, we will consider in this class the sensory perceptions of olfaction, vision, audition, somatosensis, kinesthesis, and proprioception, and the neuroanatomy underlying them. I expect you to be able to define each and every one of these terms by Wednesday. I will call upon you at random. Preparation is the key to learning, and your responses in class will by a significant determinate of your activity and enthusiasm. And will count heavily at grade time."

Garven's ears perked up.

The professor went on. "We will stick to the definable striving faculties. Secondary or acquired faculties include social dominance, conformity, obedience, religiosity—all learned phenomena. Because of his seminal contributions, we will spend a considerable emphasis on the late Sigmund Freud's work on acquired behaviors.

"We will learn about intelligence, particularly as defined by our own Stanford Intelligence Quotient evaluation—the IQ, as it has come to be known. We will separate feelings, which are temporary and weak, from emotions, which are longer lasting and powerful, more influential of behavior. We will study the phenomenon of learning—Pavlov's dog and the like. My own special interest is in mental subjective activity, conscious, preconscious, and unconscious awareness—the dynamics of personality."

Garven decided that would be his interest as well.

"A word about the laboratory," Dr. Simpkins said, looking at his watch since the hour was nearly over. "You may sign up on the sheets posted outside this hall for one of the major fields of research and for one specific ongoing faculty experiment. That will occupy time outside regular class and lab time."

There was a sub rosa groan from the two hundred students in the lecture class.

Ignoring the collective rudeness, Dr. Simpkins concluded by outlining the regular series of laboratory study—the work with fighting rats, the experiments with operant conditioning of dogs and cats, the emerging field of electronics in psychology, and the study of monkeys with various brain extirpations—done at the medical school neurosurgical labs. "You have your reading assignments, and today's list of definitions. You may sign up for your lab section anytime this week and may have two weeks to commit yourself to one of the special faculty projects. A full scholarly report will be expected at quarter's end on that project, and it will determine one-fourth of your grade.

There will be a second paper required on a topic of your choice, subject to the approval of your faculty advisor. Good day."He stepped promptly down from the raised podium and exited without taking questions, underscoring his personal importance and the exactitude of his schedule.

Garven raced the forty or so other premed students into the hallway, found the special assignments sheets, and scribbled his name in ink under Dr. Simpkins's "Hypnosis Project." He knew better than to use a pencil that could be erased by a fellow earnest premed student coming up behind him and discovering that he was too late to sign in for the professor's pet project.

After Organic Chem 201 lecture, Garven had only to sign up for his lab section, then he was free for the rest of the day until his three-thirty philosophy lecture. He had tried to get the eight-thirty lecture by Dr. Monson, the popular head of the department, but the course was filled up at that hour. That time would have given him three days a week when he would be through with classes before noon. There were too many students at Stanford, Garven decided, certainly too many premedders. He presumed—hoped—the administration would hold the student body total down to six thousand to maintain quality.

Grantland Kurze met Garven at the new eating hall by the student union. He looked bored.

"Garven, got anythin' goin'?" he asked.

"What do you mean? Like classes? That sort of stuff?"

"You know perfectly well what I mean. Like the car on the church tower—that sort of stuff. Classes? Who goes to classes?"

"Premedders, for one group. We haven't got time for all that undergraduate foolishness," Garven said, trying to suppress an impish twinkle that kept showing up in his eyes.

"Garven, you are as full of it as a dung beetle. You have quite a rep on campus, you know. The biggest caper planner and doer of them all. I just want to know what is cookin' up in that pea brain of yours."

"Well, I certainly wouldn't be involved in anything that was against the rules of the university. I love my alma mater too much for that."

Grantland rolled his eyes back in his head.

Garven ignored the elaborate display of disbelief and continued. "But there just might be a little something underway for the first set of hall dances. You never know. Not that I would have anything to do with anything, of course."

"Look, Yankee, when y'all know somethin' more about those plans you have nothin' to do with, count me in, okay?"

"I'll pass your request along should I hear more."

Grantland just laughed and shook his head.

Garven was fighting sleep when he walked into the philosophy lecture hall five minutes late. He had to sit in the back; all of the good front-row brown-nose seats were already taken. He had tried to study in his free time, but the autumn sun and the balmy breeze moving through the tall eucalyptus trees like a lullaby had been too much for him. He had one of those headaches you get from an interrupted afternoon nap.

"PHILOSOPHY 101 – LOGIC AND COMPETENT ARGUMENT HARRISON POLLOCK, INST."

The grad student giving the lecture had written the title on the blackboard about half a mile away down in front of the class. Garven thought he might need to use his glasses some time because he had to squint so hard to see even the large block letters. The college syllabus listing the courses and instructors was filled with a list of teachers known only as "staff," meaning grad student or assistant. Stanford undergraduates referred to such teachers as "Dr. Staff." It was uplifting that this "Dr. Staff" had a name.

"We will deal with a new concept for you, that of the syllogism, today and for the rest of the quarter in one form or complexity or another. This class is a preparation of your minds for thinking—correct, lucid, convincing, logical thinking—so that you can cope with the thoughts of the panoply of great thinkers of Western civilization, from the Greeks to the present."

"What's a panoply?" Garven asked the very studious-looking girl in the seat next to him.

Before shushing him, the unattractive, horsy-faced girl said brusquely, "It's from the Greek, means a 'magnificent or superlative array, like a fine collection of arms or armor.'"

Fearing to disturb the sanctuary again by speaking, Garven just nodded his thank you. The grad student was getting into the core of his presentation, and Garven knew he had better start taking notes.

"Philosophy is more than physics, more like mathematics, since it is the purest and best form of thinking, not fettered by the need for a battery of tests or experiments. The test of philosophy, of a philosophy, is how well it stands up to the test of logic. Can you make a clear syllogism out of the argument, and does the syllogism hold true?"

Garven felt himself nodding off.

"A syllogism, reduced to its essence, is a three-statement deduction. It contains a major premise, a minor premise, and a conclusion. The simplest and commonest form is a categorical syllogism, which is made up of statements without conditions. Let me illustrate with a concrete example: All horses are animals. All thoroughbreds are horses. Therefore, all thoroughbreds are animals. In this instance, the major term, that is, the one containing the predicate of the conclusion statement here, 'animals,' is contained in the statement that we call the major premise. The minor term, 'thoroughbreds,' is contained in the minor premise. The middle term is the one that appears in both the major and in the minor premise—in this example, the word 'horses.' To be valid, the statements must each be correct, and there can be no more than three statements."

"So, you couldn't say 'All thoroughbreds are stupid and high strung' then," muttered Garven sotto voce. The horsy-faced girl frowned her disapproval. He presumed she was another effete Easterner and pseudo-lover of pseudo-horses.

"The rules of syllogisms are as follows," and the grad student chalked them on his board.

Garven assiduously copied the notations, presuming he would have to disgorge them again on a test some time.

"First, a syllogism must contain three and only three terms. A corollary is that each term must be used in the same sense in each usage. Second, the middle term of the two premise statements must be distributed at least one time. Third, if a major or minor premise term is undistributed in those statements, then it cannot be distributed in the statement of conclusion."The instructor paused to allow the students to transfer his board statements to their notes. Then he elaborated. "Violation of the first rule is the Fallacy of Four Terms. The result is an impossible conclusion. It is impossible to arrive at a conclusion. The principle trouble for the listener comes when one word is used with two different meanings, and it is not stated or clarified that there are different meanings. An example will suffice: Courteous people avoid imposing their wills on others. Tall buildings are imposing. Therefore, courteous people avoid tall buildings. This is no more than a four-term fallacy because the word 'imposing' has two meanings."

Garven was becoming interested in the concept of clear thinking despite his original intention to do no more than get the information and later give it back rote to get a grade.

"Violation of rule number two is known as the Fallacy of the Undistributed Middle. This is the traditional guilt by association argument. I will give you a more serious argument, one that is becoming more and more prevalent in federal government circles all the time: Communist subversive agents supported the American Workers Party. Jane Doe, the movie star, supported the American Workers Party. Therefore, Jane Doe, the movie star, is a communist subversive agent. The critical middle term is undistributed in both the major and in the minor premises, which constitutes a fallacy. Consider this fallacy in general diagrammatic terms: All Xs are Ys. All Zs are Ys. Therefore, all Zs are As. Can you see the fallacy in the following syllogism?" the graduate-student lecturer asked with a beaming smile. "It is a statement purportedly made by the late, lamented President Franklin Delano Roosevelt. "I hate war; Eleanor hates war. I hate Eleanor."

Garven remembered hearing that when he was a kid.

There was a ripple of appreciative laughter from the conservative students.

"I take it you have some difficulty detecting the fallacy. After sober study, I must admit that I, too, fail to find a flaw in the logic."

Again, there was a current of laughing.

For once, an X, Y, and Z symbolization began to make sense to Garven.

"Violation of the third rule is an illicit process. An example should clarify this idea better than an explanation. All University of Chicago Business School graduates are socialists. No Stanford graduates are Chicago Business School graduates. Therefore, no Stanford graduates are socialists. In this example, All Xs are Ys. No Zs are Xs. Therefore, no Zs are Ys. The fallacy is that there is not a valid reason not to include Zs with Ys just because no Xs and Zs can be together. The mistake was in making the conclusion distributed when that was invalid."

Garven understood. That was a matter of curiosity to the young man because it sounded suspiciously like math, the total of which sounded as incomprehensible as Swahili to the American student.

"I will conclude by passing out a copy of one of history's great syllogisms," said the grad student with a flourish and a smile as he collected his notes and left the hall without accepting questions.

Garven received his handout. The instructions were to describe, in correct logical terms and with a letter diagram, the syllogism involved. It contained Andrew Marvell's poem, *To His Coy Mistress*:

"Had we but world enough, and time,
This coyness, Lady, were no crime.

We would sit down, and think which way
To walk, and how to pass our long love's
Day…

But, at my back I always hear
Times winged chariot hurrying near…:

Now, therefore, while the youthful hue
Sits on thy skin like morning dew…

Rather at once our time devour…"

After wrestling practice and the assorted carbohydrates of their institutional supper, Garven's friends came to his dorm room uninvited and unannounced, as usual. They did not knock, as usual. Grantland Kurze, Frosty McTavish, David Applegate, and Devon Upshire all found themselves a comfortable place to flop and laughed at Garven's frustration as he tried to study, in spite of the distracting jokes, laughter, and taunts. Finally, he gave it up.

"Whatta you guys want? This is a study period, in case you didn't know. I can only presume you guys are all done with your homework and have committed to memory your lecture notes and textbook readings," Garven said with counterfeit irritability.

"Nope," they chorused.

"So?" Garven asked.

"We need a chuckle. The whole campus needs a chuckle. The whole world needs a chuckle," Grantland replied, looking at Garven for that momentous bit of mirth.

"Look," Garven said, "I can't afford to get involved in any more larks. After the bonfire, the Greek house raids, the car on the church, and the bottle smashing last quarter, I've about used up all my escaping luck. Find someone else with a diabolically clever, ingenious, and devious criminal mind. I have to do my homework."

"But there's no one quite like you, Garven. You're infamous. The Scarlet Pimpernel, the Cisco Kid. You can't let your public down. I know you have a plan," Devon flattered and coaxed.

"I could tell tales of yesteryear that would spread your fame afar, but modesty forbids," contributed David with a straight face.

Garven was weakening.

"We have to do something memorable," chimed in Frosty.

"Somethin' I can talk about in Texas," said Grantland, unconsciously placing his right hand over his heart like a Mexican bus rider crossing himself as he passes a country church.

"I just might have a bit of an idea," laughed Garven, capitulating with theatrical reluctance.

Six eyes and six ears riveted full attention on the wiry little Arizona native.

"This all depends on whether I can con Alan Crowder into playing a role."

They gave him full attention.

"Here's my plan."

CHAPTER
Seven

The advanced German course at Stanford taught the language by immersing the students in the classics of German literature. In spring quarter of 1950, his freshman year, Garven had translated:

> *Die bunten Segel der Fischerboote sahen im Sonnenschein sehr schön aus. Die See, von einem angenehm frischen Wind ganz leicht gekräuselt, machte einen malerischen Eindruck. Ostende mit seinem schönen Strand und den grossen Hotels rückte immer ferner.*

to

(The colored sails of the fishing smacks looked very beautiful in the sunshine. The sea, ruffled by a pleasing fresh wind, gave a picturesque impression. Ostend, with its beautiful beach and the big hotels, retreated further and further away.)

He learned to laugh at the innate, overgrown adjectives of the authoritarian language:

> *Die beiden, unmittelbar zusammenliegenden und nur durch eine schmale Veranda getrennten Blockhütten bestanden auch nur je aus einem Zimmer.*

(The two immediately-lying-together-and-only-by-a-small-veranda-separated log huts were made up indeed only of a single room each.)

He had heard the only joke that Germans told on themselves as near as he could tell.

"Who is the meanest person on the world?"

"The guy that tears out the last page in a German novel because all of the verbs are there."

On the first day of autumn quarter, 1950, however, Garven started his sophomore year of German studies with the obligation to read, write, translate—and of necessity, to learn—the meaning of the German classics. On that first day, he was assigned the famous passage from Hermann Hesse:

GESPRÄCH MIT EINEM OFEN

Sonderbar? Nein, das is eines der geheimen Gesetze, weisst de. Ein geheimes Gesetz der Beziehungen und Ergänzungen, die Natur is ja voll von solchen Gesetzen. Die feigen Völker haben Volkslieder, in denen der Mutverherrlicht wird. Die lieblosen Völker haben Theaterstücke in denen die Liebe verherrlicht wird. So is es auch mit uns, mit uns Öfen. Ein italienischer Ofen heisst meistens amerikanisch, so wie en deutscher Ofen griechisch heisst. Sie sind deutsch, und glaube mer, sie warmen un nichts besser als ich, aber sie heissen Heureka oder Phönix oder Hektors Abschied. Es weckt grosse Erinnerungen. So heisse auch ich Franklin. Ich bin ein Ofen, aber ich Könnte nach manchen Kennzeichen, ebensogut ein Staatsmann sein. Ich habe einen grossen Mund, verbrauche viel, wärme wenig speie Rauch durch ein Rohr, trage einen guten Namen und wecke grosse Erinnerungen. So is das mit mir.

(CONVERSATION WITH A STOVE)

(Strange? No, don't you know it is one of the secret laws? A secret law of relationships and additions. Nature is full of such secret laws. The cowardly nations have folk songs in which courage is praised. Cold, unloving, nations have plays in which love is exalted. It is the same with us, with us ovens. An Italian stove has usually got an American name in the same way as a German stove usually has a Greek one. They are German, and believe me, they heat no better than me, but they are called Heureka or Phoenix or Hectors Farewell. It awakens strong memories. That is why I am called Franklin. I am a stove, but because of certain characteristics, I could also be a statesman. I have got a big mouth, consume a lot, provide little warmth, emit smoke through a pipe, bear a good name and awaken vivid memories. That is what I am like.)

Garven could not see any real value to what he was learning in the foreign language, but he was learning. He guessed that he might one day have to read an article from the German medical literature, but despite all he had been told, he doubted it. It was one more hole to get punched in his ticket to medical school.

The Stern Hall Autumn Quarter Dances (one for each wing), traditionally, were scheduled for the third Friday of the quarter. Stern was the upperclassman dorm, and no freshmen were allowed. The social occasion had originally been titled Balls, but the current plethora of wags made it injudicious to use a term inviting of double entendres. Exchanges between Stern and Florence Moore Halls were arranged largely to accommodate the shy, the unattractive, and the socially inept, so they could be part of the social scene. Dates were quietly encouraged, but bringing Palo Alto and Menlo Park girls was frowned upon because there were so many fine and interesting Stanford women from which to choose.

Garven did not have a date because the girl he wanted to go with refused him. He felt he could discern a depressing pattern in his social life. He made the mistake of trying to find out why.

"I thought you weren't interested in fraternities or sororities," he said, after Millicent—Milly to her friends—had given a plain and simple "no" to Garven's invitation.

She had been altogether pleasant about it, but her "no" was clearly final.

"What do you mean? What have fraternities got to do with this?"

"Well, you know. Most good-looking girls are sort of attached to a fraternity, which guarantees their social life."

"I'm not most good-looking girls," she said archly. "I have a brain, and I make my own choices. For your information, Mr. Wilsonhulme, I do not make it a practice to date in the Greek system."

"I'm Garven. My dad's Mr. Wilsonhulme."

"And you may call me, Millicent," she said with the cool note of hauteur still prominent in her voice.

"No offense intended."

"None taken, Mr. Wilsonhulme."

He got the message. "I won't bug you anymore, but could you tell me one thing, and honestly?"

"Surely. I believe in being candid. What do you want to know?"

"Why won't you go to the dance with me? Do you have another date? Do I stink? Am I ugly? Or is it just my rotten personality?" He tried to keep an expression on his face like a soda cracker, but failed enough to tug at one of Millicent's sensitivity strings.

"Are you sure you want to know?"

"Sure."

"Okay then. But remember, you insisted. I am five feet and nine inches tall. Taller in heels. You are too short. It would look funny going out with a boy shorter than me. You know what I mean?"

She tried to keep a sympathetic expression on her face.

Garven did not feel like buying elevator shoes and asking another girl to the dance. Frosty, Grantland, David, and Devon did not even try to get dates, partly because of their enthusiasm for the diabolical plan Garven had suggested to them two weeks before, and partly out of shyness. Devon was even shorter and slighter than Garven; he had to wear his hair unfashionably very long to cover the still readily discernible painted red cross on the vertex of his scalp. Grantland was overweight, and Frosty felt completely inept around girls and was overwhelmingly self-conscious about the acne pockmark scars dimpling his facial skin. David did not seem interested in girls, if the truth be known.

The guest of honor in Garven's room that night was Alan Crowder, Garven's original roommate, who would never have considered summoning up the moxie to ask a girl on a date. It irked Garven that he had to be grouped with the nerds and social misfits. His only saving grace would be his thespian ability tonight—his ability to pull off his plan; more accurately, to inveigle shy Alan Crowder into performing the key role despite his natural social reticence.

The six college sophomores sat around the diminutive dorm room table on the two chairs, a stack of books, all of Garven's pillows and extra blankets, and two boxes provided by the host. They played simple draw poker—nothing wild, nothing trump, nothing exotic—the only man's game Alan seemed to be able to grasp. He was a veritable expert at bridge, but flitty games did not count. Frosty and Devon folded after grimacing at the four new cards they drew. Garven had a full house, two fives and three queens. Grantland had a low straight in four suits, 2, 3, 4, 5, and a 6. Alan had a pair of aces, hearts and diamonds. David had nothing but decided to hang on for one more round of bets.

"I'll raise you fifty cents," said Garven.

"Challenge accepted. I'll match that, and raise you another fifty cents," said Grantland.

David folded.

"I'd better fold, too," said Alan, who actively pursued timidity in games with the guys.

"Oh, hang in there. You've won the last three hands," said Frosty, encouraging the nerdy Alan as he had all evening.

"You think so?"

"Yeah. Tell you what. I'm out of the game this hand. What if I took a look at your hand?"

"Okay, I guess."

"Okay with you Grantland? Garven? David?" Frosty asked the other three players.

"No problem. We're all gentlemen here. If we can't trust each other, well, who can we trust?" Grantland answered.

Alan sucked it in and called. At Frosty's behest, the chubby sophomore spread out his cards.

Grantland said, "Ooh, too much for me. I'm out."

Garven spread his cards and said with real disappointment hanging on his words, "I can't get a bit of luck tonight. I just have a couple of fives and queens. I can't match those aces, and both of them red, the royal colors. Alan, old buddy, do you have some cards up that loose sleeve of yours?"

Alan was pleased. His ruddy boy's face showed every nuance of his pleasure. Every other time he played poker with these guys, he lost miserably, either all of his money or had to do some noxious chore. It was about time for his luck to change.

"Let's take a break. Want to take a sneak peak at the festive ball?" Garven asked the other five.

Emboldened by his streak of good luck, Alan piped up first, "Yeah, let's. I wanna see if any of the Florence Moore girls are showing any décolletage."

The other guys laughed heartily at Alan's witty and suggestive comment. He was feeling like he was one of the guys for a change. The others were being almost too nice to him.

The six college boys quietly walked down the second-floor stairway and looked in on the entrance hall of the dorm that served as the foyer of the crowded dance hall. The dining room had been converted into a fall splendor with a panoply of dry cornstalks, bales of straw, bushel baskets of variegated Indian corn, and gold, brown, and black streamers. As it happened, two well-tabernacled high-school girls, decked out in their off the shoulder and off the upper chest formals, were standing in the entryway with their lucky dates, two jocks from the football team.

"Look at that! Will you look at that!" Alan squealed under his breath. He was entranced.

"Wouldn't you like to get that one's attention—the little blond in the red dress?" Garven asked Alan, chucking him in the ribs.

Alan would have crawled four miles over broken beer bottles just to see that particular girl bend over to tie her shoes.

"Oooh, man, would I?"

He was having a great time that night.

When the two special treats followed their dates onto the dance floor and out of sight of the collection of masculine wallflowers on the stairs, Grantland, David, and Frosty started back up to Garven's room. Garven followed. Alan reluctantly came up last; he had caught the scent of the pheromones wafting from the collection of femininity at the party, and he was reluctant to leave the charged zone.

"You know what would liven up that party?" asked Grantland, unable to suppress his inner merriment.

At least that was the way Alan interpreted the Texan's mood. Alan was becoming more adventurous with each passing minute. "No, what?"

"Oh, it's just a passing thought. A silly one at that."

"What? What? C'mon!" Alan coaxed.

"You really wanna know? Okay. I would give my left onion to see some husky guy sashay through that dance hall buck nekkid."

The other five, bored and feeling-left-out sophomore boys, laughed uproariously at the picture that idea conjured up.

Garven said, "I'd do it for ten bucks."

His friends looked at him in amusement and skepticism.

David said, "I'd probably do it for fifteen. Ten's too cheap."

"You're right. I'm too much of a chicken anyway," said Garven, looking sheepish.

"Me, too," said Frosty.

"Me, too," said Devon.

"Me, too, when you get right down to it," said Grantland. "I guess I'm a lot more hot air than anything. I'd still like to see some brave stud go through there."

Alan loved hearing the quavering of his heretofore macho companions. An idea germinated in the dormant section of his brain that handled dares. "I had a thought," he said resolutely.

"Careful, don't want to hurt yourself with that thinkin' stuff, Alan," said Grantland.

"I'm serious," replied Alan, undeterred and enjoying the repartee.

"So, let's hear it," said Garven, his ears virtually perking up with interest. "What's your idea?"

"I would do it. Walk down there naked, I mean. I would have to have a few conditions, a couple of guarantees, though."

"Such as?"

"I wouldn't do it for anything less than thirty bucks, for one thing."

Thirty dollars plunked down on the table, almost as if the other young men had anticipated such an exigency.

"I would be able to wear a sack on my head, so no one could recognize me, for another."

Garven practically leaped across his bed to dump out his sack full of necessary groceries—potato chips, Mars bars, and Twinkies, representing the major food groups—so he could present the bag to his buddy, Alan.

"No one would know your face, but your big old hooter would be famous," Grantland said with an appreciative laugh.

Alan basked in the glow. He was secretly proud of himself for coming up with the idea to walk through that crowded room nude. He had always felt left out when the other guys went out to do their great pranks. This was his chance for near total one-upsmanship on the lot of them.

"And I would have to have your solemn promises," he said, "your absolute, no screw-up, no joke promises that you would never tell on me or pull off the sack, or call security or anything like that sort of thing you'd expect from juveniles."

"Promise! Promise! Promise! Promise! Promise!"

"I'll do it," he said with a serious finality that almost shocked the other boys.

They could not believe that Garven's assessment of Alan, conveyed to them two weeks ago when the plan was hatched, could be so accurate, nor that they would have been able to engineer his acquiescence for such an insane performance in a million years of cajoling. Garven was the epitome of the campus prankster, and this would be an all-time world-class event. Too bad Garven would never be able to be famous over it. It had been a feat of persuasion that outdid Tom Sawyer and his finagling his friends into white washing Aunt Polly's fence. It was sad that no one would ever know.

To a chorus of affirmatively nodding heads, Alan indicated his solemn agreement to carry out his end of the bargain.

"One more thing."

Ten eyebrows raised in double question marks.

"I want to wear a towel."

"Boo!"

"Boo hiss!"

"I just mean to the bottom of the stairs, you guys. I already agreed to do it."

"No problem. But all deals are off if you chicken out," emphasized Devon, who had kept pretty quiet thus far.

For some odd reason, Alan became shy standing on the stairs with the paper bag on his head with its two eyehole cutouts and the bath towel secured around his middle. He insisted on walking behind Garven.

Near the bottom of the stairs, just before the final turn that would expose them all to the view of the partygoers below, Garven stopped and said to Alan, "This is it. If the rest of us walk down any more stairs, everybody will see us. Someone will know us, and it will get back to you. You are on your own from here on out."

Instead of suffering trepidations, Alan was strangely exhilarated behind the anonymity of his paper mask now. He needed no coaxing. He wanted to go. He could hardly wait to shock the socks off all the social butterflies in the name of all of the nerds and uncool, unhip, uninvited misfits of the world. Of history. With a cavalier nod of his bagged head, Alan took the end of his towel and gave it a jerk, so it fell loose. He flipped the towel away from his privates, front and back, with no more concern than if he had been ensconced in the seclusion of his own bathroom. He walked calmly down the remaining stairs and on into the dormitory entrance-hall-cum-ballroom-foyer. The other five conspirators retreated back up the stairs, where they were sure they could not be seen, and watched as Alan strode across the tiled floor and into the dining room decorated as a dance area.

There were initial small gasps and titters from the entry hall. When the chorus of shy giggles and snickers gave way to guffaws, catcalls, and shouts of "RF!" in both its abbreviated and its full-length form from the young gentlemen, and shrieks and screams from the proper young Stanford ladies,

Garven led the way back up the stairs to his room on the dead run. After an initial group convulsion of unrestrained gaiety and laughter, the conspirators resumed their seats at the poker table. The tableaux of innocence was marred by the reddened eyes and tears streaming down the faces of the earnest players and the occasional descent into uncontrollable howls of laughter.

Some of those bouts of hilarity were occasioned by the sound of police sirens, later by the tramping of Gestapo boots down the halls, and by episodic outbursts of loud voices, laughing, and girlish squealing. In about five minutes, Alan burst into the room, flushed from his exertions, and recounted his exploit: He had walked slowly through the dance hall as agreed, prepared to bolt into the night when he came to the far door. He had experienced a moment of panic when he found the door to be locked. He had tried to open the wrong half of the French doors, and, upon a moment's reflection, had been able to swing open the second of the two doors. He disappeared into the night and ran as fast as he could to the back door of D Section of Stern Hall. He was woefully out of shape, so the progress he made was not as good as he and the others might have hoped. He raced with heaving chest and gasping lungs to the third floor, down the hall, and to the front stairs.

He paused to make sure he had not been seen or followed, then ran down the stairs and cut into the second floor just as the third-floor occupants began to stick their heads out of their doors to determine the cause of all the commotion. Alan ducked into Garven's room before the pandemonium reached the second floor.

And pandemonium it was. More than one hundred fifty young partygoers, aghast faculty advisors, and caterers (who were young enough to want to be in on the action) helped the campus police in their search for the pervert and menace. Someone had seen the bright white bottom go into the rear hall door of Section D of Stern Hall. (She said emphatically.) The entire crowd of vigilantes, gendarmerie, and camp followers converged on the inadequate stairways. They pushed, shoved, and jostled their way up the stairs behind the near-retirement 280-pound chief of campus security, who collapsed at the top of the landing, blue in the face. The students found it difficult to drag him out of the way, and his fellow security officers wrangled about whether to beat on the unfortunate man's chest, to call the ambulance, or to give mouth to mouth. It fell to the chief deputy on call that night to render the life-saving breathing assistance, and he reluctantly but manfully fell to his task.

"Get away from me!" screamed the chief, his breath coming in painful little gasps. "I can't breathe! You some kind of a pervert or something?! No man never kissed me on the lips, and I ain't so down that anyone is gonna start now."

The chagrined deputy backed off double time and, with a crimson face, sought something to do that would remove him from having his manhood cast under suspicion. He detected movement in the pay phone booth located just inside the entrance door to the third floor. Someone was hiding in there. Relieved that attention could shift away from himself, he shouted to the parade of deputies, college students, and caterers rushing aimlessly down the corridor, "C'mere. Somebody's in the phone booth. I think we got our pre-vert. We got a naked guy here. I need some backup." With that dubious assertion, Deputy O'Hara stepped resolutely to the booth door and pushed the doors open. Into the bright light of the hallway from the dim recesses of the phone booth stepped a Stanford man about campus and his Menlo Park High cheerleader companion. She clutched her party dress to her otherwise naked front, and he made a puny effort to hide his own shame with a handful of her brassiere and panties. They looked like they were about to join the police chief on the floor in another series of faintings.

The Florence Moore Hall chief chaperone, the venerable Mrs. Ophelia Daybell Cruthers, with her thirty-two years of service to the university, stepped forward to take charge of the unfortunate situation since the contribution of every other onlooker was nothing more than a bemused silence. "Put that dress on, young lady. You are coming with me this minute!" the thin and severe chaperone said in a hard but quiet voice.

The humiliated girl did the only thing she could do appropriate to the situation. She started to bawl.

Mrs. Cruthers handed the poor girl her dress in a most sympathetic fashion and placed her spidery body between the rapidly dressing girl and the leering onlookers. "The show's over," she announced to the audience as soon as she could feel confident that the girl was sufficiently covered that she would not have to worry about further damage being done to the impressionable young people gathered in the hallway.

The Stanford man had gotten rid of his date's under-things and had gotten his pants on, at least. His humiliation had been complete when he stepped into his suit pants backwards in his frantic haste and had had to regroup and switch legs. His jockey shorts laid on the pile of his girlfriend's underwear.

"You may have a case of the statutory rape here, officer," said Mrs. Cruthers, now firmly in charge, to the still slack-jawed deputy. "We can't be certain of this unfortunate young lady's age now, can we?" she said by way of further instruction.

The chief deputy escorted the young man, and the chief chaperone escorted the guilty cheerleader back down the stairs. It was the first time in her life that illicit sex had raised its ugly visage so close to Mrs. Cruthers, and she was feeling nauseous. Meanwhile, the chief had regained his breath and felt strong enough to resume the search for the streaker. He deduced that the couple in the phone booth, though dressed appropriately for the alleged criminal activity, were not the culprits he sought. He directed a door-to-door search.

It took Alan Crowder about forty-five seconds to dress and to calm down enough to sit at the poker table. The chief of security and his Aryan hordes burst unannounced into room after room, floor upon floor. They found two gallons of against-the-rules whiskey, "good stuff," the security man observed; one frail young man masturbating, one against-the-rules non-Stanford female; and three rooms full of funny, sweet-smelling smoke before the minions of the law battered their way into Garven's room.

There, all was tranquility—a friendly and earnest game of cards with a pot of matches in the center and collections of matches in front of each player. Genuine surprise registered on the boys' cherubic faces. What on earth could be the matter?

"What's going on, officer?" Garven asked, starting to rise from the stack of books on which he was sitting.

"Sit!" demanded the red-faced and puffing policeman. He and the curious followers scrutinized the dorm room carefully, some tactually.

Garven wondered whether it was really necessary for the kibitzers to handle his stuff, but thought better about saying anything. Having the officialdom leave was the paramount concern of the moment.

And then they were gone. After what seemed like a safe interval, the six young men dissolved into rollicks of laughter that eased the tensions. Any worries Garven had had about the caper dissipated in the good fellowship and humor. He slept the sleep of the just that night.

CHAPTER
Eight

D avid Applegate was in Garven's organic chemistry class. He announced
officially to Garven, "I am going to cave in and be in premed like
everyone else."

"Uh oh," Garven commented. "The competition just got tougher. Maybe I
ought to go into poly sci."

"Great plan, Stan. Then you can hunt around for a crummy teaching position
or a government staffer job and make twenty K a year. Not for me, man. I am
after one of those eighty K specialist jobs. The only other real choice is to be a
corporate lawyer—that's what my dad wants me to do. He thinks I'll be the black
sheep of the family if I abandon the traditional business and law professions."

"So, let's go learn about organic chemistry; so, you can get to be a rich brain
surgeon or plastic surgeon to the stars," Garven said, moving right along in
order to get one of the front-row premed seats.

The graduate student giving the lecture looked thin and gray. He obviously
did not get out much. Chemistry did not look like the profession for Garven,
even if he were ever to have such an arrogant thought as that he might be able
to understand the subject. Garven wondered, off-hand, why Stanford bothered to have a regular faculty. The graduate students did all of the teaching;
so, why not make it official and have them be both students and teachers? It
would simplify the accounting.

"Organic chemistry is a simpler subject than your year of inorganic," the
grad student began.

Garven was glad to hear that.

"But it is more difficult," the grad student continued, finishing his sentence. Garven was not glad to hear that.

"We will deal with larger and smaller numbers, and more complicated chemical interactions. First off, let's review the S1 prefixes."

Garven knew he was going to be in a little trouble since any discussion of S1 prefixes would be new to him. He wondered how much more he wouldn't know that he should have known.

The teacher then wrote the prefixes like exa-, peta-, tera-, giga-, femto-, and atto- on the blackboard, accompanied by their respective symbols, E, P, T, G, f, and a. He indicated that the use of the prefix, added to a root unit of measurement, multiplied the root word on the high end of the scale by a 1 with 18 zeros (quintillion), a 1 with 15 zeros (quadrillion), a 1 with 12 zeros (trillion), and a 1 with 9 zeros (billion). On the small end, the multiplier was a decimal point followed by 14 zeros (femto-, quadrillionth) and 17 zeros (atto-, quintillionth). Even the grad student could not remember the word descriptor of the E and P and the f and a prefix.

"They are just too big and too small to know about for practical purposes," he opined.

"Oh boy, more useless mind fill. So why do I have to know about that junk?" mused Garven to himself. Then he remembered his dad's admonition: "You just have to do it so you can get your ticket punched, and you can get initiated into the fraternity." That was consoling.

"Now that you have that back in mind, we will learn the 'I-you-pack' naming system for hydrocarbons. That is the International Union of Pure and Applied Chemistry or IUPAC for short. I will give you the rules; you will have to memorize them, I'm afraid, because we will use them all every day for the rest of the quarter."

Garven and David groaned in concert with a low, generalized murmur from the filled-to-capacity teaching amphitheater.

"Noting the generalized pleasure that statement brings, let us begin while your enthusiasm is still up," the grad student said, adding a bit of dry humor. "Rule number one: In any compound, the longest unbranched carbon chain is called the parent chain. Let's consider the chemical class of alkanes, for simplicity's sake. This lets you come up with a principle name for the compound by using the proper prefix, like meth-, as in methane. Rule number two: The carbon atoms of the longest chain are numbered consecutively to establish the position of each atom in the chain. These important numbers indicate where, along the chain, branching takes place. The numbers are used to indicate to which carbon atoms the alkyl groups, or other groups, are attached. The direction of the numbering system is so chosen as to have the lowest numbers possible given to the side chains."

"I'll never make it," whispered David to Garven. "I will be in a coma before he gets through rule three. How many rules do you think there are, anyway?"

"Beats me," Garven whispered back. "I can't stay awake, either. Think this stuff is in the book?"

"Probably. I can only hope so."

"It isn't worth the risk. Grad students always test right out of their lecture notes. That's student rule number five. I'll make you a deal. You stay awake for the next ten minutes and take the notes, and then, I'll take my turn. What do you say?" asked Garven groggily.

"Sounds like a good idea. How come I have the feeling I am about to be screwed?" asked David in a very quiet whisper now that the students around him and Garven were giving them dirty looks.

Garven was asleep.

"…of an alkyl group on the parent chain is given by a number indicating the carbon atom on the parent chain to which the group is attached," the grad student's monotone voice droned through the microphone.

David fought the brave fight to stay awake.

"Rule number four: For compounds in which a particular group appears more…" the voice was hypnotic. "…the group appears. A carbon atom…"

David was asleep.

"Rule number seven," was the next dim auditory input that David caught. He elbowed the peaceful Garven, who woke up with a very confused and dazed look on his face.

"Your turn," David mumbled.

"And they are arranged with halogens given first, followed by alkyl groups…"

Garven struggled mightily to regain his faculties.

"So then, here is the structural formula for $C_5H_9C_{13}$, 1,1,1-trichloro-3-methylbutane."

The soporific voice stopped, and the room was quiet except for the gentle and soothing scrawl of the soft chalk on the smooth blackboard. Garven leaned his head on David's shoulder, and the two young men spent a refreshing forty-five minutes of undisturbed rest.

The rejuvenation period on chemistry day came at four o'clock, when Garven could go get tired, sweaty, and mean in wrestling practice. The first official match was scheduled the first Saturday in November, a week away.

Unlike the 1949-50 season, Garven had competition in the 144-pound class. A high school wrestler from Utah signed up and had starved down from a spindly slender six feet tall, 150 pounds to 145 just to show he could do it. Since it was early in the season, the team members agreed to make an allowance for up to one pound over the maximum weight. Although all of the returning team members were sure that Garven could beat the new guy, they still had to go through the formality of an elimination match to be fair about it. There were six contested weights with the returning juniors and seniors favored to reoccupy their first-string positions in every case against the freshmen and sophomore challengers.

Garven had gotten to know Kenny Carlile from Heber, Utah, during their workouts thus far during the quarter. It sounded to Garven like Heber was the only place in the US as small as Cipher, Arizona. He felt a certain kinship with the gangly, pleasant eighteen-year-old, whose only annoying idiosyncrasy was his penchant for proselytizing for his religion, the Mormon church. But he was not overly pushy, so nobody minded much. Garven beat Kenny twice a day in their workout sessions; so he was not particularly worried about his position on the varsity squad.

Kenny stood four inches taller and had a reach six inches longer than Garven's. The smaller wrestler found that his worst problem in dealing with the lanky Utahn was that he could be held at bay by those long arms until he either got tired or until he became frustrated and made impetuous mistakes. Learning not to commit himself until he had a real opening had been the main benefit in working out with Kenny.

The entire Stanford team clustered around the edge of the practice mat to watch each formal qualification match. Kenny had held Garven off throughout the entire first period, resulting in no points being scored. Garven was put out with himself for not being able to do better, to look better in front of his entire team. Kenny chose the down position when given his choice at the start of the second three-minute period. He spread his bony limbs, making it difficult for the smaller young man to get anything but an awkward, outstretched position of his shorter arms and legs. Pete Barnhienel was acting as the referee. He slapped his hand on the mat, signaling the start of the period.

Kenny contorted himself to leap into the sitting position as a prelude to overturning Garven. Garven was ready, leaned down towards his left side, and let Kenny's momentum carry his long body down onto its side in a precarious, off-balance position. Garven kept a vise-like grip on Kenny's left arm, pinning it against his opponent's torso. He swung his wiry body over Kenny's so they were facing each other momentarily. Kenny struggled to get fully prone but only succeeded in getting his arm ensnared in a hammer lock. Garven ground his fisted hand in under Kenny's armpit and around the back of his neck in a half-Nelson and churned his feet into the mat to drive Kenny onto his back. He kept Kenny's arm fixed firmly behind him and gave a burst of force to complete the full turn to pin the Utahn. Kenny grunted in pain. Garven ignored the signal. Kenny's arm was twisted back at an awkward angle, and his contortions to avoid being pinned were placing an increasingly severe strain on the overstretched ligaments and joint capsules. The rotator cuff twisted and began to fray.

Kenny let out a sob of pain that became more like a shriek and gave way, falling onto his back to be pinned, his shoulder inclined fifty degrees beyond its normal full range of motion. Garven, the coyote, drove his now helpless opponent's shoulders onto the mat with all his strength and weight to finish him off to pin him convincingly, oblivious to or uncaring about the desperate cries of pain. The spectator teammates on the sidelines yelled for Garven to quit, to get off. He ignored them. Pete abandoned his role as referee and rushed to the two wrestlers. His only thought was to rescue the stricken freshman from injury. Garven knew no one was going to count out the mandatory three seconds to establish the pin, so he did it himself. He did not yield to Pete's strong hands, which were feverishly trying to separate him from his conquered foe. There was a grinding crunch in the overburdened shoulder and a cry of agony that pierced the grim silence of the room. Garven knew he had gotten the pin. He pulled himself off Kenny and became very solicitous of the writhing boy. Even without medical training, it was apparent to all of the wrestlers that Kenny's shoulder was dislocated. It was a useless appendage hanging limply at Kenny's side.

Pete took charge of getting Kenny to the athletic department dispensary. One by one, the other members of the team filed past Garven, who was sitting on the mat, sweating and panting. There were looks of questioning, of anger, of concern, and of accusation. Derek van Leventhal, one of Garven's chief supporters, had a look of accusation.

"Is it that important to win, Garven?" he asked, pointedly keeping his eyes fixed on Garven's.

"It was an accident. I didn't mean to hurt him. We were both just going all out. You can't really think that I was trying to hurt Kenny!" Garven exclaimed in his own defense.

"I don't know what to think. I am going to need some time. Some of the other guys aren't going to feel that hot about it, either. We will probably have a team meeting about this injury. I'm not so sure we need anybody that aggressive."

"Cripes, Kenny is not built for wrestling. His joints and bones are too thin and long. It was just an unfortunate thing. You gotta believe me, Derek. I did not mean to hurt the guy. When he gets over it, he can take my place in the match. It's not that big a deal."

"We'll talk some more on it. I think we've had enough eliminations for one night. Practice is over. Let's let things cool for a day and then have a meeting next practice," Derek said. He was no longer looking directly at Garven and seemed anxious to be out of there.

Garven waited until the others had left the dressing room before he showered. He was not prepared to meet their gazes at that moment. Why did that stupid puny Kenny have to challenge him anyway?

"If you can't stand the heat, you'd better stay out of the kitchen," his real dad said to him when he used to get into trouble and to get punished when he was a kid.

At the meeting two days later, there was a somber, judicial mood. None of the wrestlers was overtly unfriendly, but Garven was well aware of a barrier of coolness between him and the others. He sat on the mat two body lengths away from the rest.

Pete spoke up first when everyone was on the mat. It was quiet; there was an expectancy in the atmosphere. "Look, you all saw what happened to Kenny. I checked with the docs. He had a rotator cuff tear and dislocation of his shoulder. He had to be operated on, so he is out for the rest of the year. His doc said it will depend on rehab whether he will be able to do sports again. It didn't look good for wrestling."

The team gave Garven a sullen, reproachful look.

Pete continued. "It was my fault. I take responsibility. I was the referee, and I should have realized what was happening. I should have seen sooner that Kenny's shoulder was getting twisted. In the heat of battle, the contestants can't always turn off the adrenaline."

Derek van Leventhal, the unelected, but de facto, team captain stood up to speak. "All right, you guys, I've given this a lot of thought in the last two days. At first, I just wanted to punch Garven out. Then, I wanted to get all of us together and to vote him off the team. Then, I slept on it. I can't be that sure that it was not an accident; maybe Garven did not recognize what was going on. It is possible that he interpreted Kenny's yelling as just part of a new guy's effort not to be pinned. I just don't know. I think we ought to hear what Kenny himself has to say. Agree?"

There was consensus in the nodding heads, even on Garven's part.

"I already did it. I mean, I went over and talked to Kenny after he was out of the anesthetic. He's a good, tough kid. They make 'em good out there in the mountains of Utah," Derek said.

"So, what'd he say?" piped up one of the wrestlers, impatient with the delay.

"Like I said," Derek went on, this time looking directly at Garven, "he's a good guy, a real stand-up guy. He said it was an accident. He and Garven were going at it hot and heavy, and wrestling is a body contact sport. People get hurt when the action is intense. He said he would be really upset if we kicked Garven off the team."

For a few minutes, there was a quiet among the teammates, broken only by the low murmur of occasional whispers.

Grant Casper, the heavyweight, finally said, "Let's vote on it."

"Good by me," said Derek. "Do you want a secret ballot or a show of hands?"

The team was unanimous—show of hands.

"Let's have it strictly up-front," Pete said, speaking for his teammates.

"Garven, why don't you take off for about fifteen minutes?" Derek instructed.

"If it's okay, I'd just as soon stay. I might as well know the bad news right in my face," Garven said, speaking for the first time that afternoon.

Derek swept his eyes over the assembled wrestlers. There was an unspoken, grudging assent.

"Okay. You stay, Garven. Well do it the KISS way—Keep It Simple, Stupid. Raise your right hand all the way if you want Garven to stay."

There were fourteen wrestlers on the mat, including Garven. In addition to his hand—and why shouldn't he vote? he reasoned—there were eight others, a majority. He noticed that Derek's stayed down.

"I guess it's a democratic choice. Garven stays," Derek said. "I've got one last thing to say. This is personal, not speaking for the team or anyone else, Garven. I didn't like what I saw. You are too aggressive, too intense about winning. This is just a game; we need to keep it fun. You need to watch yourself, your temper, and your uncontrolled need to win. That's all I've got to say. I know that Vince Lombardi, the assistant coach at Fordham University, said that 'winning isn't everything, it's the only thing,' but I think that's wrong. Common decency and sportsmanship are more important in the long run."

Garven failed to guard his tongue. "Lombardi also asked, 'If it doesn't matter who wins or loses, then why do they keep score?'" he said quietly, because that was what he believed, no matter what anyone else said in sports or Sunday school.

Only Derek heard him.

"Whatever," he said, shaking his head.

Garven knew enough not to say more. People did not like to hear the truth, and he had to accept that. He was relieved and kept a poker face as Derek turned and left. He did not want to get himself into a second-class position of having to be apologetic about being on the team for the rest of his career. He got up and started working out with the rest of the wrestlers when they began to limber up. The heat of the workout dispelled the overt frigidity that had characterized the earlier part of the team meeting, but there was a lingering coolness towards him. He did not find it difficult to find a wrestling partner. He let himself get beaten, though. His time would come.

The chilliness from his teammates bothered Garven. He kept the incident to himself, and made a decided effort not to allow himself to appear down with his regular friends, nor with the team. He did not write home about it, not that he was much inclined to remember to write his mother anyway. He did keep up a regular, if infrequent, correspondence with Peter Wilsonhulme. Garven had a disciplined attribute—he was assiduous about his premed aspirations, and he remembered who his benefactor was. He was not so secure in his relatively new status as the adopted son of the Arizona doctor that he felt that he could afford a snub. The wrestling incident with Kenny had defused his enthusiasm for the sport, at least for the time being. His restless energy was directed all the more into his premed studies. He was going to maintain his four-point-o average or die trying.

The hypnosis lab had proved to be considerably more interesting than it had been work. The grizzled old research professor had assured him that he would give him an A after the first session, and required, in return, Garven's undivided attention and cooperation. The hypnotist had a heavy German accent that required Garven's full attention all by itself. The professor told Garven that his accent was frankly his most useful attribute because of that.

"Just sit here in dieser comfortable chair, my poy," Dr. Gunther said. "Pe comfortable." He pronounced it com-fort-able. "Remember to pay attention only to my foice, nutting else, my poy. Just relax, forget all dose oudsite dings. Dis should pe a most restful time fur you."

Garven took full advantage of the professor's instructions, but knew that his grade depended on his cooperating, or at least, appearing to cooperate fully. He made a strong effort not to fall asleep.

"I vant you to tink furst off your pody relaxink, relaxink all ofer. Start mit your toes. Concentrate on dem. They are zo tired, zo warum. Tink off dem peing com-fort-able. Dat ist fery goot. Now tink alzo on your feet. Tink. Concentrate on dem. They are quiet und schtill, warum, com-for-table."

Garven concentrated, and it was pleasant. He could learn to like this kind of work.

"Now your lekks. Tink off the muus-kles. They are zo tiret, zo much in neet off rest. Make sure they are restful, in a goot position. They do not neet to moof this whole afternoon."

Up the body they went. Garven was relaxed, now concentrating fully on the accented voice. The lights had dimmed; it was warm and very comfort-able in his heavily padded reclining chair.

"Vash your mindt from all udder thoughts. Only ist mine voice important. Schtay mit me. Do vat I say. Rest your toughts. Do not vorry. Do not plan. Do not tink now. Nothingk ist going to disturp you here. You are safe. You feel goot."

Garven was in the thrall of Dr. Gunther's voice. He wanted to do what the old man said. He wanted to please him. He knew the old professor would know if he were resisting. He did not resist.

"Himagine a vindow in your mindt. Dis vindow ist opfen. You can look out off it. Concentrate on vat there ist to zee. Picture a mountain meadow. You like that don't you, my poy? You are movingk along in the air, seeingk the green grass, the blue and red and purple flowers, the trees coming up at the edge off the forest. There ist a bright sunshine. You feel warum, feel goot, feel relaxed."

Garven could picture the scene described by the professor as clearly in his mind's eye as if he were seeing the mountain meadow in reality.

"You are gettingk sleepy. It ist all right to close your eyes. Do so, Garven. That's it. It ist zo calm und warum und comfortable. You are asleep now, my poy. Asleep, put you can hear my foice. You are a goot poy, Garven. You vant to do vat I say. Nothing vill harm you. I vould nefer ask you to do anythingk that vould embarrass you or cause you injury. You know that. You are sound asleep. There ist nothingk put my foice. You are ready to do vat I suggest. You can answer me, my poy. Are you ready to do some tinks I ask off you?"

"Yes," Garven said dreamily from somewhere down inside himself. He was somewhere near the forest, looking back at the meadow over which he had crossed. He could think; so he was not sure he was really hypnotized, not sure how he was supposed to feel or how hypnotized people were supposed to act. He felt a kinship with the old man, with his voice. He wanted to do what Dr. Gunther asked.

"Ven I schnap mine fingers twice you vill awaken. You vill not pe able to remember anyding you do dis afternoon. You vill feel goot, relaxed, refreshed. You vill vant to come again. You vill vant to help this old man in his vork. It vill pe important vork for you to do so. Do you understand me, Garven, my poy?"

"Yes."

"Vat ist it that you vant to do ven you awaken?"

"To help in your research. It is important to learn more about hypnosis. I want to help."

"Goot. Now, count backwards from ten to zero, pleese."

"Ten, nine, eight, seven, six, five, four, three, two, one, zero."

"Fery goot. Now you see that this ist nicht hard or painful in anyvay. You are feelingk fery goot, fery com-fort-able."

Garven had ceased to be concerned with wrestling, homework, or about doing well in the hypnosis lab. He wanted to please the professor. Everything else would take care of itself. He wondered if he were hypnotized since he could make a decision. He knew he was deciding to comply with Dr. Gunther's requests as a matter of self-interest. He doubted if hypnotized people could understand such things. It did not matter.

"Now, Garven, raise your left handt slowly abofe your head. That's a goot fellow. Raise your right handt the same. Ah, fery goot. See, there ist nothingk hard about this. You are schtill zound asleep. You schtill feel zo goot."

Garven felt a little silly sitting there with his hands over his head as if he were the victim of a holdup. His hands had been up in the air for a long time, but they did not get tired. He felt relaxed even in the peculiar position. He felt funny, realizing that he wanted to keep his arms raised. It seemed the right thing to do. He wondered if he were hypnotized.

The professor had Garven extend his arms directly in front of him, raise his legs, get out of the chair, walk over to the sink, run himself a cup of water, kneel on the floor, and hop on one foot. Garven complied. He felt strange doing the silly things, but if that was what the professor wanted, who was he to balk? Garven knew it was in his self-interest to do everything the professor required, to make the nice old German man think he had been successful in hypnotizing him.

"Take this resistor in your handt, Garven. Goot. See that it is about twice the size of a thimble? It has no vires attached. You can feel that, no? Is it hot, my poy?"

"No."

"Hold fery tightly. You vill feel it gettingk varmer. Do you feel that, Garven? Do you feel the warumth?"

"Yes." It was silly. He knew the thing was not getting warmer. He was pretty sure that it was not even a resistor. But, somehow, it did seem warmer. Maybe just from the heat of his hand. He knew he was not hypnotized now, but he decided to play along.

"You vill feel the resistor getting varmer, much varmer. It ist schtartingk to get zomevat uncom-fort-able, no?"

It was warm, no, hot. He shifted the object unconsciously to his left hand. The professor had done something to the resistor to heat it up even though there were no wires. Must be batteries. It was interesting. He decided to play along. "It's getting real warm," he said.

"Now it ist fery warum. It ist gettingk even hot. Alzo, you vant to change handts. It ist too hot."

Garven switched hands again. He was beginning to feel concerned about the resistor, concerned about whether he would injure his hands. But he was sure Dr. Gunther was a man of his word and would not allow him to have any real harm. He decided to keep hold of the hot thing just to humor the nice old man a little longer.

"You can't holdt on to it any longer. It is too hot fur you. It hurts."

He was right. It did hurt. He was not going to be able to endure this much longer. Why did Dr. Gunther make him continue to hold it? He began switching the resistor back and forth quickly as if he were handling a baked potato. He was sweating with discomfort, the heat, and his efforts. He was not going to be able to keep this up. He longed to beg the professor to let him get the burning object out of his hands.

"Drop it, Garven, before it hurts you. Now!"

Garven fairly flung the resistor away. He rubbed his hands and was surprised and pleased that they were not tender or blistered. He did not feel upset now; he felt calm and relaxed. That was kind of strange. His placidity convinced him that he was not hypnotized, and he was glad he could keep his mental faculties intact so he could play the role well.

The professor's fingers snapped, then snapped again.

Garven sat quietly in his chair; he felt pretty good. He was sure the session had gone all right. He must have dozed off. Nearly an hour had passed. He hoped that he had done okay. He did not want to screw up his psych grade for some dumb pet project of an obscure professor.

"Thank you, Garven. That ist all für today. Are you feelingk all right?"

"Yes, Sir. Just fine. I think I dozed off there for a minute or so. I hope I did okay. I was really trying."

"Ach, indeedt. You ver a fery goot subpject. In fact, I vant you to consider an offer. I vould like you to vork for me in the lab. To be a subpject three times a veek. I tink I can learn somethingk from you. Vould that suit you, youngk man?"

"I think so. I have to be careful not to get too many things going; so I can keep up with my studies."

"Ach, indeed zo! I vould like you to come vor only two hours in the eveningk on Monday, Wodensday, und Fridays. The department vould, off course, pay you a dollar an hour. Pretty goot, no?"

It was pretty good. Especially for sitting around, pretending he was in a trance. He seemed to have convinced the old man. Why not? "Okay. I'd like to, Sir. When do you want me to start?"

"This veek, iff possible"

"Jake with me," Garven said. "Do I have to sign a contract or anything?"

"No, no, youngk man. Ve all trust each other here. I know you vill show up. I vill be counting on you. That ist enough."

Garven felt pretty good about being involved. It was easy; and he had to admit, it was pretty interesting stuff. Important, too. He really felt like he was going to help with some important research. He felt glad to be able to help the nice old man in his work if nothing else. He left the session feeling better than okay. He stepped on something on the way out. The professor had dropped an empty spool that had once held thread. Garven set it on the end table as he left.

Now Garven was truly busy. He had no time to brood or even to pay attention to his teammates' lack of warmth or to Devon Upshire, Frosty McTavish, David Applegate, and Grantland Kurze when they gave him daily updates on the interrogations of the students in D Section about the streaker. That all seemed like ancient history to Garven as he attacked his work, his own conditioning, and wrestling. He was going to be the best lab assistant in the history of the psych department, and would probably be able to have the department chairman, Dr. Johnathon Paternost Simpkins, write him a letter of recommendation for medical school. Now, that would be a coup. Without mentioning it to anyone else, he made a deep internal vow that he was going to be the Pacific Athletic Conference 144-pound wrestling champion. For the moment, though, he had homework.

He looked at the stack. It seemed overwhelming and endless. As he did every day, Garven bowed to the god of medical school and dug in.

Organic chemistry:

    1. Give the general formulae for alkanes, for alkenes.

    2., 3., 4., 5., ...

    6. Write brief definitions of the five major hydrocarbons—alkanes, alkenes, aldynes, alkadienes, and aromatics. Be prepared to discuss them in class and to draw an example of each in front of the class.

Philosophy:

    1. Distinguish between the types of argument: inductive, deductive, and analogical.

    2. Define and distinguish between exposition and argument.

    3. For the following passages, explain whether the narrative is an exposition, an argument, or is a mixture of the two:

    "But if the Negro is a man, is it not to that extent a total destruction of self-government to say that he too shall not govern himself? When the white man governs himself, that is self-government; but when he governs himself and also governs another, that is more than self-government; that is despotism. If the Negro is a man, why then my ancient faith teaches me that all men are created equal, and that there can be no moral right in connection with one man's making a slave of another."
Abraham Lincoln, Speech at Peoria, Ill.,
replying to Sen. Stephen Douglas,
Oct. 16,1854.

    "But then - certain professors of education must wrong when they say that they can put a knowledge into the soul which was not there before, like sight into blind eyes. The

power and capacity of learning exists in the soul already; and just as the eye was unable to light without the whole body, so too, the instrument of knowledge can only by a movement of the whole soul be turned from the world of becoming into that of being."
Plato, *The Republic*
4., 5., 6.

German:
1. Translate from the original German:

"Es ist also nur das Quantum gesellschaftlich notwendiger Arbeit oder die zur Herstellung eines Gebrauchswerts gesellschaftlich notwendige Arbeitszeit, welche seine Wertgrosse bestimmt. Die einzelne Ware gilt hier uberhaupt als Durchschnittsexemplar ihrer Art...Als Werte sind alle Waren nur bestimmte Masse festgeronnener Arbeitszeit."
Karl Marx, *Das Kapital*

2. Translate into German:

"He groped his way through the dark suburb...Through the dark suburb he groped his way back. There were no stars."

(Hint: look up Wolfgang Borchert, *Die Drei Dunklen Könige*)
3., 4., 5., 6.

It was midnight before Garven had gotten that much done. He was afraid to close his eyes for fear that he would not wake up until the next day, but he was no longer able to think coherently. His efficiency was at a low ebb. He drank down three cups of bitter, black coffee—purely medicinal; he detested the bitter, burnt taste of the stuff. He sighed and resumed his methodical attack on the pile of assignment papers.

Algebra:
1. Miltiades and his army marched to Marathon at 4 km per hour. After the Athenians won the battle, Pheidippides

made his famous run back to Athens to share the news at the rate of 26 km per hour. If the total traveling time was 16 hours, give the distance from Marathon to Athens.

2. The treasure chest that fell into Key Largo Cove when the *King's Galleon* was sunk contained 6,000 gold sovereigns. There were a total of 24,000 coins in the chest. What percent were gold sovereigns?

3. The pirate ship *The Corsair* sailed at full sail and was 30 nautical miles beyond London harbor when Admiral Lord Nelson started to give chase, traveling at twice the speed of *The Corsair*. If the admiral caught the pirate ship in 8 hours, give the velocity of *The Corsair* and of the admiral's flag ship.

4., 5., 6.

Garven hated story problems even worse than he hated to manipulate numbers, exponents, and fractions. It was two o'clock in the morning before he had the math done, and even then he was none too sure of his work or his answers. He had just about given up hope of getting an A in college algebra. He was getting to the point that it would be enough to get through it. He took a dexi and hit the next in the homework assignment pile.

Art history:

1. Michelangelo professed devotion for only one woman in his lifetime. Who and why?

2. Michelangelo expressed contempt for one of his contemporaries. Who and why?

3., 4., 5.

6. Describe Minoan art and compare and contrast it with Egyptian and Greek. Include a discussion of the Hagia Triada and of bronze daggers (200 words).

That portion of his assignments required a plethora of writing. He found it quick and fairly easy because he had been careful to get the reference books cited in the lecture from the library before anyone else from the class could get there. It was one of those things he learned from a fourth-year student in premed who lived down the corridor from him in Stern Hall. He felt the effect of the dexi peter out just as he finished the last question. It was three-thirty. He took another of the little white helpers.

English literature:

1. Discuss the quandary posed by John Locke in his *A Letter Concerning Toleration* (no more than 500 words).

"But some may ask: What if the magistrate should enjoin anything by his authority that appears unlawful to the conscience of a private person?… I say, that such a private person is to abstain from the action that he judges unlawful, and he is to undergo the punishment which is not unlawful for him to bear."

2. Discuss the controversy between science and the humanities in light of George Berkeley's *Principles of Human Knowledge*. Consider especially this passage (300 words):

"Arithmetic has been thought to have for its object abstract ideas of Number; of which to understand the properties and mutual habitudes, is supposed to mean part of speculative knowledge… It hath set a price on the most trifling numerical speculations which in practice are of no use, but serve only for amusement…and attempted the explication of natural things by them."

3. Argue for the value of the humanities based on this excerpt from *Learning the River* by Mark Twain.

"Now when I had mastered the language of this water, and had come to know every trifling feature that bordered the great river as familiarly as I knew the letters of the alphabet, I had made a valuable acquisition. But I had lost something, too. I had lost something which could never be restored to me while I lived. All the grace, the beauty, the poetry, had gone out of the majestic river! I still kept in mind a certain wonderful sunset which I witnessed when steamboating was new to me. A broad expanse of the river was turned to blood; in the middle distance the red hue brightened into gold, through which a solitary log came floating, black and conspicuous. [In another place] the surface was broken by boiling, tumbling rings, that were as many-tinted as an opal… I drank it in, in a speechless rapture… Then, if that sunset scene had been repeated, I should have looked upon it without rapture, and should have commented upon it;… those tumbling boils show a dissolving bar and a changing channel there; the lines and circles in the slick water over yonder are a warning that that troublesome place is shoaling up dangerously…"

4., 5., 6.

It was four forty-five. He scrawled the last line on his paper and did not proofread it. He was too tired. He lamented not having a typewriter. He drowsily mused that it would not do any good to have a typewriter since he did not know how to type. There was still psychology to do. He was sitting in the hard-backed chair, pen and paper in hand, and the *Principles of Psychology* textbook open to the section related to the homework assignment. An inquiring neighbor, peering in, would have marveled at the fortitude of the premed student perched there in such a diligent posture. But he was asleep.

CHAPTER
Nine

"I'm tellin' y-all that they are closin' in on us, Garven," said Grantland with more of an indication of anxiety than usual when he made this pronouncement to his friend. His Texas accent seemed more pronounced under stress.

"What's different?" asked Garven without irony.

"My spies tell me that the Gestapo has interrogated everybody on the first floor and most everybody on the third. Strange how they left the second floor till now, huh?"

"Think a little birdie has been giving them hints?"

"Most likely."

"You mean, like one of us five?"

"Nah. That doesn't make sense. I firmly believe that people don't do things that are not in their own best interest."

"Me neither. But some people are weak."

"Like Alan," they both said at the same time.

"He has the most to lose of any of us. That really doesn't make sense."

"Unless some busybody saw us do it and tattled; then, the Gestapo paid our Alan a visit and scared the crap outta him."

"And he made a deal to get himself off. A deal to rat on us," said Grantland with a ring of sudden enlightenment in his voice.

"Yeah—acting in his own self-interest. That's called a plea bargain in Dick Tracy circles, I think," Garven added for emphasis.

"Maybe somebody should have a little chat with our exhibitionistic pal. Maybe even several somebodies wearing white sheets and hoods. Like that," Grantland groused.

"I'll talk to him," said Garven. "I probably know him better than anyone. But I'm telling you, he is crafty, that one. I am just as likely to come away with nothing as something."

The stress of midterms was well past, and Garven had aced them. He was sailing along with A's in every class so far. He was doing decently in his wrestling now that the furor over Kenny's broken shoulder had subsided, but he was too chronically tired to excel.

"Nobody's perfect. Nobody's superman," Garven said to himself from time to time by way of self-consolation.

Alan was not in his room, or at least did not answer the door for the next three days when Garven went there to talk to his old roommate. Finally, Garven caught Alan in the communal bathroom on the third floor. It was difficult to make the encounter seem casual and by chance since Garven would naturally be expected to use the facilities on his own, the second, floor.

"Hey, Alan. How're they hangin'?"

"Down," said Alan, looking surprised and less than thrilled to see Garven.

"I don't see you around much lately."

"Been busy."

Real communicative.

"I guess. Look, Alan, I'd like to talk to you for a minute."

"So talk."

"Maybe in your room. I want to talk privately, you know. The walls have ears, and you never can tell what the walls might want to say to the wrong people."

Alan looked really reluctant.

"Any problem with us having a private conversation?"

Alan drew in a long deep breath and sighed quietly. He kept his eyes averted from Garven. Garven could hear the alarm bells going off in his own head. Alan kept his student-issue towel bunched up in front of his privates, as if to protect them more than for modesty. He was shivering slightly from the cool air drying his wet skin after his shower. There was an awkward pause.

"Well, Garven, to be frank about it, I remember how aggressive you can be sometimes. Like when we were roomies. They said… I mean, I don't know if it is such a good idea for us to go to my room."

"You worried that I might beat you up? Whatever for?" Garven asked, his voice laden with incredulity. His face was as bland as he could make it, but there was a hard, inquiring look in his hazel eyes.

"Why should I be?"

"Yeah, why should you be? You haven't done anything against me. Not that I know of anyway. Why should you be nervous? Why *are* you so nervous?"

Alan was trembling slightly, and he was sweating despite the coolness of the morning air. "So promise you'll leave me alone if we have this little talk you have in mind."

Alan's face had a craven, ratlike appearance, Garven thought.

Out loud, he said, "Of course. We're buddies, no?"

The two young men walked to Alan's dorm room, with Alan leaving a faint trail of water drops. The room was as it always was, filthy and so cluttered that there was no place to sit. Garven presumed the other boy only used the room for sleeping, eating junk, and as a trash receptacle. What, if any, studying Alan did must have occurred elsewhere. It would be impossible to think in this mess. He waited patiently until Alan finished putting on his dirty tee shirt, pants greasy with hand wiping, and old moccasins. He did not wear underwear or socks, Garven noted with no particular interest.

"So what's this grand inquisition all about?" Alan asked in a mildly defiant voice. His confidence had increased in the security of his own familiar junk.

"No grand inquisition, Alan. I haven't seen you around. None of us have seen you hardly at all since your grand streak. We were wondering how you were doing."

"*Our* grand streak?" Alan emphasized the "our."

"Right. 'Our' grand streak," Garven replied in his most conciliatory voice. "You okay? They been on your case?"

"Which 'they'?"

"The Gestapo!"

"The who?"

"Oh, c'mon, Alan—*the* Gestapo, the administration, campus security, the dorm monitors, all of the forces for good in the community. Anyone and everyone investigating our dark deed!"

Alan's eyes averted again. He was all of a sudden absorbed in the stains on his throw rug. Garven could easily envision the course of any interrogation of Alan. No bamboo splinters under the fingernails required here.

"Well," Alan said with a reluctance that amounted almost to a stammer. "Well…"

"You already said that," Garven pointed out, a little less friendly now.

"Well…yeah, somebody came by my room."

It was like pulling teeth.

"Such as who?" prodded Garven.

"It was Ivan Winkler."

Garven showed no indication of recognizing the name.

"The assistant dean of students."

"Oh." It was time for Garven's crest to fall a bit.

"They call him Ivan-the-Terrible. He's the troubleshooter for the administration. For students, I mean. He wasn't so bad, though."

"And?"

Garven was getting tired of this. What did he have to do to get Alan just to come out with it?

"He said somebody had seen me, recognized me. He wanted to give me a chance to confess. He said it would go easier on me if I did."

"And did you?"

"I asked him who saw me. Didn't I have the right to confront my accuser? That kind of stuff."

Garven was not fooled by Alan's awkward non sequitur. Despite the slowness of the process of divulgence, Garven's heart was sinking into a marsh of growing suspicion. "So, go on."

"That's about it. Jeez."

Alan might just as well be standing there with his nose getting longer. He was a rotten liar. Garven knew he was not going to get anything much more from the slimy fat rat. He asked anyway. "Just one more question, Alan. I'll get off your back. Did you give up the rest of us? Did you tell your pal, Ivan-the-Terrible, about us?"

Alan sniveled and squirmed. He had a mean, devious look on his face when he answered, which did not exactly jibe with what he had to say. "What do you think I am? You guys are my friends, isn't that right?"

Garven controlled his overpowering urge to answer Alan's first question, but instead, responded only to the second.

"We are friends, and friends stick together, right?"

"Yeah…yeah, sure."

"Okay, friend. I have to get to psychology. See you around."

"Yeah."

It took real effort to calm himself down for the psych lecture. The sonorous monologue was boring enough to be soothing, enough to let Garven convince himself of the fiction that Alan probably had not turned him and the others in; he was still probably okay.

"Although we do not touch on the subjects of abnormal psychology until spring quarter, we should have the foundation for understanding disorders in the autumn and winter terms. My own field of special interest and practice, clinical psychology, has, at its core, the elements of psychoanalysis. Today, I will briefly present an overview of Freud's landmark discoveries and will introduce one of the major tools of the psychological discipline. I speak here of hypnosis," Professor Dr. (as he liked to be addressed) Simpkins lectured.

Garven was grateful that he had heeded his premedder's instincts and had gotten into the hypnosis research section. He was now working regularly, and, if he did say so himself, he was getting to be well liked by his hypnotist and research professor, Dr. Gunther, and the staff.

Simpkins droned on in his self-important delivery, "Psychoanalysis is primarily a system or method of clinical psychological practice that concerns itself with the effort to interpret and to treat various visceral, nervous, and mental disorders based on the understanding of their most fundamental causes growing out of the thought processes, nature, and life of the individual."

Garven scribbled the definition in his notes. Definitions were prime test material. Knowledge of that fact always stood him in good stead.

"While we are not yet ready at our fledgling stage in this class to cope with abnormal psychology and its treatment—that being best left to those of us who are experts in the field—we can begin to deal with the underlying cognitive and experiential basis of the factors that lead to both normal and to abnormal behavior. We can learn somewhat of the science of the psyche, the mind. Your readings will include selections from the pioneer in this field; I refer, of course, to the late Professor Dr. Sigmund Freud of Vienna." His voice dropped several decibels in deference and in modesty. "I, of course, had the privilege of working with Sigmund."

Dr. Simpkins met the aging psychoanalyst in the receiving line of a seminar social function in 1938 in Berlin, a year before Freud's death. Dr. Simpkins remained among the legions of followers who did not call him Sigmund to his face.

Garven despised the whole phony name-dropping routine and just wanted Simpkins to get onto the stuff worth taking notes on for tests.

"My mentor has been misunderstood, and I would like to ensure that those within the sound of my voice…" And the voice was becoming more sonorous and Shakespearean with each paragraph, "carry with them an appreciation of his greatness. The uninformed dwell on the sexual side of his discoveries. At this juncture, I am reminded of an amusing story." He chuckled, appreciating the timeliness of the anecdote and the anticipated approval of the audience for his jocularity. "It seems that young Sigmund (Simpkins was now pronouncing it Zigmond) took a romantic fancy to a fashionable young lady in Berlin." Simpkins chuckled for a moment, unable to contain himself. "And the proper young lady approached her aristocratic father for his permission to allow her to attend functions with the newly famous physician." Simpkins had to pause to regain full control, he was laughing so heartily. "'Oh, my,' said the careful father, 'Not the Freud boy, he has a dirty mind.'" Simpkins's rich laugh filled the hall. He was proud of another successful delivery of his favorite joke. It had been similarly successful for twenty-seven years.

The audience of students laughed appreciatively on cue.

"*The sucks*," thought Garven. He laughed harder than the rest, but his laugh was at the pomposity of the professor.

Dr. Simpkins caught Garven's eye as they both laughed since the premed student was in his usual seat on the front row. "Freud worked with Breuer in hypnotizing patients and found this method to be a most useful tool to ferret out the hidden factors of the mind and psychopathology that eventuated in the observed behaviors. We will begin to examine hypnosis today. Since this subject can only occupy an abbreviated place in our extensive introductory course material, I expect you to take careful notes and to pay close attention," Professor Dr. Simpkins warned.

Enough said for Garven. "A word to the wise is sufficient" was an adage that was made for the premed student. He wrote down every word.

"My mentor, Sigmund—and I don't want to hear any of you referring to Professor Dr. Freud with that unearned familiarity—first learned that certain mental factors lay unremembered, hidden deep in the mind, in what he called the subconscious, and hypnosis was a most useful tool to explore the subconscious psyche and to bring to consciousness the long suppressed and covert thoughts and feelings in those who could submit to hypnosis. One of your members, Mr. Wilsonhulme, has been working in our laboratory and has proved to be a most apt hypnosis subject. We will expect a special written report from that student before quarter's end."

Garven blushed. The few students sitting around him who knew Garven looked at him briefly with the pleasure that fans get out of basking in the presence of a celebrity.

Those premed students within sight of him looked on with undisguised envy and whispered, "Brownnoser."

Before that afternoon's hypnosis session began, Garven made it a point to broach the subject of his getting paid for his two and a half months of work as promised by Dr. Gunther.

"Jess, my poy," Dr. Gunther said matter-of-factly. "Indeedt you shall pe paid as soon as the next accounting period. I presume that you haf kept the record off the hours that you haf spent in the laboratory."

Garven withdrew a paper from his pocket to show the professor. Dr. Gunther made a dismissive gesture.

"Not necessary to show me, youngk men. Just take that accounting to the departmental secretary alongk mit this note from me, and all vill pe vell, not zo?"

He hurriedly wrote a note:

> *Elizabeth,*
> *Please to record the wages for this young man, Garven Wilsonhulme, who has worked in the laboratory on the hypnosis project. He is to have payment at the rate of .60 per hour.*
> *P. Gunther, Prof.*

Garven got back into the work without another thought about his salary until the following day, when he delivered the note to the imperious departmental secretary.

In an extensive display of her disregard for his paltry problems and of her interest in more pressing and weighty matters, Miss Elizabeth Thorton-Mulberry took the two papers from Garven and said, "I will file them with accounting. They will be taken care of in proper order."

Garven hesitated, not realizing that his audience was over.

"Is there more?" Miss Thorton-Mulberry queried with a frosty look that bespoke the concept that it had better be very important if he did have more.

"No, Ma'am," Garven said submissively and backed out of the heavy, dark, oak-lined office.

By the time he put on his vile-smelling sweats for his wrestling workout, Garven had had a crawful and was looking for the release of his body contact sport. He ran six miles in a little under thirty minutes and was soaked with sweat while he moved through his routine of jumping jacks, push-ups, pull-ups and free weight lifting. He was still feeling the adrenaline or testosterone or whatever it was when he went at Pete Barnhienel in a bout to build up his skills against faster opponents and against Derek van Leventhal to build up his endurance against stronger competitors.

"You are as fast as me, Garven," said Pete when he finally signaled that he wanted to quit. Wrestling the somewhat larger opponent had worn him out.

Garven beat Derek three falls out of four even though the senior outweighed Garven by two weight divisions.

"You're lookin' good, Garven. I think you are almost as good as Hector already. I'm lookin' for you to take the conference this year."

"Oh, c'mon," Garven said, embarrassed.

"I mean it. Keep up the work, and you will be there. You won all three matchups so far this quarter, right?"

"Um hmmh."

"You're in great shape. You ought to be about perfect by the conference matches in March. I still got to say something, Garven. It's great to win, but it isn't everything. Remember, we represent Stanford, and that means something; all I'm trying to say is to remember that wrestling, like any other sport, is still just a game. Winning isn't everything."

"Um hmmh," Garven said. He thought, "*First place is the only acceptable thing. I think Vince Lombardi said it, and he was right. And I am going to win. I don't get that same warm and fuzzy feeling about Stanford as old Derek. It's about time Stanford stopped being so lovey and kissy, and started winning a few games. The football team is pathetic.*"

Garven won the next three matches, against UC Berkeley, UCLA, and College of the Pacific. Pepperdine was next up, and so far as Garven had heard, they did not have anybody any good in the 144-pound class. Pete told him the scuttlebutt was that they might not even have a guy in the 144-pound division, so he would get a bye. Garven was feeling good, what with his dual successes in his college studies and in his wrestling for a change.

CHAPTER
Ten

The good feeling was destined not to last, however. Garven had told Grantland, Frosty, David, and Devon about his conversation with Alan the same day that it took place.

Frosty said, "It's only a matter of time. They must be taking this stuff pretty seriously to be making such a slow process out of it."

"Maybe that's good news," ventured Devon, ever the optimist.

"I think it's more a matter of what my daddy says: 'The millstone of God grinds very slowly, but exceedingly fine,'" Grantland suggested.

"Thanks, Grantland, I needed to be cheered up," said Garven sourly.

"Ah, shucks," replied Grantland. "It wasn't nuthin'."

The week before dead week in mid-December, Garven received a knock on his dorm room door.

"C'mon in, its open," he called, reluctant to leave the German passage he was finishing.

Instead of entering, the knocker rapped again. Garven pushed his cane-back chair away from the small writing desk, keeping his eyes on the German phrases until he had to turn to open the knob.

There stood a uniformed campus security cop, a rent-a-cop, as they were derisively referred to by the students. This man was seventy if he was a day. He reached out a wrinkled and freckled hand to Garven without speaking. The hand held an envelope with Garven's full name typed in bold capitals on its front. To be difficult, Garven did not take the envelope.

"You Wilsonhulme?" The rent-a-cop pronounced it Wilson-huulmee in a drawn-out and irritating drawl.

"Yeah," answered Garven. He still made no move to take the envelope.

"This here's for you, then. Official," the security officer said. He thought, *"Snotty punk, I hope it's a good kick in the balls."*

Garven finally took the envelope from the officer's hand. He said, "Okay, so what do I do with this?" He thought, *"Your big activity of the night is over, back to your donuts, Sarge."*

The security policeman had already made an about-face and was into the hall without answering.

"Jerk," Garven said low enough so the man would not be able to hear him. "Big shot."

But he could feel his blood racing.

The message was typed under the letterhead of the office of the assistant dean of students and was signed legibly in bold stroke black ink by I. Winkler, Ivan-the-Terrible himself. It was terse:

> *Present yourself at the office of the dean of students on Wednesday, December 17, 1949, for a meeting of the utmost seriousness. Your failure to attend will constitute grounds for expulsion.*
> *I. Winkler*

Garven involuntarily held his breath. Then, he gulped. As ridiculous as it could be, he felt the sudden sting of tears welling up behind his eyes. He felt the muscles in the back of his neck knot up, and a headache clamped onto his forehead. He felt panicky, almost faint. It was hard to think. All he could think of was his whole career going down the drain. All because of that stupid streaker incident. A flash of bitter hatred for Alan Crowder rose through him. He knew exactly what had gone on, as exactly as if he had been an eavesdropper on the conversation between Ivan-the-Terrible and that sniveling snake, Alan.

He sat down and consciously strove to get back his control. He had to talk to the other guys, and he could not look like he had flipped out. He had to be cool.

A second knock came on his door. Now, what?

He walked to the door and met Grantland, David, and Devon as they entered.

"Have a visitor?" Devon asked as soon as the door was closed.

"Yeah. I take it the three of you did, too."

"Um hmmh," the other three answered.

"Now what do we do?" Grantland asked. He did not seem overly worried; he was just being practical.

"You mean after we kill young Crowder?" asked Devon with venom dripping off every word.

"First of all, we need to go see Frosty. And we can't be absolutely, positively, completely, perfectly certain that our friend, Alan, is a gutless, reptilian, conniving, self-absorbed, quisling of a rat fink, though, can we?" said Grantland in sweet, assuaging tones. His eyes, like those of Devon's, spoke of mayhem and murder.

The three of them appeared at Frosty McTavish's door and shared the camaraderie of the identical letters with him.

Frosty said, "I don't much relish getting kicked out of here. Won't look too good on the old scholastic record, don't you see? I plan to eat crow or anything else they want to dish up; to crawl, beg, cry, or promise. Whatever it takes."

"Me, too," offered David disconsolately.

None of the others had any better ideas.

Grantland said, "We can do a Stonewall Jackson on them—just don't tell 'em nothin'. Deny everything. Blame scuzebag Crowder for everything. Stick together."

None of them had any good ideas, including Grantland's poor effort.

December 17 was a week away; it seemed like tomorrow. Garven summed it up for the condemned coconspirators. He said, "One of my favorite songs is '*On the Grand Canyon Line*' by Burl Ives. The bank robber has just been caught and condemned to die by hanging. He said, 'Five hours to live, boys. How the time it does fly.'"

"And on that cheery note, let's all go home and drink hemlock," said Grantland.

"*Forsan et haec olim meminisse juvabit* (Maybe we'll laugh about this one day)," Garven said, dragging up his old Latin.

"Don't stand around on one leg, waiting for that day," said Devon.

The more Garven thought about it, the madder he got. It colored his every thought and emotion. He became short-tempered and irritable. The next day, he got a c-s speeding ticket from the stupid campus cops—it just so happened that the fat old man who had delivered the note to his dorm room had the opportunity. The ticket would cost him twenty corp yard hours or a forty-dollar fine. He did not have forty dollars, so there would go his weekends for a month. Great.

Garven was seething at this latest contrary turn of events when he got into his workout clothes. They were still wet from yesterday's and probably from last week's sweat. Garven usually did not notice, but today he was appalled by the smell. It seemed impossible that his own body could generate such a stink. It made him madder. It started to rain outside, so he could not do his running. He had a load of pent-up frustrations and angers to get rid of, and the inability to vent them by running made him madder. He would have to jog in the field house, slowed down by the crowd of all the other jocks, jostling and getting into each other's way. That made him still madder.

The wrestler moved onto the already overcrowded inside track.

No sooner had he done so than an announcement came over the loud-speaker: "*All non-track and field personnel, clear the track immediately. The track is for official runners only. Sorry!*"

Garven was getting really mad now. He complied with the egregious demand, but with a wounded spirit at the unfairness of it. Wrestling was every bit as important a sport as track and field. His temper was at a strong simmer, and the temperature was still climbing.

He found a place to run around the second-floor bleachers. The aisles in the old indoor stadium were narrow, and even when he was not being interfered with by other jocks with the same idea, he barked his shins on the benches. That made him a little angrier each time. He remembered an incident his dad, Dr. Wilsonhulme, had told him about. A small circus had had a pretty good collection of animals and a well-known animal training act. The bears, the lions, and the tigers lined up on stands all along the entrance into the performing arena and had been taught to sit on their hind legs while the cougars pranced through to where the trainer had them do their tricks—jump through hoops, lay on their backs, dance with each other, and the like. One particular cougar had a streak of malicious mischief, and every single day, when it ran through the line of bears, lions, and tigers standing on their truncated cone stands, it would flick out a claw and nick a bit of flesh off the foreleg of one particular bear. Day after day, the cougar clawed the bear's leg, and day after day, the bear perched stoically on its stand. One day, and Dr. Wilsonhulme had happened to be at the circus that day, as the cougar trotted blithely through as usual, and raised its paw to cut the bear's leg again, as usual, the bear suddenly whipped out its massively powerful forelimb, claws fully extended, and struck the cougar full force on the side of its head. The cougar was decapitated, and the head rolled up the aisle in front of the trotting cougars. The bear otherwise did not move from its stand. That was one of Garven's favorite stories. Each time he deviated a little from his course down the narrow aisle and barked another little bit of flesh off his sore shin, the story came back to him and fed his anger.

The football team's number one running back, campus heartthrob, local newspaper's sweetheart, and one of Garven's big pains, though he had never met the man, happened to be obliged to run along the same difficult aisle track as Garven to get his aerobic exercise done on that drizzly December day. The football star ran the opposite direction to that of Garven, and each time they passed one another, one of them would have to jump up on the benches to allow the other to get by. It did not make Garven any too happy to have to break his stride and rhythm once every round of the building, but if it had been a fair exchange, he would have tolerated the inconvenience without incident. As it was, however, he was obliged to do most of the jumping onto the benches as Mr. Touchdown, who even wore a workout sweatshirt emblazoned, "MR. T," threatened to run Garven down in a game of pedestrian chicken. That little injustice, unfairness, and indignity made Garven all the angrier, an anger that grew by increments every trip around the stadium, just like the bear in Dr. Wilsonhulme's circus story. His temper temperature was approaching a low boil.

Garven felt testier as his anger grew. He ran closer and closer to collision each round until, finally, the football hero felt obliged to shove the smaller wrestler out of the way on one encounter. He did not feel obliged to take a turn jumping awkwardly onto the benches.

"Watch it, creep. This area is for the football squad," was all he said and continued his imperious run around the stadium aisle.

Garven was beyond thinking. He was at a rolling boil. He did not remember the rest of his run around the improvised indoor track except that he was moving much faster than before. He no longer felt tired. He did not see the periphery, only a blood-pink haze coloring the path directly in front of him. He weighed 140 pounds and Mr. T weighed 206. Garven ran right over the top of him. Coyotes took down bulls. Garven was barely aware of his attack on the far larger man.

The football player was stunned, as much by the surprise of having the worm turn as by the actual collision. He struck his occiput, elbows, low back, and butt on the benches and floor. He felt dazed, but was awake enough to see a staccato drum roll of sharp fists fire out of the haze and into his face before he lost consciousness. The whole encounter took no more than five seconds, and there were no witnesses. Garven's blood was so up that he stepped back from punching the downed athlete and then proceeded to run right over the inert man's legs and torso. Had the campus heartthrob and media hero not come to and dragged himself off to the side under the benches, Garven would have come back and run over him again and still again until he felt like he had had all of the aerobic exercise he needed for the day.

The hero was still sitting in bewilderment, nursing the lumps on his face and body, when Garven trotted nonchalantly down the stairs, along the first-floor aisle, and out of the stadium into the rain. He did not notice that he was getting wet, and his adrenaline surge did not fully dissipate until he had wrestled three matches. His teammates said he had never looked better.

The twelfth of December was a cheerless dull day that saw the air fill with the characteristic Northern California rain that was so fine and dispersed that its quality was somewhere between a dense haze and a drizzle, not quite a real rain. It was cold, a marrow-chilling, penetrating wet cold for which there was no dressing. The university's response was to turn the temperatures in the class-rooms to the thermostat mark, "stifling," which was two marks above "stuffy," and one mark above "too hot." Garven presumed this kindness was for the sake of the women; they constantly complained of being too cold, it seemed to him.

He found himself seated in the front seat, drowsily listening to the soothing, cultured voice of Dr. Edith Brawlbecker, associate professor of English. Sweltering alongside him in the next seat on the front row was Forest McTavish, who was equally somnolent.

"Last period, we divided into two sections—the first group choosing to analyze for us Conrad's *Heart of Darkness*. The reports on that allegory are due at the end of the period today. No later," Dr. Brawlbecker announced.

Garven and Frosty had been so preoccupied with the gathering streaker scandal that they had both chosen to concentrate on the second of Dr. Brawlbecker's two choices, Herman Melville's *Moby Dick*, because it would not be due for another week. They had had a week to prepare their comments and had known that their in-class oral participation would be tallied as part of their overall grades. Nevertheless, neither had prepared adequately and banked on the improbability of being called on to wax eloquent at any length.

"Now, we turn to Melville's work. For purposes of discussion, let me read to you an excerpt. I want you to evaluate the allegorical implications of this passage as a prolegomenon to our class discussion today," the professor said.

Garven spelled "prolegomenon" phonetically as best he could on a small note sheet and included a question mark. He showed the note to Frosty, who returned a negative shrug of his shoulders.

"For those of you with the *Official Stanford Reading Series*, I will be reading from page 385. I will skip about, so follow closely:

> "Oh, my Captain! my Captain! noble soul! grand old heart, after all! why should any one give chase to that hated fish! Away with me! let us fly these deadly waters! let us home! … What is it, what nameless, inscrutable, unearthly thing is it; what cozening, hidden lord and master, and cruel, remorseless emperor commands me; that against all natural lovings and longings, I so keep pushing, and crowding, and jamming myself on all the time; recklessly making me ready to do what in my won proper, natural heart, I durst not so much as dare? Is Ahab, Ahab? Is it I, God, or who, that lifts this arm?…
>
> "Ahab crossed the deck to gaze over on the other side; but started at two reflected, fixed eyes in the water there. Fedallah was motionlessly leaning over the same rail."

Dr. Brawlbecker paused to let the power of the passage have its effect. As she had done for seventeen years, she looked out over the vapid, disinterested faces, hoping against hope to see an upturned set of eyes burning with her same passion. She thought she caught a glimmer of interest from a small young man on the first row. She made a quick check of her seating roll and said, "Mr. Wilsonhulme," and was glad to see the appropriate head bob in her direction in response. "Mr. Wilsonhulme, what can you tell me about this whale? What is the meaning of *Moby Dick*?"

Garven was moved to ask what there could possibly be about whales that would interest a professor of humanities. As he really saw it, there were whales, and there were whales. He liked the book, all right, but saw it only as a great story. Somehow, English teachers all felt the need to ruin a perfectly good yarn by analyzing it to death, by seeking the deep inner meaning. It was just a story about hunting a big white whale for cripes sake.

He was about to speak when Frosty leaned toward him and quickly whispered, "Hey, Garven, why don't you tell old Dr. Ballbreaker that you think Moby Dick is some kind of venereal disease?"

That struck Garven as hysterical, and he had to choke to suppress an uncontrolled and disastrous laugh. "Excuse me," he coughed out. "I know this is supposed to be a big allegory and to have a deep meaning, but couldn't it be like Upton Sinclair said—just one of the world's great stories, a tale of men and whales and the sea?"

She was offended, disappointed. Garven could see that. He knew better than to suggest that something in English class was just a good story and to hint that the search for its meaning might be futile, or worse, that it might spoil the story. He wanted to kick himself. He remembered the time at Burton-Cagle, when Mr. Harcrest had gotten all enthusiastic about William Blake's poem, *Tyger, Tyger*. Harcrest quoted the first verse:

"Tyger, Tyger burning bright,
In the forests of the night,
What immortal hand or eye,
Dare frame thy fearful symmetry?"

"Billy," Harcrest had asked, singling out Billy Dell Geodes, the most concrete-thinking person on the planet. He was an Okie. "Billy," he had said, "Tell us what this poem is all about."

"It's about tigers."

"What kind of tigers, Billy?" Mr. Harcrest had prodded.

He was after that hidden deep meaning; Garven had known that.

"What kind of tigers are there?" Billy had asked innocently.

"Well, there are tigers and there are allegorical tigers," Mr. Harcrest had pursued, becoming a bit put out, like all English teachers did when somebody could not get that deep inner-meaning stuff.

"Jeez, and I thought there were just tigers and tigers."

Billy had not fared well in English. He never did get it. You just had to get all warm and fuzzy over the deep inner meaning, then the teacher would eat it up. You could get a good grade anytime just so long as you could come up with the hidden meaning, no matter how goofy. It occurred to Garven at that moment that he had better start coming up with something about the deep inner meaning, or he would be in Billy's boat.

"It was Sinclair Lewis, Mr. Wilsonhulme," Dr. Brawlbecker corrected him.

"Oh, that's right, thanks," Garven said even though he had no firsthand idea of what the critic had said. He just threw in that bit from *Cliff's Notes – Study Aids*, the condensed version and explanation of the hidden meaning put out for guys like him who just wanted to get through it.

"I am sure you see Ahab as more than just a whaling boat captain out to catch a whale for the market. Ahab represents mankind in a sense. He sought to capture the great white whale to assert his own, and therefore, man's, supremacy over evil, or as Ahab termed it, the monomaniac incarnation of a superior, oppressive, and evil power. Ahab spent forty years on a great quest, one taken for all mankind, to subdue the evil of the universe, a desire possessed by us all. Here is how Ahab described it:

> "I see in him outrageous strength, with an inscrutable malice sinewing it. That inscrutable thing is chiefly what I hate; and be the white whale agent, or be the white whale principal, I will wreak that hate upon him. Talk not to me of blasphemy, man; I'd strike the sun if it insulted me."

Garven identified himself fully with Ahab's sentiment.

"Now, Mr. Wilsonhulme, I am sure you comprehend the magnificent allegory, the very purpose of Melville's timeless book!"

She was really into it now.

Garven knew better than to miss his chance to show the lady professor how sensitive he was to the inner meaning, how genuine his feelings were about the moving piece of literature. He said with quiet conviction, "And more than that, Dr. Brawlbecker, maybe Ahab saw that the great evil represented by the white whale had contended with his own soul. Remember, in that passage you read to us, where Ahab looked over the rail into the sea and saw the two reflected, fixed eyes in the water? I think he was seeing the eyes of the devil, or at least the reflection of evil itself, and it was his own eyes he was seeing."

Dr. Brawlbecker quietly clapped her thin hands. "Bravo, Mr. Wilsonhulme. I think there is hope for you yet. I hope the rest of you can capture the majesty of this allegory and that your insights will be well presented in your papers. They are due one week from today." She was thrilled that, at last, one out of the hundreds of insipid students who had sat in her classroom, because it was required of them, had apprehended the vision. It was a memorable day.

Garven basked in the glow of her praise. He was especially pleased with himself because his last insight had not even come from the *Cliff's Notes*. Frosty made a gesture of sticking his finger down his throat and gagging theatrically. Garven chose to ignore him, the insensitive clod.

"I so want you to get into the marrow of this work, as Thoreau would have termed it, that I will make you an offer of an alternative," Dr. Brawlbecker enthused. "You may choose to write the paper as previously assigned and take the final, or you can write a double-length paper comparing and contrasting the two allegories, *The Heart of Darkness* and *Moby Dick*. I will look more favorably on those who choose the more industrious second option."

That was simple enough for Garven. Between Frosty and the *Cliff's Notes* and himself, they should be able to come up with enough hidden meanings to melt her heart.

Like all impending dooms, the seventeenth of December came. It was an appropriately gloomy day when Garven, David Applegate, Grantland Kurze, Devon Upshire, and Frosty McTavish made their way into the foreboding outer office of Dr. Howard Taft Winslow, dean of students. Alan Crowder's absence was conspicuous and ominous. They were five minutes early.

"We have an appointment with the dean," Garven announced to the severe head of the dean's secretary, who had not deigned even to look up to acknowledge their presence.

She looked to be in her sixties and had her hair pulled hard enough back into a spinsterish bun to flatten the wrinkles of her forehead. She wore a plain gray business suit that covered her from ankles to mid-neck to her wrists. She was altogether reminiscent of Elizabeth in Dr. Simpkins's office, all warmth and helpfulness.

They must have to attend a special school, Garven mused to himself.

"Please wait in the seats provided," she said simply without looking up.

"When will we see the dean?" Garven asked, wearying of his role as group spokesman already.

"When he is ready. Now, if there is nothing else, I will get back to my work." They sat for an hour.

"Think he forgot about us?" David whispered at four-thirty.

"You wish," answered Frosty.

Shortly after this conversation, the only words to pass between the nervous boys as they sat fretting for the hour, Ivan Winkler, assistant dean, swept into the antechamber, checking his watch.

"Is The Man in, Miss Haverport?" he asked.

Somehow, Garven knew she would be amiss.

Miss Haverport evidently did not consider the assistant dean important enough for eye contact, either.

She said into her stack of important papers, "Dr. Winslow is finishing a meeting with the alumni board. He should be through any minute. They are running a bit late."

There was no place for Ivan-the-Terrible to sit. Grantland got up and politely offered the assistant dean his chair. Dr. Winkler got a cup of coffee from the side table near nice Miss Haverport's desk and accepted Grantland's offer without thanks or comment. Presumably, he considered it an accepted privilege of his rank.

The quiet of the antechamber office was broken by the decorous buzz of the intercom from Dr. Winslow's office. A deep voice sounded through the microphone on her desk, asking, "Is Winkler here?"

"He is, Sir."

"Send him in then. I'm running a little late (sixty-seven minutes). Tell him we will have to make this brief." In the quiet room, the announcement was clearly audible.

"You may go in now, Sir," came Miss Haverport's pleasant and correct voice, unhurried and disinterested. "And he wishes for me to convey the message that he is running a little late and your meeting will, of necessity, be abbreviated."

She kept her lips pursed the whole time.

It was like an echo. Under other circumstances, and perhaps at a different time, the echo might have been mildly amusing, but today, Garven had no inclination to be mildly amused. He was not sure whether the idea that the meeting would be brief was a good one or a bad one for them. In fact, at this point, he was not altogether sure that he and the other sophomore men were even going to be included. The five young men kept their seats as Dr. Winkler got up and proceeded towards the inner sanctum door.

"Come along. Smartly now," commanded the assistant dean.

The students all reacted as if the idea of following the administrator was entirely novel. With surprised expressions, they each straightened up out of their chairs and trotted obediently, single file, into Dr. Winslow's office.

"Greetings, Ivan," said the dean, rising to shake his assistant's hand.

He gestured to a comfortable padded chair next to his desk, and Dr. Winkler sat down. The boys remained standing in awkward, fidgety silence.

Ignoring the boys, who might not even have been there for all the attention they attracted, Dean Winslow asked Winkler, "Refresh my memory. What is this business all about?"

Assistant Dean Winkler gave a three-minute, detailed rendition of the whole sorry, sordid affair of the streaker, naming names, accurately outlining the roles played by each of the names.

"Ah, yes, the public disruption," was the dean's only comment. "And in the course of your investigation, did you find evidence of a history of perversion on the part of the perpetrators?" was his only question.

Garven was not at all sure that he liked being referred to in the third person and being treated as if he were not even there. He was altogether certain that he did not like the reference to perversion. He could see that this had gotten way out of hand.

"Here is the report, Sir. Your question is referenced here," Winkler told the dean, pointing out a paragraph in the middle of the several-page document.

"Um hum," Dean Winslow commented. He still had not bothered to glance at the perpetrators. The dean took another two minutes to thumb through the report. "Good job, Ivan. Thorough. What is the recommendation?"

"Expulsion. I don't really see any other alternative."

Gulp. An infectious lump caught in each of the young men's throats at the same moment.

It must have been the sound of the quartet of swallows that attracted Dean Winslow's attention. He looked at the young students as if he had only just realized that they were in the room. "What have you to say for yourselves, gentlemen?"

None of the students spoke. They could not really think of anything useful for their cause to say right then.

"Don't all speak at once," the dean said. His voice was not as angry or as dictatorial as they expected.

The boys all looked at Garven.

"*Who died and left me in charge?*" he thought to himself.

The silence was awkward.

"Uh, Sir. We, uh, don't know what's in that report. We're not quite sure what all of this is about," Garven began.

"Coy, eh?" came the dean's sharp reply.

Ivan-the-Terrible just snorted.

"Sir?" Garven decided to brazen it out a bit for a moment. Not too much, and not too long.

"And you are Mister…?"

"Wilsonhulme, Garven, Sir."

"Well, Wilsonhulme. We have irrefutable evidence that the four of you were behind the perverted episode at the Stern Hall dance some weeks ago. We have several eyewitnesses. It is a waste of all of all of our times for you to deny your complicity. Back to my original question: What do you have to say for yourselves?"

Garven looked from one coconspirator to another. Their unspoken facial and body language message was to confess, to beg, to grovel. He said finally, "I guess it's true that we had something to do with it."

"You guess?! Something to do with it!? You had everything to do with it!"

"Begging your pardon, Sir, but that is not quite accurate."

The dean and the assistant dean pierced Garven with their gazes.

"None of us had *our* clothes off. Might I ask, since this is all so thorough, but where is the streaker himself? The alleged streaker?"

That seemed to give the administrators a moment of pause.

Garven filled the pause. "I am not sure I understand, Sir. What it is that is so terrible that we—I mean the four of us here—have done? Your note and Dr. Winkler just now said that we should be expelled for whatever it was we did."

He was assiduously polite, and kept his eyes downcast and inoffensive. But his assertiveness seemed to break the seemingly irrepressible juggernaut of catastrophe planned for his and his friends' careers.

"You needn't trouble yourself over the other fellow," said Assistant Dean Winkler authoritatively.

"Alan Crowder."

"Um, yes."

"It's fair to ask what is going to happen to him, right? I guess that everyone wants to be fair, right?"

"I think it in the best interest of the young man if we were to limit any discussion of his involvement," said the dean. "I guess it is proper for you to know that we have had the boy and his father in. He will be receiving some counseling before returning next quarter."Winslow regretted saying that as soon as it was out.

"So, I take it that you would not think expulsion was a fair punishment for us. We were only peripherally involved, after all." Garven's voice had lost its earlier faint trembling borne of trepidation.

Young Wilsonhulme had him, Dean Winslow had to admit it. Ivan-the-Terrible had a dour look.

"Let me turn the tables on you, young man, and don't be too smug," said the dean. "You are entirely mistaken if you think this is a democracy. I assure you that we can do as we well please. This is our province, and you will get nowhere butting heads with me. Now that that is settled, what do you think I should do about you?"

Without hesitation, Garven said succinctly, "Give us a few corp yard hours. Teach us a lesson. Make us an example for the rest of the students. You have done your duty; we go back to being the regular decent students we have always been. The university gets its due, and you don't have to ruin some young guys' lives just to make a point."

He avoided catching Ivan-the-Terrible's eye.

"Again, young man, don't get cocky. You are still in an execrable position."

Garven knew that for sure. He just hoped he was not making things worse, but he was in the slime water up to his lower lip already, no use trying to back off now.

"I will propose a take-it-or-leave-it set of options," the dean intoned brusquely. "You can leave the school at the end of the quarter and for good, or you can opt either to do fifty corp yard hours or you can paint every bicycle rack on campus. The time for this meeting is up. Make your choice as a group."

Garven inclined his head to his fellows, and they came together for a very brief huddle.

"The bicycle racks. Nobody says we have to do a good job. And nobody is going to monitor how thorough we are after a while. I hate the corp yard," Grantland urged with a suspiration, desperate not to be overheard.

Evidently, he spoke for all of them, including his deep sigh.

"The racks for all of us," announced Garven.

Winslow laughed. Winkler did not catch the joke.

"Just the bicycle racks. Our punishments are not more medieval than that. Report to Dean Winkler then," the Stanford dean of students said.

In the antechamber, Assistant Dean Winkler, trying to recoup his small loss, said, "Start tomorrow."

He flattened his lips in what, for him, passed for a smile. It was more like an accidental slit in his lower face. There was malice in that expression.

"That's not fair, dean," remonstrated Garven. "You know that means certain failure for every one of us. Finals are ten days off. There is no way we can do that work and do finals as well. I am sure you agree that finals are more important, Sir." His tone was conciliatory, not begging, but not contentious, either.

It seemed to abrade Winkler to say it, but he finally relented and agreed.

"Okay. Report day one of winter quarter to the grounds maintenance building for your paint and brushes. It will be a pleasure to see you little Lord Fountleroys dirty your pristine hands."

The Crowder Rare Books Section of the Stanford University library came into being, on paper, and in the bank, before Christmas, 1950. There were contributions from the Applegate Foundation, from Dr. Peter Wilsonhulme, from the K and H Oil Company of Fort Worth, Texas, and from the law firm of Harrolsen, McTavish, Leland, and Compers of Boston, Massachusetts. There were substantial tax write-offs involved.

CHAPTER
Eleven

Garven Wilsonhulme was becoming accustomed to confrontations. When he found out in casual conversation with the psychology lab techs that they had been paid for the last accounting period, he became less concerned and more angry. He was owed for more than two and a half months of work in the hypnosis study by the time autumn quarter finals were completed, and if it required of him to have a confrontation with Dr. Gunther, then so be it, he thought.

"I need to have a word with you, Dr. Gunther," he said to the old professor.

"Anytime, my poy," answered the German researcher.

"I would like it to be now, if that's okay. Something has been bothering me, Sir. I think we should get that settled before we start work this afternoon, so I can concentrate."

The two walked into the book and paper strewn untidiness of Horst Gunther's office and took seats facing each other. Garven disliked having to bring this subject up again. He thought a lot of Dr. Gunther and enjoyed the project. The professor was unfailingly polite and respectful of Garven and of the research staff, and Garven was loathe to disrupt that relationship. Still, he had to speak up for himself.

"Dr. Gunther, this is awkward, but I still haven't been paid for my work in the project. It has been quite a while now. Nobody even seems to acknowledge that I am involved, let alone employed."

"*Ach du lieber!*" the professor ejaculated. He was genuinely surprised, bordering on being shocked. "I hat no idea. Der muss be zome mistake at vork here. Alzo, I vill speak mit the bean counters in the department this fery day. I myself remember my starving student days. It shall be attended to. You haf my vord on it, my poy."

That was enough said. Garven still harbored doubts, not of Dr. Gunther's good intentions, but of his memory for prosaic details. The scholarly Old World gentleman was the very model of the absentminded professor—mismatched socks, stained shirts, letters from creditors scattered on his desk with snippets of lab data, facsimiles of journal articles, discomposed stacks of unread journals, and graduate student papers and tests waiting to be graded. The chaotic disarray of the office, indicative of a cluttered mind, did not inspire confidence in the young man, who, even at his tender age, was becoming increasingly compulsive about the orderliness of his own desk.

His lab session was his last responsibility before leaving for Arizona for the Christmas vacation. There was not much devotion to duty by anyone in the lab that close to the holidays. The staff had made some chips and dips, cookies, punch, and, for the professor, one of the braver women had made a *Gugelhupf,* a molded cake with a hole in the center filled in with raisins and almonds. The confection was not quite up to German standards, but it was very good, and delighted Dr. Gunther that such an attempt had been made. He and Garven spent the afternoon in a casual instruction in the art and practice of self-hypnosis, which was not in the direct line of the research grant.

"I can tell you, youngk man, that this vill standt you in goodt steadt in the future. In my natif *Deustchland,* der are practitioners who can teach dose in pain to utilize the techniques I am teachingk you today to get away from the suffering, as to take a vacation from the pain, don't you see? Even *kinder*—the children—can learn it. This I have seen mit mine own eyes. In this country, satly, there is no entusiasm fur the practice."

Garven was an interested and apt pupil and subject. By the end of the day, he was able to put himself into and out of a trance at will so long as there was not too much background distraction.

"You are the fastest learner and the best subject I haf known," praised the old man.

Garven felt that he had learned a useful stratagem. He could transport himself to a high mountain meadow or to the company of a sweet-natured and ample-bodied blond with ease when the ambiance of reality became disagreeable. That had to be worth something, he decided.

It continued to be the season for confrontations when Garven arrived in Emmett, Arizona, to spend the first portion of his Christmas vacation with his adopted father, Peter Wilsonhulme. Usually indulgent, and with a history of considerable forbearance when it came to his son, whom he had come to regard as both spoiled and selfish (his fault), but now, Dr. Wilsonhulme's patience had been strained to its limit.

Shortly after Garven had settled in and had eaten a large second helping of venison roast, the doctor fixed his adopted son and protégé with a firm look and said, "Garven, I have something of a serious note to discuss with you. I am not one to beat around the bush, so I will be direct."

Now what have I done? thought Garven.

His father went on. "You have gotten yourself into another scrape, Garven. A foolish boy's prank. And if I do say so myself, one that can be misinterpreted as involving a perversion."

Garven started to protest in his own defense, but Dr. Wilsonhulme put up a hand, indicating his desire to finish before he heard from the young man.

"I know the details. I also know that you were more or less the mastermind. Don't bother to deny it; that's water under the bridge. You will pay for your indiscretion with the dean's punishment. You might as well know that I have had to pay as well. There was one of those smug and veiled phone calls from the assistant dean, Winker, I think."

"Winkler," Garven contributed quietly.

"Yes, that sounds right. The upshot of that call is that I have made yet another contribution to an institution of learning on your behalf. That was to keep all of these antics off your record. That record remains spotless; you can thank me."

Garven nodded his appreciation on cue.

"Young man, that was not the first time. Did you know that? Did you really presume that your pranks, which are, no doubt, making you famous with your fellow students, were unknown to the faculty and the cops first at Burton-Cagle and now at Stanford?"

What could he say? Garven had, indeed, been unaware of the behind-the-scenes protections of his dad, which gave him all the more reason to feel a bond of gratitude and fealty to the man, but also a disturbing sense of obligation. He recognized the great difficulty of keeping a secret, and made a mental note to be more scrupulous about secrets in the future. He shrugged his confession. He was at the mercy of his angry father and would have to sit there and take the reproach.

"I said it was not the first time, but by heaven, boy, it will be the last. It is time for you to grow up. You are nearly twenty years old. By your age, I had been on my own and making my way for two full years."

"And walking four miles to school in Pennsylvania through six feet of snow, uphill both directions," thought the disrespectful young man, realizing that the reprimand was beginning to take a familiar turn.

"I'm not sure you fully appreciate what it takes to get into medical school, Garven. You cannot have something like this on your record. Grades and good family are not enough. There are boys with good grades coming from good families at a dime a dozen applying for the scarce places in medical schools. You have to have a perfectly clean nose; then, you have to convince the interviewers and admissions board that you will be the greatest doctor in the country. You can't let down for a minute. You have to be prepared for this new Med CAT test. I didn't have to contend with that, thank heavens. They're even starting to let more girls in—wasting the places—but since FDR and Truman, the liberals have been getting all the say. But I'm getting off the subject. No more foolishness, young man. Do you understand the significance to your life of that piece of advice? Do you?"

"Yes, Sir, I do. I'm sorry."

"Sorry won't do. What would you do if you didn't get into medical school? Go to law school?" Dr. Wilsonhulme shuddered slightly at the latter suggestion. "They let anybody in law school so far as I can see. Look what comes out! Maybe that's the kind of man you will turn out to be. Would that suit your fancy, Garven?"

He was getting insulting now. The worst thing the doctor could call a man was a lawyer, which he pronounced, "lie er."

"No, I am going to be a doctor. No matter what. Look, I fouled up; I admit it. It won't happen again. Listen, I'm doing okay otherwise. I just let these college jokes go too far. I don't really see why everybody is making so much out of them. Nobody got hurt. They seemed pretty innocent to me. But I have to admit, that kind of thing can hurt my chances to get into med school. I won't do it again, promise."

Dr. Wilsonhulme was sure he had gotten his point across, but added one final salvo. "I won't pay another exculpatory donation."

Garven was sure he meant it.

Rachel was pleased to see her son, surprised that he had come to Cipher earlier than usual in the vacation period. Garven kept a low profile, content to loll around the house and to sunbathe in the yard. He seemed amused by such small pleasures as the novelty of getting a suntan in the last week of December, the incongruity of decorative sleighs on paper snow in the bleaching heat and aridity of the desert, and the sign hanging in Big Lyle's window: "Happy Birthday, Jesus."

He rode into the craggy red mountains with Edward Sespootch, who seemed less animated, and more paunchy now even than last year. Garven knew his Indian friend had been drinking steadily; his mother had filled him in on all the local gossip over their first meal. He wondered if his friend was beginning to show the early signs of disintegration that characterized so many of the reservation men and if alcohol were not the root cause. Garven was neither a deep thinker nor a moralist. What Edward did was his own business, but still, he felt some concern for his friend's puffiness, lethargy, and depressed attitude. He worried about what things would be like when Edward's youthful reserves were used up. But for now, he contented himself to gallop over the dusty mountain trails, kicking up puffs and plumes to trail behind him and his old friend.

The early part of winter quarter was a chastening experience for Garven and the other infamous four. Painting the scores of bicycle racks all over the Stanford University campus, combined with the rigors of a demanding curriculum and his wrestling aspirations, left no time for a social life. Even doing a crummy job, the painting seemed to take forever. When the end of the task seemed in sight, the maintenance workers took perverse delight in turning up another hitherto unknown grouping of the metal bike stands. As they slapped on the thick paint, Garven and his friends could not help but observe that, in most cases, it was not necessary that more paint be applied to the racks that had paint approaching half an inch in thickness. It was abundantly evident that they were not the first nonprofessional painters to work on the rapidly multiplying structures. Alan Crowder was never seen at the painting sites even though David swore he had seen the streaker going into a class in the same building where his physics lecture was held. That evoked some nasty thoughts on the part of the young men paying their debt to society. Garven mused about what it must have cost to keep that creep in school and away from the comeuppance he and the others were enduring.

Two weeks into the quarter, the hypnosis project was completed, and Garven was out of a job, not that he was paid anything. He gave up on getting Dr. Gunther to do anything effective; what did the busy professor care? Garven was determined to get paid, as much for the principle that he could not be misused as for the actual money. He made up his mind to go to the psych department office as soon as he could see his way out from under the mountain of homework, term papers, idiot painting job, and wrestling. The wrestling was the only thing that kept him sane, and he was looking like the upcoming PAC champ. Garven needed the lift to his ego; so he continued to expend the necessary practice time, growing progressively more tired by the day.

The whole Stanford wrestling team was beginning to look like competitors, unlike their performance the year before. Their win-loss record was positive so far through autumn quarter of '50 and early winter quarter of '51—barely positive, but enough to hold their heads up. The quarter's first match had been against the University of San Diego, and Stanford had squeaked out a win. The two teams had evenly split the number of wins by their members, and Garven's pin of his opponent, the only pin by any wrestler in the entire match, had given Stanford the one extra point to make them the team winners. Only Derek had looked askance at Garven when his opponent had gotten a very bloody nose. Garven had been peeved at the questioning, sort of accusing, look and had insisted that he and the San Diego guy had just bumped heads. He did not mention that the force of the head bump had broken the San Diegan's nose.

Garven had won every match thus far and had the best official record in his weight class in the entire PAC. Only one other wrestler—Don Lomas, the heavyweight from UCSF—had a perfect record. Garven was full of vinegar when the Stanford team signed up for the yearly San Francisco AAU tournament. There were thirty-six registered teams and another eighty-two individual registrants in the huge tournament held in the Cow Palace. Everyone warned Garven that he would have to meet the perennial champion, a sixty-six-year-old hotel doorman from Oakland.

Garven tried not to scoff, but sixty-six? The guy had no business trying to hold on against the young bucks. It would be kind of fun to meet the old guy in the finals. His name was as proletarian as you can get, too, Bill Houseman. Garven checked out the first-round pairings and found that he was not matched up with Houseman. He was with one of the independents, not even a college guy. Garven knew better than to get too cocky, however—the tournament was a single elimination contest.

Garven pinned his man—a Chinese fellow who had never been to a wrestling match before—in the first period. In the second round, he beat a hugely strong but dumb stevedore who lived in the French neighborhood. He had meant to watch Bill Houseman wrestle, but their bouts had been going on at nearly the same time, so he missed it.

Pete Barnhienel said, "Hey, man. You had better check the old guy out. He is as tricky as a weasel. Everybody who goes against him is sure they won't fall for any of his funny moves, but they all eventually do. He has pinned every opponent he has met for the past ten years, they say."

Pete looked like he was going to win his division. He had already beaten the most highly touted wrestler in his class.

Garven caught the end of Houseman's third-round match—the part where the older man pinned his adversary. It didn't look like he was much of a wrestler, just the other guy looked worse. Garven became aware that the older wrestler was watching his own third-round match, which came half an hour later. There were six mats going at once, and the AAU officials were extremely efficient. By the four o'clock in the afternoon break, every division was down to four men in each weight class. Garven was paired up with the wrestler from San Diego whom he had already beaten twice in the college circuit. Bill Houseman was paired against the USC guy whom Garven had picked to win the tournament if he didn't win himself. He just did not envision Houseman winning that round and facing himself for the championship.

"Listen," Pete warned again, "you gotta keep away from him when he stands out there on one leg. I've been watching him all day; he kills everybody with that trick. Make him wait and come after you. I'm tellin' you."

"Hawthorne?" Garven asked, his USC opponent.

"No, dummy. Who cares about Hawthorne? It's that old geez, Bill Houseman, who you are gonna meet at nine o'clock or so tonight," Pete urged, getting exasperated that Garven did not seem to be listening to him.

"I have to fight one at a time, Pete. Get off my case. Hawthorne is an okay wrestler. I am not going to underestimate him."

That was apt advice for himself. Hawthorne was charged up, determined to beat his nemesis, Garven Wilsonhulme, from Stanford. He very nearly did, too. Garven won by a score of 11 to 9, one of the points from riding time. He was pooped when the match was done. His overly long hours of work and study were beginning to tell on him. He did not seem to be bouncing back as fast as he had earlier in the day.

Bill Houseman pinned his man. Garven now had a niggling suspicion that there was something to all the whisperings about the tricky hotel doorman. He hoped the old guy was as tired as he was. Houseman had to be; he had wrestled four times, just like Garven. Garven did not tally the minutes of wrestling in his comparison. Houseman had pinned most of his opponents in the first period after dancing around with them for a minute or two. He had paced himself so that his actual down and dirty wrestling time was half that which Garven had put in. He was not as tired as his younger competitor.

Garven's recuperative powers were in better tone than Houseman's, but Houseman had less from which to recuperate. Garven guessed that the two of them were about equal in terms of condition and tiredness, given their separate disadvantages of age versus the necessity of keeping of late study hours.

All other factors notwithstanding, Garven Wilsonhulme stood face-to-face with Bill Houseman for the championship at nine o'clock sharp. Bill had a surprisingly large and devoted following. He was something of a local newspaper hero, and the photographers and reporters from the *San Francisco Chronicle* and the *Oakland Expositor* were there, making themselves evident.

The ref dropped his hand in the signal to begin. Different from the college matches, the AAU officials used a whistle as well. It was hard for Garven to get used to the startle of the sudden shrill noise. He felt tired, almost drowsy, right at the time when his system should have been full of adrenaline. Nothing happened. Bill stood quietly, almost disinterestedly, waiting for Garven to bring the action to him. Garven resisted, heeding Pete's warning, although he was not about to admit that to Pete. When Garven did not rush in where angels should fear to tread, Bill did the most peculiar thing. He stood on one foot, the opposite leg fully extended in front of him.

It was weird. The invitation to attack was as overt as it could be. It was very, very tempting.

Pete's admonition rang somewhere in his head, *"Don't fall for it!"*

The time was passing. Garven could feel the ref's attention on him. He was going to get called for stalling. Houseman was stalling every bit as much as he was. There he stood like a mechanical toy with his right leg up in the air. The only movement the older man made was to pivot to face Garven every time the younger man circled around him. Two of the three minutes of the first period were gone. Garven had to do something.

He closed off his mind to the calls from his teammates to be cautious and to wait. The opening was there, inviting and seductive. Garven suddenly went for the standing leg. In his mind, he saw the old man topple over on his back, the breath knocked out of him. Garven could almost feel himself pinning the thin man with the tufted white hair on his chest. He could hear the shouts of victory from his own small gallery of fans.

What happened in actuality was quite different. Bill moved with the speed of electricity. Garven did not even see the leg disappear. Instead of lying on the man's back, pinning him, Garven found Bill around on his own back, taking him down to the mat. His surprise and consternation were so great that he did not have time to think or plan. He hesitated for a fraction of a second. Then, he found himself lying on his back, ensnared by an octopus with stringy arms and legs. He did not really know how he had gotten into that position. It had happened too fast. His mental image had to shift drastically. Now, he had to envision himself wriggling out of the half-Nelson and the second arm encircling his chest.

Garven bucked and squirmed. He bridged his neck to keep his shoulders off the mat. The more he moved, the tighter the coils of the human octopus coiled around him. Garven felt a sense of confusion, dread, something akin to panic. He started to hope that the time would run out. He could hold out until the period ended, then he would cease and desist forever from making idiot mistakes. He twisted and surged against the older man's sinewy body. First one shoulder, then the other hovered a fraction of an inch from the mat. He saw the ref's hand raise in a brief cadence of counting several times. He knew he could hold out. He bridged until the veins on his neck stood out like miniature garden hoses. He dug his heels into the mat and started to churn his way towards the edge of the mat.

That was it. He could get off the mat. There could not be much more time. He was suffocating. The ref had to call this a choke hold. He could not breathe. The time was racing by. He was getting very tired. He found his mind wandering, thinking about being somewhere else. The ref slapped the mat. The time was almost up. He was almost to the edge of the mat. Houseman must be getting tired; his grip was loosening. Maybe he was hurt and had to let go. The pressure on his chest began to lessen; Garven set himself to do a roll-out to get two points. He could still win on points.

Then his mind cleared up. He remembered vaguely that the ref had slapped the mat. That could not mean what he thought it meant. He was so tired. The old man stood up. Garven wanted to cry, really wanted to cry. He felt humiliated. The other man's hand reached down to help him up. The realization of what had happened rushed in on Garven. He had been pinned. Pinned in the first period of his match. Pinned in the first period of his match by an old man, by an old man he had been warned about by everybody. He really felt like crying.

The raising of the perennial champion's hand, the brief medal ceremonies where he got a silver AAU medal on a red, white, and blue bunting ribbon, and the bus ride home were dim memories as surrealistic as the match itself. Garven could not get over it. He had been pinned in the first period by a man old enough to be his grandpa. There must be a lesson in this, but Garven's mind was in no shape to benefit from it.

CHAPTER
Twelve

Quantitative chemistry was not as difficult as either the inorganic or organic chem classes had been conceptually. It was just a matter of determining what elements or compounds were present in what quantities, and how pure it was. However, for the first time in his life, Garven, like his classmates, was required to do something with precision, exquisite four-decimal-point precision. He and his classmates now had to concern themselves with such questions as the validity of the sample and the accuracy of the result of the analysis. They learned something of the methods of analysis and even of the cost of the processes in terms of time and even money. It was not a matter of doing extensive and boring reading. Two-thirds of the class time were expended in the lab. He became dependent upon, if not exactly fond of, the Mettler Scale (number 6204) to which he was assigned.

He and his lab partner, contending with the rest of the cutthroat premed students, spent hours measuring out small quantities of unknown chemicals and weighing them to a ten thousandth of a gram, preparing the sample for analysis, then performing the day's experiment and weighing the residue, again to .0000 place precision. They made indicator blanks—the amount of reagent needed to affect the indicator—cleaned and calibrated their own pipettes, burettes, beakers, Erlenmeyer flasks, watch glasses, and crucibles; prepared and preserved standard solutions; analyzed, hoped, and often guessed.

"It is the opportunity to learn the chemistry world's work," the professor stressed.

Over and over again, the patient professor and his small army of grad student lab instructors reiterated the critical character of the weighing and measuring. It did no good, they said, to speculate about chemical reactions and the results of their interactions if you could not prove your work with accurate measurements. Every experiment required four independent determinations. For Garven, it was his first introduction into the exacting work of real science.

It also did no good for your grade if you got careless, like dropping some of the unknown or the resultant, or if you contaminated one chemical with another, even with the dust or moisture that collected on the instruments. The quant lab was the cleanest and driest place on earth because the premedders' grades depended on that freedom from dust and contamination. It also did no good to have one of your desperate competitors in the class water your unknown or add a little chalk dust to the vial of a white unknown or combinant reagent to increase the weight, or to filch a wee bit to lower the final weight. The premedders learned not to be careless very soon into the quarter. It was considerably harder to learn how to prevent having the extra weight of the chalk or water, or the loss of weight from the final weighing, than it was to learn the formal procedures of the working chemistry world. There was a hint of blood in the air in the quant class all the time.

Lab partners covered each other's backs, making sure they never left their unknowns or their burbling beakers, or their precisely drawn up pipettes, or their scales unattended. Every lab period, every lab-partner pair recalibrated their Mettler Scales, and every lab period, two or three of the scales were found to be grossly off, either high or low. A small quiet war was being waged.

Grading was on the curve. There would be twelve A's, twenty-two B's, forty-one C's, twenty-two D's, and four E's. The professor did not like to use the connoting and emotive F symbol for failure. He was soft hearted enough to overweight the grading scale on the upper end so he did not have to listen to the inventive and mournful complaints of too many recipients of E's.

The result was that all was considered fair in war; there was no love. "Do unto others before they could do unto you" was the class motto. The idea of causing another student's work to be wrong by contaminating it was roundly condemned; anyone caught at it would be penalized two full grade points for the first offense, and kicked out of the class altogether for the second. So far as Garven was concerned, it would be a capital offense. He and David Applegate, who had signed up for the same lab with him, arranged to be partners to cover each other's backs and to guard the results of their hard work with unrelenting vigilance.

The Pacific Coast Athletic Conference wrestling finals were scheduled for the last week in March. Garven had a month to prepare for them and realized that the most important hurdle he had to surmount was his chronic tiredness. He and his coconspirators in the streaker incident finished the odious punitive painting task by the beginning of the last week of February, so Garven was granted three to four hours a day of extra time, which helped immeasurably. He now wrestled in practice with a dedication that his teammates admired and resented. He was too rough, too aggressive in practice matches. He was heedless of the growing coolness manifested towards his win-at-all-costs athletic philosophy. He added fuel to their smoldering embers of discontent and estrangement from the 144-pound class wrestler by repeating what had become his fighting motto: "Winning isn't the most important thing; it's the only thing." Derek gritted his teeth when he heard the phrase and suggested to Garven that he get some new material.

Garven was impervious to the atmosphere of implicit criticism and to the near disenfranchisement by the rest of the wrestling team. He was correctly aware that he was the only man on the team with a reasonable chance to take the conference championship, and he felt himself mildly magnanimous because he had the generosity of spirit to attribute the growing level of disregard on the part of his fellow wrestlers to envy.

Winter quarter was largely a writing period in Garven's scholastic career rather than one of amassing and learning facts to be regurgitated back on midterm examinations and finals. Art history became more history than art appreciation. Garven found that he had something of a talent for expression, and the work became easy, especially since the library had so much source material. His term paper had insured his success in the class since it, by no coincidence, had expanded on an anticlerical theme privately espoused by the associate professor, Georg Antonino, who taught Garven's class. David Applegate had attended a coffee house lecture in San Francisco given by Dr. Antonino (at Garven's pleading) and had come away with some highly useful quotes and tidbits. Garven was not slow to learn that no student ever seemed brighter than when he appeared to be in independent agreement with the private opinions of his teacher.

Garven followed up on a lead given by David. Antonino had quoted a sculptor, Lorenzo Ghiberti, to make his point in the coffee house. Garven obtained Ghiberti's *Commentaries* from the library and, liberally using quotes from the fifteenth-century artist, came up with his own title, "Deleterious

Effects on the World of Art by the World of the Ecclesiastics." Garven's pre-amble included a passage in full that Antonino had quoted in part:

"And so in the days of Emperor Constantine and Pope Silvester, the Christian faith gained the upper hand. Idolatry suffered so fierce a persecution that all the statues and paintings, of such nobility and antique beauty, were smashed and torn to pieces. And the volumes, treatises, drawings, and precepts which had been used for training men in these great, noble, and gentle arts also perished with the statues and pictures. And in order to do away with every ancient idolatrous custom, it was enacted that churches should be white throughout... Once art had ended, the churches stayed white for about six hundred years."

Garven quoted Leon Battista Alberti's *Treatise On Painting* (1436), to document the pervasive influence of the Catholic faith and its particular attitudes on painting:

> "It is fitting that a painting should exhibit gentle and agree-able attitudes, suited to the action represented."

Leonardo Da Vinci was hands down Prof. Antonino's favorite artist, not just because of the magnificence and timelessness of his word, but because he was articulate in his defense of art against the opponents of representational artistry in the Church. Garven included a twist in his paper to indicate that even Leonardo was under the ecclesiastical restraint of the age:

> "...So therefore we may justly speak of it [painting] as the grandchild of nature and as related to God Himself. THE PAINTER HAS THE UNIVERSE IN HIS MIND AND HANDS. If the painter wishes to see enchanting beauties, he has the power to produce them. If he wishes to see mon-strosities, whether terrifying, or ludicrous and laughable, or pitiful, he has the power and *authority* to create them."

Garven borrowed a phrase from his teacher, as faithfully related by David Applegate, that provided a clincher for his standing in the art history class since it represented such insightful perception. He concluded that Leonardo, for all his protestations of the independence of art and the value of the artist's mind in the creation of his imagery, was only a small measure removed from the command of his benefactors and their all-pervasive Catholic religion for his subject matter and for the style in which it could be represented. Garven highlighted the word "authority" in his discussion. He said that Leonardo could not escape the influence even if he had had an inclination to be irreligious, because the purse strings of the benefactors were held by fingers dependent upon currying favor with the all-powerful Church.

On his own, Garven found the examination of Paolo Caliari (Veronese) before the Sacred Tribunal (Inquisition) on 18 July 1573 and used an excerpt for his conclusion:

> "He was asked his profession.
> A: I paint and make pictures.
> He was asked whether he thought it suitable that in our Lord's Last Supper one should paint jesters, drunkards, Germans, dwarfs, and similar scurrilities.
> A: No, my lords.
> He was asked, 'Are you not aware that in Germany and other places infected with heresy there is the custom of using strange and scurrilous pictures and similar inventions for mocking, abusing, and ridiculing the things of the Holy Catholic Church, in order to teach the false doctrine to the illiterate and ignorant?'
> A: Yes, my lords. That is wicked…"

His efforts in the art history class sealed his disbelief in and disdain for organized religion, which, to that time, had been nascent and unformed. He was now a convinced atheist, but not a publicly antagonistic one. That, he knew, would not have been a socially advancing opinion to espouse, and he kept it to himself.

Garven and David collected their day's unknown, a bluish compound that they had been warned to keep tightly covered because it was hydrophilic and would quickly add water weight from the air and yield erroneous weights to the initial and final results. Garven presumed it was some sort of cupric mixture. As he mingled in the gaggle of other students hurrying to get their day's lab work started, Garven observed an open container of similar colored, although not identical, blue chemical on a low shelf. No one was paying attention to him. He wet his forefinger with a little spit and dipped it into the smoked-glass jar. As he walked back towards his scales, where David was already setting up their experiment, the compound dried to a fine powder. He had not actually planned it, but one of the student pairs, who were known to be in active competition with Garven for two of the precious twelve A's, worked with a single-minded purpose at a table on his route to his own workplace.

As he passed them, his peripheral vision caught sight of the open glass plate upon which rested their compound, very carefully deposited so as to be sure than none was missed in the transfer. Garven lingered for a moment in transit, gave in to what seemed to him to be a sudden and momentary irresistible urge, and rubbed his fingers with the blue powder between them over the bluish compound on the gleaming, clean glass plate. A few specks from his fingers fell on the other students' compound, and Garven walked by without looking about. In a few seconds, he was busy at his own workplace, setting up the burners and the spiralated glass tubing for the distillation process required in that day's experiment.

He did not think about the effect of his addition to the other premedders' experiment. His education in classical history had taught Garven the efficacy of hard attack and the crucial value of seeking his own advantage, his own profit. He recalled that there had been a sign over the gates of ancient Carthage—the perennial foe of Rome during the two thousand years of the Punic War—that "nothing that produces profit can come of evil." So far as Garven was concerned, that was a worthy mantra for himself as a premed student. The day's work did not lend itself to moralistic ruminations, and Garven was constitutionally disinclined anyway. He put the incident out of his mind in a matter of a few minutes. The mundane aspects of the daily routine did not require much actual thought, and Garven found himself concentrating on his wrestling, his solid geometry assignment, and on his problem with the psychology department, and not feelings of guilt or such nonstarters as repentance or confession.

He was doing great in the psychology course, and was reluctant to jeopardize his standing by antagonizing the department for the money they owed him. However, it was just not right. They were rich and powerful, and he was poor and occupied a position of weakness and inferiority, so they felt they could just rob him. He fretted over the question and the injustice, and decided that today was the day he would brave it and confront the lion in his lair. Right after class.

Dr. Simpkins was concluding his lecture. "The working principles of psychoanalysis are contained in the acceptance of an unconscious or subconscious reservoir to the mental or psychic life that forms not only a real, but the greater portion of any individual's life. This unconscious material is the resultant accumulation of reserve material conserved from the past, including the emotional overlay, lying fallow, ready for intermittent and continual passage back into the more superficial, conscious portion of life, furnishing a reservoir of material for thought and action. It is the storehouse, if you will, of all past experiences in all their complexity and the sum of feeling and tendency that constitutes individual character. In normal individuals carrying out their ordinary lives, both mental and physical, the way into consciousness is sufficiently open, but controlled, that such subconscious material may be selectively chosen according to practical and creative needs, and yet so well guarded that superfluous information cannot thrust itself distractingly into the field of conscious thought and action. Therefore, a certain amount of repression is necessary to hold this psychic material in productive control

"This leads us into the subjects of the id, ego, and superego that will be covered in the next two lectures. The text covers these subjects in an altogether too brief a fashion in chapter twelve. You will need to commit those definitions and explanations to memory as a minimum for this class. I invite you to read, in advance of my lectures, the source material outlined in the reading syllabus you were given on the second day of class this quarter. A word to the wise should be sufficient."

Garven was seated in the professor's office, feeling tense, when Prof. Dr. Simpkins hurried in through the antechamber, past Garven and Elizabeth, his secretary. Garven brazenly followed the important academic into his inner chamber before Elizabeth could protest successfully. The department chairman looked at the young intruder with an expression of mild annoyance and incredulity.

"And what is important enough to warrant the discourtesy of this intrusion into my office unannounced?"

Garven momentarily thought better of his decision to pursue his righteous claim right to the top of the pinnacle. But here he was. He said, in as polite and unemotional voice as possible, "I will only take a minute, and I will come right to the point. My name is Garven Wilsonhulme, W-I-L-S-O-N-H-U-L-M-E. I worked in your hypnosis lab for three months under Dr. Gunther. He contracted to pay me, and I have never been paid. I have made every effort to communicate with everyone up to you and have gotten nowhere. That is why I am here, to see the man in charge."

Professor Dr. Simpkins looked at the young man before him first with incredulity that anyone so minuscule as he should trouble anyone so momentous as the occupant of the Rockwellian-endowed chair of psychology with such a mundane irrelevancy. Then his gaze hardened with undisguised disdain for the small-mindedness inculcate in such a requester, and finally, with anger at the effrontery. "I will have it looked into, young man. In the future, kindly give credence to the proper channels of authority." There was a mantle of frost on every word.

Garven continued to stand there. Dr. Simpkins turned to occupy his desk, a clear enough signal that the uninvited interview was at an end. But Garven continued to stand there.

"And what is it now, young man? You are pressing your luck."

Garven knew that. "Would you please give your secretary, Elizabeth, instructions; so we can have done with it; so, it will happen?"

Dr. Simpkins's face reddened, and he gritted his teeth in an effort to control an unrestrained outburst of pique. "If that is what it will take to get you out of my office!"

In response to an unseen push of a button, Elizabeth, with her tight face, appeared in the room.

"Deal with this young man's financial problem. Scrutinize it carefully to be certain we are not being made to be the victim of an extortion or a flimflam artist. You can never tell in these uncertain times," he said more for Garven's sake than his secretary's.

CHAPTER
Thirteen

The remainder of the quarter leading up to the wrestling championship tourney was occupied in a feverish assortment of unrelated academics.
Translate:

> *Und wenn dich das Irdische vergass,zu der stillen Erde sag:*
> *Ich rinne. Zu dem raschen Wasser sprich: Ich bin.*
> Rainer Maria Rilke – *The Sonnets to Orpheus*
> (And when the earthly forgets you, say to the silent earth:
> I flow. Speak to the rushing water: I endure.)

Solve:

In a bird watcher's paradise, 3,000 pink egrets and whistling swans filled the air. The number of egrets was 1,800 times greater than 3 times the number of swans. Solve for the number of each kind of bird.

Prove:

If X, Y, and Z are real numbers, show that XYZ = ZYX using givens, associative, and commutative properties.

Define:

Transference, ego
Comparative psychology, id, psychopath
Behaviorism
Neurosis

Argue:

> "If, then, no cause or reason can be given, which prevents the existence of God, or which destroys his existence, we must certainly conclude that he necessarily does exist. If such a reason or cause should be given, it must either be drawn from the very nature of God, or be external to him; that is, drawn from another substance of another nature. For if it were of the same nature, God, by that very fact, would be admitted to exist. But substance of another nature could have nothing in common with God, and therefore would be unable either to cause or to destroy his existence.
>
> "As, then, a reason or cause which would annul the divine existence cannot be drawn from anything external to the divine nature, such cause must perforce, if God does not exist, be drawn from Gods own nature, which would involve a contradiction. To make such an affirmation about a being absolutely infinite and supremely perfect, is absurd; therefore, neither in the nature of God, nor externally to his nature, can a cause or reason be assigned which would annul his existence. Therefore, God necessarily exists. Q.ed."
>
> Spinoza – *The Ethics*

Discuss:

> "For out of olde feldes, as men seyth,
> Cometh al this newe corn from yer to yere,
> And out of olde bokes, in good feyth
> Cometh al this new science that men lere."
>
> Geoffrey Chaucer – *The Parliament of Fowls*

Having feverishly done all of the writing, graphing, translating, proving, solving, defining, arguing, and discussing required of him for two days, Garven was able to put all else aside, and to concentrate on becoming the Pacific Coast Conference wrestling champion in the 144-pound weight class.

Garven entered in first place in his mid-conference region, having won every conference match. His ignominious defeat by the elderly hotel doorman did not count in the standings, and Garven had studiously neglected and effaced the distasteful event from his consciousness. His reward was to be pitted against the fourth place seed from another region. Staqland Garrison—a sophomore from the University of San Diego in the southern region, ranking fourth place because there were only four schools in the region—had the misfortune to be Garven's first victim. He was pinned in the first period. Garven complimented the ardent but inexperienced wrestler on a game try. Staqland was sure that Garven would be the champion; if not, he would have hated to meet the guy who could take the Stanford man.

In the second round (of four), Garven defeated the first-place winner of the northernmost region, Henry Takler, from the University of Washington. Henry was very good and lost on points—six of them, in a full, three-period match. He, too, took solace in the observation that he had been beaten by the wrestler who would be the champion, and would probably be given the grand championship for the tournament, if Henry was any judge and if the conventional wisdom among the wrestlers was worth anything.

Garven won his semifinal match by twelve points from an opponent who got the flu and was drooping before the match. It was the luck of the draw. The guy was so sick that he had to drop out and could not come to the mat edge in the consolation event, so he had to forfeit even his chance at third place.

The final rounds started on Sunday at eight o'clock in the morning. Garven was pleasantly surprised at how good he felt; the long, hard hours of workout were paying off in reserves of stamina. He ate a sparse breakfast of cornflakes with the minimum of milk, fruit slices, a banana, and half a piece of toast at seven o'clock a.m. to be sure he would have the calories and energy level, but also to avoid wrestling on a full stomach, which always made him feel sick and faint. His bout should take place at about ten, if the matches went off on schedule. The heavier weight division matches were left until late in the afternoon.

Garven knew about his opponent, Clyde Nartle, a senior from UCLA, although the two men had never met in competition. Clyde had started in the 136-pound class, but grew so much during the year that he would never be able to make that weight again. He, like Garven, weighed in at 143 without dieting. Clyde was tall and angular, more like a basketball player, where Garven was short and wiry, a small version of a muscular athlete. Clyde was known for his foul mouth and temper, and Garven knew from his after-match discussions with his UCLA teammates that Clyde had been disciplined on two occasions for poor sportsmanship.

The match started early—at eight fifty. It was a Mutt and Jeff match. Clyde Nartle was six foot three in height and appeared spindly until you looked at the fat-free, well-defined musculature and the washboard abdomen closely. Garven Wilsonhulme was slender with wiry, knotted, tense muscles. Unless he was compared to another man of known height, it was hard to be recognize how short he was—five foot nine. The referee, having been forewarned about the history of aggressiveness of the two contenders, gave them a short lecture before officially starting the physical hostilities.

"Now look, boys, remember this is a sport, not a fight. You represent your schools, and you want to do that as good sports. When I caution you, I want you to separate. If I have to do it twice, it will cost you points. I will pay close attention to pressure holds, choke holds in pinning combinations, and to elbows and knees and fingers. I have been around the block a couple of times, so I don't miss much. Unsportsmanlike conduct will cost you dearly. Make this the match what it has been advertised to be. May the best man win."

"*I can agree to that,*" each wrestler thought to himself, knowing that the description applied to him.

There was a 180° difference in their understanding of who that best man was.

"Shake," the ref instructed.

"Good luck," said Garven.

Clyde just nodded.

Down dropped the ref's arm. Clyde had coiled his emotional tensions and finely toned muscles into a tight spring for the five-month wrestling season in anticipation of this culminating moment. He sprang like a panther, intent on effecting a paralyzing and demoralizing surprise on his smaller opponent. He aimed his head and shoulders at Garven's upper thighs, designed to tackle him and to get an immediate point advantage. Two points could mean the difference between winning and losing.

Garven's legs were not there. The quick smaller man made himself horizontal in the air, three and a half feet in the air, and came down on Clyde's back. Clyde had held nothing back and was fully extended with both feet off the mat, touching only with his mat shoe toes, when Garven came down on his back. They landed with Garven facing the taller man's feet. Clyde stretched out flat on the mat with no interposition of his arms for protection of his chest. His breath escaped in a sudden whoosh, and he felt momentarily as if he would suffocate or black out.

In that moment, Garven spun around so his chest and belly laid on Clyde's back with Garven's head now facing the back of Clyde's head.

"Two points, red!" shouted the ref to the scorekeeper, signifying the takedown.

Clyde could do nothing but keep himself from being overturned and pinned until he got sufficient breath back to let his muscles and brain begin to work again. Garven jammed his hand into the protected right armpit of Clyde, but Clyde was experienced and too smart to leave Garven an opening. Clyde stubbornly kept his legs fully extended and widely outspread, and his torso straight and pressed to the mat, so Garven could not get him on his back.

After Garven struggled futilely for a full minute to get another point, the ref said sternly to Clyde, "Do something, or I will start giving out points. You are stalling, and I won't warn you again."

In Clyde's mind, he was struggling to keep from being turned over and pinned, and he resented the stalling call. He fought to his knees, thinking to sit out or to roll Garven over. Garven had a practiced knack of keeping his weight on his opponent in such a way that the opponent never felt comfortable. When Clyde thought his opening was adequate, he started a sit out, only to find that Garven had shifted his position, and at the end of the move, Clyde found Garven's arm in position under his to start the turnover for a pin. He made his second mistake of the match at that moment. Clyde decided at that instant to go with the roll and to move so fast that he carried Garven on over for a reversal and two points. Garven had anticipated that move, and when he felt the muscles under him tense for the roll, he stretched out perpendicularly to Clyde with his own legs outstretched and widespread, and stopped the UCLA wrestler halfway. Clyde had made the classical beginning wrestler's mistake. He had turned onto his back. Garven took advantage and pressed his body down on the struggling man beneath him with all of his strength.

The scoreboard now showed Stanford leading by 3-0; two points for the takedown and a full-minute riding time. Clyde bucked and lurched, and arched his neck to keep Garven from locking in a secure hold on his sweat-slippery body. Neither wrestler wore any kind of shirt. He finally struggled to the edge of the mat, and the referee awarded Garven another point for having gained an advantage. Garven thought it should have been a near pin for at least two points. The score was now 4-0. The first period ended.

The coin was tossed; Clyde won. He had the decision to select either the up or the down position. He knew that it was usual to select the down position in the second period, while he was fresh, in order to be on top in the critical third period, when he was tired. However, he was not doing too hot being down so far, and he knew that he was in great physical condition, so he took the top to see if he could not change the course of history for this match. He needed a pin. His height was a real advantage now.

Garven blinked the sweat from his eyes and concentrated with every fiber of his mind and body on the ref's hand. He was kneeling in the prescribed position but held his knees a fraction off the mat. He was ready to launch himself. The ref's hand swooped down to slap the mat. A fraction of an instant prior to the hand actually contacting the mat, Garven executed a powerful uncoiling front roll, and before Clyde could react to counter the move, Garven had rolled out of his grip and was gaining his feet.

"One point, break away!" shouted the ref.

Clyde knew Garven had started an instant too early, and would have protested, but Garven was boring in on him, trying to get hold of one leg to add insult to injured pride by turning him over for another two-point loss. Clyde started to lose his grip on his temper.

Unseen by the ref, Clyde flung his fisted hand down alongside Garven's head ostensibly to get a protective limb between himself and his relentless adversary. The knuckles crunched against the skin of Garven's cheek, where it laid without padding over the cheekbone. The blow was a total surprise to Garven, and it hurt with a harsh sting. The bruise would not appear before the match was over. Garven's head reflexively jerked to the side, away from Clyde's leg, and the UCLA wrestler jammed his long arm like a lever alongside Garven's neck. Clyde propelled himself into the onrushing Stanford wrestler and toppled him to the mat.

"Two points, takedown, yellow!" the ref shouted.

The score was now showing as 5-2.

Garven's head was smarting, and now he was in the disadvantaged position with the much longer body fairly enveloping him. He struggled to his knees, only to be knocked down again. He did it again and was knocked to his stomach again. He lurched from side to side and finally got to his knees again, this time in a stable and defensible position. Garven began to sit out, again and again and again. Each time, Clyde knocked him back down, but at the expense of getting tired. Clyde felt it was only a matter of time before Garven would sit out and get a full turn out of his arms for a two-point reversal. Garven could sense Clyde's feeling.

He started to sit out again and felt the characteristic tensing of Clyde's muscles to stop him. This time, however, Garven hooked Clyde's right elbow in the crook of his own right arm and rolled hard to the two wrestlers' right, carrying his long opponent over with him. Garven was now on top, and Clyde could do nothing but squirm out of the supine, pinnable position and into the prone position.

"Two points, reversal, red!" shouted the ref.

The scoreboard showed 7-2 and the time read 0-0, end of the second period.

Garven could see victory; it was almost palpable. All he had to do was to hang on and avoid doing anything stupid. He could see the intensity, or anger, he was not sure which, in his rival's face. There was a mean set to the young man's jaw. Garven was on top. Clyde did an inside sit out that completely fooled Garven and caught him unprepared. He had never seen that move before. His hesitation cost him the reversal: 7-4. Garven was down and there were two minutes, fifty-two seconds to go in the match. Now three points did not seem like very much.

Clyde was desperate. This was his last chance to take a championship, and he was not going to let any rich shrimp from fancy Stanford keep him from being the champ, no matter what. Each time the ref came around to the wrestlers' right, he jabbed his left fingers across Garven's closed eyes and over the tender bridge of his nose. Every time the ref circled to their left, he ground his fist into the tender cup of Garven's axilla. Garven did not believe in protesting. He was trying not to get mad by concentrating on how to get even.

The pain was distracting. Garven allowed Clyde's insistent hand, then his arm, to get insinuated into a half-Nelson around the back of his neck, and despite desperate efforts at pulling away the arm and at spreading his free arm and both legs to prevent being turned over, Garven was deposited on his back. As he hit the vulnerable supine position, Clyde drove his hard forehead into the fragile bones of Garven's nose. Garven heard the crack of the nose bones almost as soon as he felt the blinding flash of pain. He sprayed a fan of blood droplets as he tried violently to breathe. He was strangling on the blood gushing down the back of his throat. The ref was about to slap the mat when he saw the spread of blood on Garven's face and the spray on Clyde's back.

"Time!" he yelled.

Clyde was furious. "I was pinning him! You can't stop me now! I could have won the match right now! What do you mean 'Time'?!"

The ref helped Garven to a sitting position, and his teammates ran out to the mat to bring him a towel and an iced washcloth.

The ref turned to Clyde and, in a low-pitched, quiet, angry voice, asked, "Do you want to lose this match right now for unsportsmanlike conduct?"

Clyde did not; he indicated by a vigorous head shake.

"Then shut up," snapped the ref with finality.

Clyde shut up. He did not like it, but he shut up.

The ref signaled with upraised three fingers and yelled to the scorekeeper, "Near pin, yellow!"

The score was now a 7-7 tie with forty-nine seconds left in the third and final period.

The Stanford team laid Garven on his back and placed a compress on the back of his neck and on his forehead, as they had been taught. It was sickening; there was so much blood. Nothing they did worked. The blood continued to gout out of Garven's crumpled nose. He looked terrible. The boys carefully avoided touching the nose; they knew they were not supposed to pinch it for some reason.

"I'll give you one more minute to get that bleeding under control. If you can't, then I'll call the match in UCLA's favor, and we'll get Wilsonhulme to a doctor," said the ref to the frantic trio of helpers in red tights.

Garven was not about to lose this match. He reached up and blew copious clots of blood out of his mangled nose, which started the bleeding to erupt where before it was just a vigorous flow. He then took the nostrils between his thumb and forefinger and pinched as hard as he could. His eyes glazed with the pain. It was blinding. He was afraid he would pass out. He was nauseated from the blood he had swallowed. It took all he had not to give in to unconsciousness, but he clung onto his frightfully tender nose for the full minute.

The ref looked up from his watch, having counted off a precise minute.

"Well?" he asked. "How's it going?"

Things looked better.

Garven let go of his nose. There was no bleeding. Pete raised his right arm in a gesture of triumph. He and Don Tunnel washed off Garven's face as best they could without disturbing the nose.

Garven, who looked like the wrath, said to the referee, "I'm ready. Let's finish." He looked up at the scoreboard with all of its evidence of impending doom for Garven's chances of a championship and gritted his teeth. It wasn't over until it was over.

"Red down," instructed the referee.

Garven assumed the position. Clyde fitted himself on top, leaning too hard and clasping Garven's arm with a full prehensile grasp instead of the rule book flat hand and no thumb grip. The referee caught it and warned Clyde. They repositioned. The ref's hand slapped the mat for the start of action. Not willing to accept a tie and mandatory overtime, Clyde sprang up to throw his legs around Garven's chest. This threw Garven facedown. Clyde jammed his arms under Garven's to put the smaller wrestler into his favorite hold, the "Cloverleaf," as he liked to call the well-known figure four and double arm bar. Garven was churning his legs, keeping the long lower limbs of his rival from encircling his abdomen. Clyde drove his head down hard and painfully against Garven's shoulder to knock his Stanford opponent flat to the mat.

But this time, Garven did not fall to the mat. He could feel the awkward, off-balance position of the lanky man on top of him. Instead of letting his arms collapse under him, as he was expected to do, he reached up over his shoulder and grabbed Clyde's occiput. The grip on the back of the head and the forward momentum of Clyde's body were his undoing, and he neatly rolled forward, and over and off Garven's back. Garven's nose was starting to bleed a little again. He snuffed hard to keep the ref from noticing.

Now Garven was on top, and the two wrestlers were in the standard man-up, man-down position, with Clyde planted on his knees.

"Two points, red!" shouted the ref over the din in the cheering auditorium.

The scoreboard lights changed to 9-7, Stanford.

Clyde was thrashing violently. He was going to get up, go for a tie, and go into overtime if nothing else. He was not going to lose. There were thirty-one seconds left in the period. Garven hated the very thought of an overtime. The broken and bloodied nose had cost him a severe loss of reserves. He was dizzy, nauseated, and light-headed. He had to hang on, had to get more points, had to win.

Clyde spread his long legs wide and began to back up into a standing position in a spiderlike motion. Garven felt, rather than saw, his chance. He, too, had a new trick or two for the edification of his violent opponent. He swiftly coiled his left leg around Clyde's left leg and locked his foot in dorsiflexion around Clyde's knee. At nearly the same instant, he threw his entire body forward over Clyde's back. Clyde instantly felt the far off-balance forward positioning of Garven's body and recognized his final chance to take advantage of this flagrant strategic error of his opponent.

As Garven's weight shifted still further in the off-balance position, Clyde suddenly whipped his right arm back over his own shoulder and around Garven's neck to roll him neatly over onto his back for a reversal and maybe even for a pin.

Which was exactly what Garven wanted him to do. Garven stretched out his own body, knocking both of Clyde's legs out from under him, and at the same time, he ran his left arm back around Clyde's neck, locking the lowermost wrestler's arm in a painful and awkward position above his head and behind his back. Using the arm as a lever, Garven easily turned Clyde over onto his back and fixed his own arm around Clyde's neck so Clyde's shoulders were obliquely inclined towards the mat.

Clyde recognized his error even though he was unfamiliar with this terrible new hold. His first priority was to prevent himself from getting pinned, and he squirmed with every ounce of energy, strength, and reserve to get out of the hold. He still held out hope that he could turn Garven over in the same direction they had rolled and could achieve a reversal and win the match. There was still time— twenty-one seconds.

The movements were calculated into Garven's practice with his new and invincible hold. It was called the "Guillotine," or by some, the "Cobra," because the more the victim struggled, the tighter he was coiled in the locking limbs and the more his circulation and room to get out were cut off. Garven lengthened himself as much as he possibly could and squeezed as hard around Clyde's neck as he could get away with. The pain on the neck and around the torso were terrible, and Clyde cried out. He could feel himself being rent apart at mid-chest. In the last fifteen seconds of the match, instead of trying to squirm his way out and increase his pain, Clyde fought unconsciously to flatten his shoulders out on the mat to escape the tearing of his overstretched torso.

He was successful. The pain began to subside, and the fear and suffering reduced to a manageable degree. And the referee slapped the mat, signifying the pin. He would never have imagined saying so before today, but Clyde breathed a sigh of thanksgiving that he had been pinned as he felt the other wrestler unwrap himself from around the bruised and aching ribs, and off his throbbing neck and numb leg. One small compensation was that he saw the hemorrhage from Garven's nose flowing full force again.

Garven's nose was straightened by the stadium doctor with nasal forceps crammed up into the swollen, battered breathing passages in a swift wrenching of agony and blood. The doctor pinched Garven on the end of the excruciatingly tender nostrils until the bleeding stopped. Garven did not notice the pain so much because he passed out. It took him a space of a week to decide that winning the Pacific Coast wrestling championship was worth it. His main regret was that he would always have something of a flattened pugilist's nose.

CHAPTER
Fourteen

G arven was acknowledged by his student peers to be one of the twelve A's in the quantitative analysis chemistry course. Besides doing great in the lab because he and David managed to protect their territory so well from the attackers who would wreck their experiments, he had gotten near-perfect scores on the midterm written exam, one of the highest percentage scores in the professor's memory. Garven had answered the trick questions about not analyzing heavy metal samples in an iron mortar, nor storing alkali metals in glass vessels, nor exposing silver compounds to light and the technicalities of achieving a representative twenty-five-gram sample of wheat from a twenty-five-ton ship load. He and David considered their main aim from then until the end of the quarter to be protection of their lab materials from saboteurs and became justifiably paranoid in the process.

The midterm laboratory examination was entirely open book, just a matter of determining quantities of known chemicals in a compound. Each pair of lab partners was assigned a chunk of dolomite limestone and required to ascertain to three-decimal-point accuracy the quantities of silica, magnesium, calcium, combined oxides, and carbon dioxide. The test was a project expected to take a week, using platinum crucibles for the ignition of the contained calcium-oxalate precipitates and to determine loss on ignition. Porcelain crucibles were needed for the magnesium-ammonium-phosphate precipitates. Meker burners, blast lamps, and muffle furnaces, all of which were in short supply in the student laboratories, had to be employed, and there was going to be a lot of standing around.

It was David who first observed the big, athletic-looking blond guy in the vicinity of their scale. He mentioned the fellow's presence to Garven, so they could be on the lookout for him if he were up to no good. Garven recognized him as one of the high scorers thus far in the class, and further, knew that the guy's scale was located all the way across the lab. He did, indeed, bear watching.

It was Garven who saw the big athlete move by the scale (number 6208) next to his and David's (number 6204) and dip a moistened pair of tooth-picks into the white powder sitting on the brass balance of the Mettler Scale. Garven did not care over much personally since it wasn't his scale and had to wonder why sabotage a lab pair who were in the middle of the pack in the class. Both he and David had seen similar alterations of the next-door part-ners' work over the last two weeks of class. David was for turning the guy in.

Garven said, "It's against my religion to turn somebody into the cops. It's always better to take care of your own problems. We can tell the poor schmucks at 6208. They can take care of it any way they like."

David was dubious, but agreed.

Scores were posted weekly by listing the results next to the assigned Mettler Scale numbers to preserve anonymity. For two weeks, 6204 had gotten per-fect scores, and David and Garven were all smiles and tranquility; 6208 got abysmal scores and were all scowls and discomposure. The big blond student was all perplexity.

He finally could not contain himself, and heedless of the likelihood that he might be self-incriminatory, ventured to ask, "How'd you guys do?"

He had a peculiar accent that Garven could not place.

"Okay," replied David. "You get your unknowns?"

"Pretty close," the big fellow said, still uncertain of why the two lab partners were so cheerful in view of their terrible lab performance. "But I thought you hadn't done so hot."

"Actually, we were pretty lucky—got perfect scores the last two weeks," David added, watching the known saboteur's face.

He looked confused, unpleasantly so. "I don't get it," he said, forgetting his resolution to be subtle and not to give himself away. "I kind of thought 6208 did lousy."

"They did," David told him, unwilling to give out more explanatory information.

"I thought you had 6208."

"Nope."

The guy's face was earnest now. He was trying to be crafty and subtle, but it was a little late in the day for that. He did not see it, though. He kept on.

"So what number are you guys?" He was so determined in his detective work that he could not see how dumb his question was.

"Who wants to know? And how come?" asked Garven, who had been standing to one side until now. He was in a bad mood from the chronic pain in his face, and he did not like the big jerk making an obvious attempt to find out his and David's place so he could sabotage their work. The dummy might just as well have come right out and told them his plans.

The big guy knew he had kind of painted himself into a corner. He figured, as he always did with his superior size, that a good offense was better than a good defense, so he retorted, "Looks like you thought someone said stand up when he said shut up." He took some pride in his mastery of the American idiom. He was a relatively new citizen, an African-American, originally from South Africa.

Garven was in no mood to accept, with any measure of forgiveness, references to his raccoon's eye, spread nose, purplish-colored face, and especially not from some jerk who was trying to wreck his GPA and was clumsy about it. "Why don't you just go and see if you can screw up somebody else's unknown and butt out of my business, cretin?"

A small crowd was gathering, including a couple of lab instructors who had chanced to overhear the reference to sabotage. The over muscled student was becoming uncomfortable. He did not like the reference to screwing up unknowns and the implications for his own well-being in the class, and furthermore, he did not like being called a "cretin" even though he was not quite sure what it meant. "How would you like to make me, little man with the messed-up face?" he sneered in a something-less-than-adroit rejoinder.

Garven felt the eyes of the gathering crowd on him. "Anytime, anyplace." He was angry now. He turned to his fellow students. "Watch this guy around your lab stuff if you want to pass this lab. Ask number 6208."

There, it was out.

The lab instructors locked eyes with the big guy, and he studied his shoes. His face was scarlet and his masseter muscles were clenched.

He slowly looked over at Garven. "I'll be seeing you around, brownnose. This isn't over. Not by a long ways."

He stalked off, leaving an aura of smoke and poison vapor in his trail.

******

Grantland offered the social solution for his academically harried premed friends that weekend. "Listen, you prospective young doctors, how would you all like to go over to Berkeley with me Saturday night?"

David and Garven looked too tired. It was Friday, and the only thing that seemed appealing to either of them was to get some rest.

"I have lined up some girls, nice loose moraled Berkeley girls."

David and Garven weakened a little.

"Good-looking, non-Stanford-looking girls," he said as an added incentive for his two reluctant friends.

They looked as if they might be ready to give in but were still more tired than horny.

"And besides, I have two medical school pals from Odessa who can give you two some pointers about how to get in. Isn't that all you types ever think about? Hmmh?" he needled. "They'll be goin' with us."

David and Garven did not need much coaxing. After all, it was a day's rest away, and the business about the med students was a nice little clincher.

"Okay, you twisted our arms," David said after a confirmatory glance from Garven.

The three young Stanford undergrads left for the Oakland Bay Bridge at six-thirty Saturday evening. They needed plenty of time to be sure they could get a seat at the Hungry i for the night's recitation of beatnik poetry. Not that any of them cared a whit for any of the non-rhyming drivel, but the ambiance was exciting, and most of the time, there was some nutty girl who did not believe in brassieres in the crowd who made the trip worthwhile almost by herself. Garven looked forward to getting the straight skinny about medical school from the med students.

At the toll booth, Grantland held out a fifty-cent piece, and the toll taker, a middle-aged Negro man, who looked as if he had been in the toll booth his entire life, took it into the palm of his hand with all the animation of a cigar store Indian with hinged elbows. The three Stanford students joined the traffic over to Berkeley. Grantland picked up the two girls he knew at their sorority house, and they fitted themselves comfortably among the boys, unconcerned about the disproportion in the respective genders. The carload met the two med students in front of the UC Berkeley Medical School Administration Building.

"Jeff Williams," the taller of the two introduced himself as he worked his way into the back.

"Hey, y'all," said Grantland. "Tell these ol' horn toads your names, boys," he said, cricking his neck around to take in his Stanford friends.

They gave their names. The two Berkeley girls gave theirs.

"C. Patrick Donaldson," puffed the softer, rounder, and shorter of the two med students.

"Hi, Grantland," Jeff and Pat greeted their old Texas high school mate with genuine warmth.

"Annabel Potter."

"Susan Crenshaw."

Back through town, the talk was of California versus Texas girls, the unseasonably high rainfall that year, Stanford's pitiful football team, Berkeley girls, the football scandal involving Midland and Odessa that fall, Stanford girls, and the vacation from decency they had planned for that night. Garven noticed that the two young women were as open and as foulmouthed and suggestive as their male counterparts. The car was crowded and his arm rested comfortably on one of the girls' accommodating breasts. He was sure this was going to be a great night.

Garven asked the two med students if they liked medical school, particularly if they liked UC Berkeley.

Jeff answered, "Nobody likes medical school. It's like bein' pulled through a knothole sideways. It just has to be done, that's all. Berkeley is as good as anywhere else, not as well known as the Mayo Brothers, but just as good."

Jeff added, "We had a tour group of undergrad premedders visiting our gross anatomy lab one time last quarter. Some girl asked how we liked med school, and one of the flitty guys from San Francisco told the girl, 'It's fun.' Bug crap! He's a dork, one of those guys who actually likes givin' up his playtime, drinkin' time, screwin' time, daytime, and workin' his nuts off in a room that stinks of formaldehyde. The rest of us real people just get by day to day, do what has to be done, and plan to stick it to some rich patient someday when we get out to get a payback for all the misery."

At the toll booth, Jeff said, "Hey, Grantland, lemme give the guy the toll. It's the least we can do."

"Y'all think I'm some kina cheapskate?" Grantland responded good-naturedly.

"Surely not, but I would be obliged to you if you would grant me this courtesy," said Jeff with exaggerated Southern courtliness.

The car paused at the toll booth and pulled ahead just enough to let the medical student's arm protrude from the driver's side back window. He was wearing a sport jacket, and none of the other occupants of the car paid any attention to him. The Negro toll taker could have been a clone of his opposite number on the other side of the bridge.

Garven made that observation, and Pat commented in a whisper, "They all look the same, you know. I can't figure how they tell each other apart, most times."

The car began to pull away from the booth when the go light came on.

"Hit it!" shouted Jeff to Grantland.

"Huh?" asked Grantland.

"Drag this heap outta here, right now!" Jeff exclaimed.

The other occupants of the car looked at him as if he had taken leave of his senses.

For some strange reason, the Negro toll booth man started to scream, long, loud, and horrifyingly at almost the same time as Jeff first spoke to Grantland. The driver jammed his foot to the floorboard and squealed rubber getting out of there. The black tire marks were evident for fifty yards. The last thing Garven saw of the toll man was that he was clutching his chest and had fallen bug-eyed back against the booth wall.

Jeff and Patrick were howling with laughter. Grantland had started to laugh uproariously, too, but he had no more idea of what was going on than any of the other Stanford students or the girls. It was David who finally found an opening and queried Jeff.

"Out with it, what's going on? What happened back there?"He was infected with the hilarity and began laughing as soon as the last word was out of his mouth.

It was like a car full of insane asylum inmates on their night out. All five young men and two women were crying with laughter, and only two, if that many, had the foggiest reason why.

"Did you see that?" was the best Jeff could manage.

"That expression," Pat howled, "looked like he'd seen a ghost!"

"Bug-eyed as a frog in heat!" added Grantland.

They all laughed until it was painful.

Pat gasped and moaned, trying to stop his uncontrollable laughter.

"Y'all deserve some sort of an explanation. Young Dr. Williams here finds gross anatomy his favorite subject."He broke down for a few moments more. "He even likes to take some of his work home with him."

Again, the narrative was interrupted with undisciplined gaiety. He could not go on.

"Lemme tell it then," said Jeff. "You are making a regular display of yourself, Dr. Donaldson. I declare that you have chosen the right specialty to pursue. You will fit in right well with the rest of those crazy psychiatrists."

And he started to laugh.

Garven despaired of ever finding out what had taken place.

Pat got hold of himself first.

"Anyway, where was I? Oh yeah, Dr. Williams, our budding orthopod here, took home his cadaver hand to study over the weekend. It is something of a no-no, but he didn't think anybody would be the wiser, and he could slip it back in place come Monday. The devil took him over and whispered that he should take that withered-up old hand along tonight to give the girls a thrill or something."

"It waren't my doin'; the devil took aholt a me," Jeff interjected in his deepest Texas, hard-shell holy-roller Baptist drawl.

"Hush up," insisted Pat. "I'm tellin' this now."

"I'm hushed," sighed Jeff, tired and sore from laughing.

"As I was sayin' before I was so rudely interrupted, the intention was to put the cadaver hand in one of the girls' handbags or somethin'. But an even better opportunity presented itself when Jeff saw the toll booth. So this villain put the quarters on the palm of the cadaver hand and stuck the nasty thing out from under his shirtsleeve. When that colored man took the quarters, Jeff left the hand hangin' in the man's hand along with those coins," Pat said, rushing to complete the story before another fit of unbridled laughter overcame him.

The picture was so vivid in Garven's head that he howled with unrestrained hilarity. It was a wonder they did not wreck because no one seemed to be paying any attention to the driving. The rest of the evening was forgettable, but Garven remembered the event with clarity even as years passed. It was one of those convincing experiences that made the boy from Cipher, Arizona, all the more certain that he wanted to be a medical student, as if he needed any further incentive.

CHAPTER
Fifteen

David tugged at Garven's lab coat sleeve. When he had Garven's attention, he pointed at the large blond athlete who was hunched in a concentrated attitude over the chemical-stained lab table. The big student was
very carefully measuring a pipette full of water, then scrutinized the test tube
of light-amber fluid in the tube holder. He took admirable care to drop one-
half cubic centimeter of the water into the tube, and only then did he look up
and around at his area. The devotion to the scholarly pursuit would have been
laudable except for a couple of elements of the activity that caught David and
Garven's attention—the blond African-American was sitting in the work area
of Mettler Scale 6204, and there was nothing in the midterm test experiment
that called for H_2O. Garven's fury was mitigated by the fact that he had left a
tube of highly diluted Coca-Cola as a protective decoy.

"Go left, and I'll go right," whispered Garven.

"Why not just get the grad student?" whispered David in return. "We've
got the guy red-handed."

"It's better to deal with our own problems ourselves," Garven said firmly.
Even he was not sure why he had such a natural aversion to including the
establishment in his affairs, especially when he was so obviously in the right,
but had never really gotten over being the coyote from Cipher.

They circled the Johannesburg émigré, who was returning the additionally
diluted tube of Coca-Cola to its original mesh square in the test tube holder
and was unsuspecting of his having been detected.

"This your place?" snapped Garven in a theatrically loud voice as soon as he
had sidled up to the blond student's side.

The Afrikaanner jerked in a severe startle.

"Who wants to know?" snarled the trapped student.

He could feel the presence of David standing slightly behind his left arm and was sure he could feel the eyes of every student and lab instructor in the room boring into his big back.

"I do," growled Garven. "This just happens to be my work area, as if you didn't know. Do you think everyone in the place is blind and stupid—like they wouldn't see you pipette water into the test tube with my unknown?"

He was now speaking intentionally very quietly, below the threshold of the straining ears nearby.

"You and me have to finish dis," said the South African, his accent suddenly pronounced because of his tension. "I am sick of you and your accusations, you little shrimp."

"I'm busy with my quant experiment until four. How 'bout we have a little get together in the basement of the Encina Gym? Nobody's there this time of year after the wrestling season," Garven said in a near whisper.

Relieved at the unexpected reprieve, and invigorated by the additional prospect of murdering the smart-mouthed little know-it-all, the big blond backed away from his guilty work and malevolently said, "I'll be there—don't chicken out, you little creep!"

He did not look at the other students as he slunk his way out of the lab and attended to his important business in the men's room.

It was only after the congratulatory back pats and "attaboys" from the rest of the lab students faded away, and he had finished his cleanup after the day's work, that Garven allowed himself to take stock of his situation. He concluded that he had been a fool, and that he was now obligated to fight a much bigger man. He could have been a minor hero, and now, instead, he was just going to get the crap beat out of him. It also occurred to him that his penchant for making trouble for himself had just cropped up again. He felt very annoyed with himself, had a sense of potential trouble for his premed career, worked up a froth of malevolence towards his opponent, and wondered why he was not afraid of the impending fight in which he was at a decided size disadvantage.

David went with him into the inner recesses of the athletic building, its dark, close, and smelly lower rooms in contrast to the brilliance of the sunny early spring day outside. The hallways, stairs, and side rooms were all familiar to Garven, and evidently to the South African, because he was waiting in the wrestling room with only his admiring girlfriend as a second. The large wrestling mat was rolled up against the far wall, away from the door, leaving a capacious empty cement floor for the contest. Garven and David stepped into the room and closed the heavy door behind them, effectively isolating themselves from all knowledge and hearing of the outside world.

The Afrikaaner seemed genuinely surprised to see Garven. He had been exercising and showing his muscles to his appreciative girlfriend and had no more than repeated his bluster for the tenth time that the shrimp would never show up, when the two boys entered and closed the door. The big blonde's unbounded self-confidence deflated slightly at seeing Garven and especially at seeing the businesslike intensity in his manner. Garven walked up to the Aryan and his girl, and the Afrikaaner could feel the malignant rays emanating out of Garven's eyes.

"Didn't think you had the guts to show up," he said when Garven was standing near his face. "You can still turn around and get out, and we forget the whole thing," he added.

Garven, with concentration in his eyes, on his face, and in the way he held his body, seemed somewhat larger. He said simply, "Did you come to talk or what? You gonna fish or cut bait?"

The larger young man looked from Garven to David and to his girlfriend. He shrugged his shoulders, indicating to one and all that he had done everything he could to avert the disaster that the little man had brought upon himself. He smiled with bravado as he turned to follow Garven to the middle of the bare floor. He gave one last toothy grin over his shoulder to the excited girl when he stopped near where Garven was standing with his back to him. He did not see the first blow come hurtling out of the void.

Garven sensed exactly where his opponent would be standing and depended on the surprise of his first blow to equalize his standing with the larger fellow. He had not counted on that last moment turn of the head, which would leave his foe totally unseeing of the un-Marquis of Queensbury blow. The effect was deadly accurate and devastating. Garven's fist connected with perfect accuracy on the point of the upper lip just above the front teeth and just below the end of the big man's nose. Before the Afrikaaner's eyes could adjust to the incoming fist, the crack of bone on bone occurred. Garven's fist took out the two top front incisor teeth and continued upward to unhinge the slender Aryan nose. The blonde's head jerked backward with an audible crack of the neck bones and a sickening crunch of teeth and nasal cartilage.

Garven's knuckles were cut by the teeth, but he did not have time to feel the pain. Blood erupted in a spray from the shattered teeth and gums, and from the torn nose. The fine bones and cartilages accordioned into an amorphous swollen mass. The South African's body jumped back involuntarily, and his arms flew open in an awkward and unprotected aerial balancing act. The message flew from his brain toward his hands to make fists and to strike back, but before the order could be executed, Garven had driven his brogan of a shoe with full force into the outstretched and vulnerable shin of the dismayed opponent. The addition of a second horrible and sudden pain in another part of his body caused a momentary disassembling of the Afrikaaner's defensive coping mechanisms, and he stood almost motionless and defenseless for a fraction of a second.

Garven had the fighting momentum, and had a plan that was working with unanticipated perfection. His fighter's eye and wrestler's kinesthetic sense caught the image of the precarious stance of the South African, and with a fluidity of movement that would have inspired congratulations from a black belt, he swept his right toe full force between the legs of the large, blond young man.

The Afrikaaner almost crumpled to the floor, stunned, nauseated, in great pain, and in chagrin that no more than a second or two had elapsed, and he was in complete danger. He was tough and not entirely a stranger to fighting, having bullied the Kaffirs in Soweto for sport with his mates. He withdrew into a protective stance and felt two or three blows to his head and abdomen that did little damage. His main fight now was to maintain consciousness; at times, he felt he was losing that battle. He swung his large fists where he thought Garven must be, but always, the quick little man had moved somewhere else.

Garven ducked under the flailing fists and arms and tackled the larger man's one remaining uninjured leg, toppling him backwards onto the hard cement floor, knocking the breath out of the South African. Before the powerful arms could envelope him, Garven sprang up and away. He landed a solid kick to his opponent's kidney, causing an involuntary grunt of pain. The South African was now a mass of pain.

The big blond, rage and frustration distorting what remained of his facial features, staggered to his feet and lumbered after Garven, swinging his fists like a windmill. Garven circled around him, taunting and evading the beef-roast-sized fists. From time to time, he got in another punch on the already excruciatingly tender broken nose or a kick on one or the other of the big fellow's already hurting shins. The blond African-American was wearing down rapidly, and Garven, still in supremely good condition from the wrestling season, was flooded with adrenaline and was feeling a progressive exhilaration.

Garven ducked to the left to fake out the flying fists aimed at him. He outsmarted himself that time and took a bell-ringing blow on his left ear. The ear swelled up like a red cauliflower, and Garven felt dizzy. He danced well away from the enraged animal that his opponent had become. All was deadly now. If the big man ever got hold of him or connected with a blow that knocked him down, Garven knew that he was sunk. The girlfriend shrieked in horror at what was happening to her hero. David felt a sick fascination at the study in primitive violence unfolding before him. As the South African's face came into view from time to time, he felt himself getting sick. He had never seen a real fight before.

The girl's shriek slightly distracted the big blond, and he hesitated. Garven's singleness of purpose was not susceptible to anything as flimsy as an auditory distraction. He bore in again and pounded the now pulpy face with a rain of quick jabbing blows. The Afrikaaner was starting to fade. The punishment was too fast and too much. He vomited a nasty mixture of blood and bile, and began to whip his head back and forth to clear some sort of breathing passage. He spotted the floor with gouts of blood in a twenty-foot-diameter circle. He was nauseated.

Garven caught a hard but glancing blow to the gut that stopped him in his tracks and made him jump away. The centripetal velocity and forcefulness of the big man's windmill blows were beginning to wane. He was stumbling about rather than moving with clear purpose. He had blood in his eyes; he was choking. He was crying with rage, pain, and humiliation. He could no longer think; he was unable to move air through his nasal passages, and he fought for air. He could just react.

Garven sensed, as do all predators, that the moment of the kill was growing nigh. He spiked the big man's shins again and again with the heavy shoes he had worn especially for the duel. The Afrikaaner fell down, got up, received two smashing blows on his ears, and went down again. He was gasping for breath like a proverbial fish out of water. Garven smashed the sole of his shoe into the man's chin. He had been aiming for the throat. He slipped, off balance, and the Afrikaaner slugged Garven's leg as hard as he could, raising an apple-sized knot on the tender inner thigh. Garven fell to the hard floor.

The larger man turned slowly towards Garven to take advantage of the more promising circumstances, but Garven was still able to move with aggressive speed. He drove the bottom of his foot full into the face of his weakening opponent, then lifted and dropped the heel of his other shoe into the corner of the man's mouth. Two more teeth cracked and broke, leaving a jagged sawblade of teeth remaining. The Afrikaaner now began to choke in earnest. There was no more fight in him. He could only struggle against his retching and choking, and inability to get a clean breath. He was losing consciousness.

Garven leaped to his feet, a look of bloodlust on the contorted features of his face, giving him a demonic look. He poised himself for the kill and lifted his foot to stamp on the Afrikaaner's neck, which was now open and unprotected. David hurled himself at Garven, knocking him completely off balance and away from the floundering blond student. The girlfriend sobbed.

"Stop! You'll kill him! You will have more trouble than you ever dreamed of! Stop it! It's enough!" David shrieked and flung his arms around Garven's, pinioning them to his sides momentarily.

It was finally enough for Garven to see that he no longer had an opponent. He allowed David to move him well away from the stricken fighter, who was heaving and gasping for air. The other fellow had made it to his knees and was gaining a measure of control now that the copious blood from his face could run out onto the floor instead of back into the nasal and throat passages. The girlfriend made her way to the door and ran headlong out of the room.

David made Garven wait long enough to see that the big South African-American student was likely to be all right, then the two of them walked out, leaving the other man staggering and weaving in the center of the wrestling room floor, very slowly traversing towards the exit.

It was two weeks later, into dead week, before Garven and David saw the very docile Afrikaaneer again. There was no more trouble over watered unknowns, no more aggressive challenges, no more ferocious academic competition in the quantitative analysis class that quarter.

No one made any reference to Garven's or the South African's battered faces—the students ignored them, glad to be able to do their work without the constant need to defend their chemical unknowns, and the lab instructors turned the other way, glad that they did not have to know about it and did not have to deal with the unpleasantness of challenging a student for sabotage or cheating. In aggregate, the quarter ended well for Garven.

Spring quarter found Garven feeling burnt out. He felt lethargic, wanted to sleep, wanted to play. His bruises and sore and swollen spots were healing. He had to force himself to study or even to attend classes. It was gorgeous outside. There was sunshine, bright blue skies, frolicking girls, and non-premedders playing touch football everywhere. He had trigonometry, German, biochemistry, creative writing, psychology, and philosophy classes to plague him and to interrupt his pleasant reveries. It was a hill for a climber to buckle down to his academic work in the midst of such a bacchanalian sensory surround. He was only partly successful. Devon Upshire provided the most unfair and seductive distraction.

CHAPTER
Sixteen

"Absolutely, absolutely, genuinely, completely not," Garven said when Devon introduced his "greatest caper yet."

"You haven't even heard the plan yet," Devon protested as he, Garven, Grantland, David, and Frosty sat around Grantland's room that was now festooned with poster-sized hangings of *Punch* cartoons in keeping with an English country gentleman phase through which Grantland was currently going.

"Don't even want to *hear* about it," said Garven emphatically. "Every time any one of us says, 'I've got a great idea,' I get into trouble. My dad told me, in no uncertain times, that one more 'trouble,' and he would cut me off. I presume he meant my nuts!"

"Oh, come on. Let's just hear it. I'm bored out of my skull," said Grantland.

"Don't go encouraging him," said Garven in protest, working to maintain the weak hold on his resolve to do his work and to keep out of scandal and trouble. He was feeling as if he had used up all of his luck for the year by not getting into any kind of difficulty for his thrashing of the guy in quant class. The big South African had proved to be a stand-up guy—never breathed a word of the fight and had laid off Garven entirely after that day.

Frosty, usually of the words-are-precious-and-I'm-a-thrifty-guy category, spoke up, apparently driven by boredom and an attack of spring fever. "I want to expand my mind with great ideas. Go ahead, Mr. Upshire, expand me."

Garven started to protest.

"Don't be a wet blanket, Garven," Frosty calmed him. "What can it hurt to listen?"

Garven had a pretty good idea, but held his peace anyway.

"Well, since you insist," Devon said with mischief seeping out of every crevice and movable part of his face. "This is the grand plan of the spring quarter of 1951 at our beloved alma mater."

Garven groaned both at the grandiosity of the pronouncement and at his own weakness for not plugging his ears or getting on Shanks's pony and getting out of there.

"Relax, Garven, you'll like it. You really will," Devon insisted.

That was what Garven was most afraid of.

******

Trigonometry was not as bad as Garven thought it would be. It was much worse. Compared to trig, college algebra had been only obtuse, and solid geometry downright understandable. From the first day of class to the last, Garven was sure he did not understand a thing said. He battled sleepiness so much that he was sure something was wrong with himself, and he went to see the doctor at the student health office. The doctor had just laughed and told him he would be fine in two months.

"Drink some coffee," was his only therapeutic advice.

"To begin with, you will need to memorize the fundamental identities of trigonometry," the grad student in charge of his section of trig had ordered. He wrote them on the board:

> *"Reciprocal identities: sin theta equals the reciprocal of csc theta, cosine theta equals the reciprocal of sec theta, and tangent theta equals the reciprocal of cot theta. And, by deduction, csc theta equals the reciprocal of sin theta, sec theta equals the reciprocal of cosine theta, and so forth."*

"Clear, right?" Garven groused. *"What's a cosine?"* he murmured to himself.

"Tangent and cotangent identities: tangent theta equals sin Ø/cos Ø while cot Ø = cos Ø/sin Ø."

Whoever made up words like 'cotangent'? thought Garven.

Still, the words were better than the numbers and made-up symbols. Pythagorean identities—Greek. Appropriate choice of languages.

"Sin squared theta plus cosine squared theta equals one; one plus tan squared theta equals sec squared theta, and also one plus cot squared theta equals csc squared theta."

"One plus cotangent squared theta! There is absolutely no way that can mean anything!" moaned Garven to himself. He felt very sleepy. Outside the window, he could see the greenest grass and the bluest sky he could ever remember. A frat man and his coed semi-slave walked past the window, holding hands, oblivious to "csc squared theta." His friends, the hawks, the coyotes, the desert rats, and the Indians never thought about such stuff, and they got along just fine.

The class period ended with the definition of periodic functions and a set of graphing assignments. Moan. Garven hated graphs as bad as he hated story problems.

"A function f is defined as a periodic function if there is a positive real number z such that $f(x + z) = f(x)$ for every value of x in the domain of f. The smallest such positive number z is known as the period of f. The period corresponds to the length of one cycle on the graph of f," patiently explained the grad student, glad to be done with the odious introductory teaching assignment.

To save his life, Garven hastened to the math lab to find a senior student nerd math tutor. It troubled him considerably that he had no idea what the definitions meant, and even more so that the problem-solving assignment, based on those definitions, was entirely inscrutable. The book was full of definitions, to say nothing of numbers. He would never be able to memorize them all. Maybe this stupid class would be his downfall.

The resident nerd for the day was a thin, bespectacled gum chewer with premature balding. Garven was prepared to dislike the man but to put up with him for the sake of salvation in trig. After introductions, he got right to the point. "I hate math. I can't understand a thing about it. I am not particularly dumb in general, but without a miracle, I will flunk trig and can kiss medical school good-bye."

"Funny thing," the nerd said. "But everybody I tutor is in premed. I don't know why you guys can't just flunk trig like everybody else and get on with life." He sighed, knowing that Stanford used trigonometry as the cut class to weed out the non-math, non-physics, non-chem majors who wasted so much of the educational time of the math department faculty. "But, I know, you have to get into med school—it's life or death—no?"

"That's about it."

Garven was not sure whether he would decide to like this guy or not. The guy's sarcasm was a plus, at least.

"Let's see. You hate graphs, right?"

Garven nodded sullenly, almost angrily, at the thought of graphs.

"And…oh, yes, you hate story problems even worse."

He pressed his forefingers to his temples like Presto-Chango, the magician, to emphasize his prescience.

Garven nodded again. He had to smile a little. The nerdy senior knew exactly what it was about. "Think you can help, doc?" he asked.

"Ach, ya!" he said in a mock German professor accent. "Your problem is in getting the understanding of the concept of the equation, how you always have to have the same thing on both sides of the equal sign. You know, like the famous old equation, 'the heat of the meat equals the angle of the dangle.'"

Garven laughed at the corny joke. The nerdy guy was okay.

The tutor was pleased at having gotten a smile and a little laugh out of the too-serious premedder. They were the most uptight single group of human beings on the planet, definitely the all-work-and-no-play-makes-Jack group.

"Okay," he said. "Let's try a sample story problem, all right?"

Garven looked dubious, but said, "Okay, you're the boss."

"I like to see that attribute of humility in premedders and jocks. Gives me a sense of power. Now, for the problem: If a locomotive weighing 888 tons is going up an 8 percent grade at 8 miles an hour, burning 8 dollars' worth of coal to the mile and puts out 8 cents' worth of wasted coal dust up the smoke stack every 8 miles…" He paused.

Garven waited, trying to figure something out from the information he had received, but nothing seemed to come to mind. It disturbed him that the problem sounded familiar.

"How much would it cost to blow the whistle?" the senior asked in all seriousness.

Garven looked perplexed. He thought about the story problem seriously, knitted his brow, frowned, then figured it out. "You're pulling my leg," he announced, feeling foolish that he had taken the joke seriously.

It all seemed very funny to the tutor, who laughed richly at the success of his gag.

"Okay, let's get down to serious business of learning more than you ever wanted to know about triangles. I don't have time for this foolishness," the tutor said with a mock-severe expression.

Garven decided that he liked the guy. He spent nearly two hours with his new tutor, who finally got too frustrated to go on and went away talking to himself. Garven felt a little bit better about triangles and definitions, and thought he might even squeeze out a C if he could keep working with the same senior tutor.

Philosophy 103 would, he presumed, like the two quarters of philosophy before it, be Garven's saving grace. He seemed actually to understand the stuff, the professor liked him, and the papers he wrote were now being accepted as a matter of routine. Garven was fairly sure that some of his papers did not even get read since they came back with the pages entirely unwrinkled. He took pains to make sure he typed in plenty of pages; so the cursory glance would reveal a full paper that looked as if the work had been done, as usual.

"We will complete our survey of philosophical metaphysics with this current chapter from my book. There will be no midterm exam, just a term paper from the vast compilation of metaphysical literature. I would prefer that the paper deal with ideas emanating from the thought of Western civilization, but I do not insist on it. Because of the lack of a careful and critical literature study, even the major Eastern philosophers, I will be giving extra scrutiny to any paper on the Asiatic or Oriental metaphysics," said Dr. Pollock.

That simplified matters. A paper about Royce, or Spinoza, or Hume, or even Plato, decided Garven. The more obvious and uncontroversial, the better. "*Probably end up writing about Plato's Republic, like everybody else,*" he thought. "*At least I don't have to listen to or read anything about the other old dead philosophers if I don't want to, but I'll have to know Plato cold.*"

"We have covered Plato's *Euthyphro* and his *Republic*—that's one of my personal favorites, in case you hadn't noticed," Dr. Pollock said with a smile.

"*No question about it: Plato's Republic it is for the term paper,*" Garven mused.

"We have finished Spinoza's *Ethics*, Lord Hume's *A Treatise of Human Nature*, and Rene Descartes's *Discourse on Method*. If that is not enough to chew on, come by my office, and I will give you some more materials. For now, consider the following passages…"

Garven was impressed that the professor recited the excerpts without resorting to notes.

> "The mind is a kind of theater, where several perceptions successively make their appearance; pass, re-pass, glide away, and mingle in an infinite variety of postures and situations… The comparison of the theater must not mislead us. They are the successive perceptions only, that constitute

the mind; nor have we the most distant notion of the place, where these scenes are represented, or of the materials, of which it is composed."
David Hume – *A Treatise of Human Nature*

And,

"But, you say, is not, then, all this faith of ours after all well founded? Isn't there really something yonder that corresponds in fact to this series of experiences in us? Yes, indeed, there no doubt is. But what if this hard and fast reality should itself be a system of ideas, outside of our minds but not outside of every mind?… For, after all, isn't this precisely what our analysis brings us to?… Isn't it plain, then, that if my world yonder is anything knowable at all, it must be in and for itself essentially a mental world?"
Josiah Royce – *The Spirit of Modern Philosophy*

Garven got all his schoolwork done by seven o'clock. Not having wrestling saved him a big chunk of the day. He broke down and wrote letters to his mother and to his dad. It was then still only seven thirty; balmy and sleepy warm, and there was considerable horseplay going on in the dorms and out on the grounds. Garven felt restless.

As if he had rubbed the mental magic lantern, the genie of wishes for creative time wasting, Devon Upshire, entered Garven's room, without knocking, as usual, and plunked himself down on Garven's other chair. His face was full of enthusiasm, fun, and rascality. He radiated happiness; Garven had learned to fear that look. He tried not to see the posters and papers with scribbles, line drawings, and diagrams that Devon settled down in Garven's plain sight. He knew they were plans. He did not trust those potential plans. He knew, of course, that it was himself who he could not trust. His "will" was strong, but his "won't" was weak, as one of the middle-aged Mormon women used to say back in Cipher.

"Greetings, fellow conspirator!" enthused Devon.

"Forget it, count me out; *ixnay!*" replied Garven, but his "*ixnay*" sounded a little weak. He made the anti-vampire sign of the crucifix directed against Devon.

Devon ignored him. "I've not come to tempt you, that wouldn't be right." He smiled. "I have come to educate you."

"I'm sure."

"Indeed, I have. Tell me, what do you know about Roman and medieval siege weaponry, old friend?"

The inclusion of the phrase "old friend" was a dead giveaway. Garven knew that he must not succumb to this latest blandishment.

"Next to nothing," he said. "And I think, at this point, I should add that that is about all I want to know."

"Come on," Devon coaxed and wheedled.

"Catapults." Garven thought for a second. "And pitards, as in being 'hoist by your own pitard.'"

"Very good. I knew you could dredge up something if you really tried."

"And I haven't got a clue what a 'pitard' is."

"Well, a pitard was a bucket of hot coals or hot oil that was hoisted up a castle wall by soldiers laying siege. The plan was to flip the burning stuff over on the defenders behind the wall. Sometimes, the bucket would tip over the wrong way and spill the hot stuff on the soldiers hoisting the pitard and burn them. That was called being 'hoist by your own petard.' But I only mention that to prove to you what an expert I am in these romantic, old knightly weapons."

"I accept your superiority in those matters. Now, go home."

"That is rude, Garven. I will ignore the discourtesy, knowing that studying has unhinged your mind. I have seen the symptoms before. I have come to help."

Garven laughed. "This still sounds like trouble to me, but do go on. What kind of trouble can I get into by just listening?" He knew perfectly well the weakness of that argument for himself almost before the words had left his mouth.

"What I really came to teach you about is this," and now Devon unveiled his most elaborate poster, a to-scale, carefully drawn rendition of a siege machine, complete with arrowed labels.

"A catapult," said Garven. "Nice piece of work. Wish I had time to fritter on such projects."

Ignoring the implicit criticism of his study habits, Devon corrected Garven. "To be technical, this is a medieval trebuchet, also known as a mangonel. They used this machine to fling big rocks or buckets of hot coals and the like over castle walls. It used a counterweight—this thing here—instead of a tension rope like a bow and arrow or a catapult. The Romans made a distinction between their ballista, which threw stones, and their *catapulta*, which shot arrows or spears, but they were essentially the same thing. They depended on the sudden release of the tension on a tie-down holding the throwing arm—this lever pole here."

Garven found himself taking an interest in spite of his better judgment about his own best interests.

"I also have a diagram of a catapult."

"Nice work. I can see everything about it," Garven observed with growing enthusiasm.

He scrutinized the drawing more closely and found out that the picture was not truly of an historical device. The labels had inscriptions for modern materials like, "1/2 in. nylon rope, plastic hose pipe, and industrial rubber banding." He may not have been any kind of genius at mathematics, but the implications of the drawing were rapidly becoming evident to him.

"Ah oh," he said, looking hard at the sketch. "The thick plottens."

Devon laughed.

"What is this missile? Says, 'latex chemical bag.'"

"That is an extra thick balloon for all practical purposes," Devon answered.

"And what goes into the balloon?"

"Water. Under pressure from a common garden hose."

Garven could see the trouble brewing.

He knew he should not go on, but nevertheless, he asked, "And where does this missile go? What kind of target did you have in mind?"

"You know how those silly little freshmen boys are always throwing balloons full of water on us when we walk between Wilbur and Stern Halls?"

Garven did. He also knew that the upperclassmen were not above such foolishness themselves at times. This particular spring season—more commonly referred to as the "silly season" (like the election cycle)—definitely was one of those times.

"Um hmmh," he drawled with skepticism, coloring the tone of his voice noticeably.

"I have a bit of one-upmanship in mind," Devon announced, now getting to the heart of his plans.

"I can just imagine." Garven knew that what he should be saying was "No, no, a thousand times no!"

"With a properly made trebuchet or catapult, we could fling a water balloon clear from Stern to Wilbur. With a little practice, we might even get accurate enough to target a specific person or at least a specific group, like a touch football huddle, something like that."

"Who's this 'we,' paleface?"

"Why, my best buddies. The cleverest and most capable and most promising historians, engineers, and military science students on this campus."

"You are so full of crap, Devon."

Devon gave a modest little bow, acknowledging the compliment. "So, I presume I can count you in—in on the procurement, construction, practice, and eventually, on the military trials, old friend, old buddy?"

"No way, never, not on your life. No, not, negatory, *ixnay*, impossible," announced Garven firmly.

Devon smiled beatifically.

CHAPTER
Seventeen

This was Garven's sixth and last quarter of German. The university course now concentrated on German philosophers and on the classics. He spent most of his time translating, discussing, and writing short explanations and treatises on the deep meanings of the German works. In that regard, the study of German had become very much like the study of English literature—find the deep inner meaning even if the author did not consciously intend such obscurity. For this week, Garven worked on *Faust*. He set out to translate Goethe:

DER TRAGÖDIE ERSTER TEIL
Nacht
"In einem hochgewolbten, engen gotischen Zimmer Faust, unruhig auf seinem Sessel am Pulte.
Faust:
Habe nun, ach! Philosophie,
Juristerei und Medizin
Und leider auch Theologie
Durchaus studiert mit heissem Bemühn.
Da steh ich nun, ich armer Tor!
Und bin so klug als wie zuvor;
Heisse Magister, heisse Doktor gar,
Und ziehe schon an die zehen Jahr
Herauf, herab und quer und krumm
Meine Schüler an der Nase herum—

Und sehe, dass wer nichts wissen können!
Das will mir schier das herz verbrennen.
Zwar bin ich gescheiter als alle die Laffen,
Doktoren, Magister, Schreiber, und Pfaffen;"

(THE FIRST PART OF THE TRAGEDY)
Night
"In a high-vaulted, narrow Gothic den, Faust, restless in his
armchair at the desk.
Faust:
I have, alas, studied philosophy,
Jurisprudence and medicine, too,
And, worst of all, theology
With hard endeavor, through and through—
And here I am, for all my lore,
The wretched fool I was before.
Called Master of Arts, and Doctor to boot,
For ten years almost I confute
And up and down, wherever it goes,
I drag my students by the nose—
And see that for all our science and art
We can know nothing. It burns my heart.
Of course, I am smarter than all the shysters,
The doctors, and teachers, and scribes, and
Christers."

The third and final quarter of psychology—the introduction to psychopathology—was proving to be more interesting to Garven. It seemed to him
more practical, more useful, more like what he had envisioned medicine and
psychiatry would be. That had become for Garven the test of the worth of a
class, of virtually any endeavor, for that matter. He, like his premed competitors, was an ultimate, well-defined, task-oriented pragmatist. The class had to
contribute to getting into medical school, or it had actually to teach something the aspiring young physician deemed appropriate to his future practice
of the healing arts, or the class was nothing more than another hurdle to be
passed, then ignored, and finally forgotten.

Dr. Simpkins lectured with enthusiasm on the psychology of the abnormal,
the stuff of his practice of psychoanalytically based clinical psychology. His

definition of normal included all those behaviors, conducts, and expressions classed by the informed, particularly Professor Dr. Simpkins, as "usual," "conventional," "appropriate"; well, "normal." By the psychology of the abnormal, he meant the actions of those individuals who were classed, by the same august body of determiners, as abnormal or whose ideas and responses stamped them as differing from the usual, the statistical average; those who lay at the edges of the bell-shaped curve.

"In this distinction, we clinical psychologists tend to exclude mere eccentrics since their behaviors are not necessarily deleterious to their ability to cope with the problems of their lives. The abnormal attribution would, therefore, be applied to such deviant behavior as homosexuality, to use an obvious example of psychological disease. The study of such individuals, of their deviant and self-destructive behavior patterns, is only an extension of the study of normal psychology. We seek an explanation, incidentally, a non-judgmental one, as in the case of homosexuality or other perversions, of the various kinds of failure of adjustment.

"An individual should be considered with the same objectivity by the psychologist as an iron bar would be evaluated and studied by the engineer. That bar of iron may be tested by having forces applied to determine the amount of stress that it can endure before it bends, and then what force is necessary to cause it to break. The engineer may take into consideration the components of the bar, its diameter and length, the temperature, the effect of previous stresses. He may note the site of the bend or break and examine the cause of weakness at that point.

"The psychologist examines the patient, the individual, to come to a helpful understanding of why that individual should fail to cope or adjust to stresses that others take in their stride. What is it in the past history, in the personality, in the character type that determines that this person will respond abnormally—to bend like the iron bar in our analogy? Take our homosexual, for example. Why is it that some men, and even a few women, exhibit the illness and depravity of seeking sex with their own kind? An interesting new theory has been put forth, to wit, that homosexual boys fail to have an adequate father or male figure in their developmental stages and therefore develop ambiguity about their sexuality. For my part, it seems this hypothesis needs a great deal more study."

Garven took his usual careful and copious notes on the exogenous and endogenous causes of failure, on the elements of personality failures that led to cumulative failure of adjustment, on the manifold frailties of humankind that lead them to behave so abominably and pathetically—so pathologically. Simpkins listed inherited influences, acquired ones from illnesses, infections, injuries, or the happenstances of life from which the individual could not escape. The lecture covered, in a cursory fashion, the results and pathological coping mechanisms of abnormal psychology—delusion, delirium, hallucination, neurosis, phobia, retardation, and psychosis. Garven felt like he was, for once, getting at the meat of his education.

Dr. Simpkins concluded with the comment, "Intelligent people have ever observed and tried to understand deviant behavior. As far back as the first century BC, Cicero bemoaned, '*O tempora, O mores!*' I'm sure those of you with the requisite background can translate, but for the rest, 'Oh, the times. Oh, the behavior!'"

Garven also felt a gnawing frustration at having been wronged by the Department of Psychology. He had never been paid for his work on the hypnotism project despite all of the assurances of staff workers, professors, secretaries, and even the Man himself. Mid-quarter, he made one last effort with regular channels to get his pay. He determined to be a paragon of civility and humility, but at least to make his request assertively, as if he had not been assertive enough when he barged into the office of the department head at the end of last quarter.

Garven stood quietly in front of Elizabeth, Professor Dr. Simpkins's all-powerful secretary, until she finished what she was doing and looked up.

"Yes?" she inquired, showing no apparent recognition of having seen the young man before.

Garven thought that had to be good. "I have come to get you to clear up an error, probably one in accounting, so I can get my pay for the work I did on the hypnosis project."

"I am sure you are mistaken, young man. There were no paid students or subjects on that project. Were you one of the subjects as part of your class assignment, perhaps?" There was condescension and suspicion that she was facing a cheap confidence man by the tone of her voice.

"I was involved as a class assignment, and I was also hired by Dr. Gunther to work regularly for more than a quarter in addition."

"Have you time cards or other indication of your work hours?"

"I gave everything to you to use to get me my check."

"A moment. I will peruse the files."

She hurriedly fingered through a row of manila folders in her large three-drawer metal file cabinet, then shook her head.

Garven gritted his teeth.

"Nothing, I'm afraid. I do not find you listed as an employee, nor is there any record of work time. I do not have a contract agreement."

Garven held his temper. "But Dr. Gunther—"

"Dr. Gunther will return from sabbatical next March. Perhaps you can take it up with him then. Now, if that is all, I really must get back to my work."

Garven had more to say. His face showed his strain.

The secretary finished the interview. "There is nothing I can do for you, son."

Garven hated to be called "son" by anyone.

"I strongly advise you to drop this effort at extortion."

She said it with tightly pursed lips as if she had been forced to divulge her opinion and leave this matter alone hereafter.

"Dr. Simpkins is not without influence. Perhaps you can envision the consequences of incurring his enmity."

Garven could see the possibilities and knew that neither the money nor the principle of the thing were worth saying more. Elizabeth returned steadfastly to her work, making a production of ignoring Garven.

The undergraduate student could see that there was nothing more to be gained in that office. They had won; he had lost. He had worked for nothing. He had been screwed. It occurred to him to consider that he had learned a valuable lesson and would be less likely to be the screwee in the future and to drop the whole thing. But that was not what he did. He was young, unused to the ways of the establishment world, and full of himself. That was why he wrote the fateful letter.

> *April 14, 1951*
> *Dallin T. Cheevers*
> *President,*
> *Stanford University,*
> *Stanford, California*
>
> *Dear Sir:*
>
> *I am a Stanford student who was employed by the Department of Psychology in the hypnosis project. My problem is that I was never paid, and now I cannot find anyone in the department who will recognize that I am owed my salary. The money is important to me, but more important is the idea that those in*

power should not be able to treat me this way just because I am
a student.
Since even the department chairman, Dr. Simpkins, will not
help me, I am appealing to you to use your high office in my
behalf. Thank you for your consideration.
Respectfully yours,
Garven C. Wilsonhulme
Class of 1953

Weeks passed and Garven heard nothing; so, he admitted final defeat and gave up further tries to collect his rightful wages. He made an effort to tuck the incident into the back of his mind, so it would be a worthwhile lesson, but his mind was too busy, and he simply forgot it altogether.

******

Devon had, by the fifth week of spring quarter, mounted a well-designed plan to bombard Wilbur Hall. He, Frosty, Grantland, and David had built a prototype catapult and were planning with great secrecy to test it out with the launching of a few nightly missiles. Garven refused to lay hands on the war machine himself to maintain an alibi and a credible fiction of innocence should the conspirators be exposed. He did consent to be the purchasing agent, making surreptitious trips to San Francisco to get two by fours, two child's wagons to get the wheels, heavy latex balloons, industrial size and strength rubber banding, glue, and assorted hardware. The country lad from Cipher, Arizona, became adept at haggling, scrutinizing the quality of materials, measuring and figuring amounts of materiel, collecting and disbursing funds, keeping records (never to see the light of day), inventing plausible cover stories, secreting materials so that they were hidden in plain sight, and at lying, especially at lying.

Garven carried his role so far that he adopted disguises and became fairly adept at altering his features by the time the project was over. He acquired two wigs, one red and one black; a pair of elevator shoes; an oversized trench coat, into which he secured cotton batting to make him look sixty pounds heavier, and an assortment of hats and glasses. It would have taken a team of G men to follow his tracks. He convinced himself that it was not silly.

The pesky freshmen from Wilbur Hall were carrying on increasingly daring and provocative raids against the Stern Hall upperclassmen without a satisfactory answering being forthcoming from the older men. One day, there would be a hose left running down a first-floor hall; another day, a group of innocent touch footballers would be set upon by a well-organized band of ambush water bombers. Then there was the incident of the cow locked on the third floor of Stern that Sunday night. It was becoming humiliating, and more than one council of war was held by the men of honor in the dorm. It was unacceptable, and by extension, retaliation was altogether justified.

Devon and his conspirators maintained their secrecy and declined the invitations to contribute to the plan, to any plan, of retaliation offered by anyone else. The other sophomores, juniors, and seniors shook their heads in sad disbelief that the famous pranksters of the class of 1953 had turned conventional and law abiding, as bad as if they had become actual grown-ups. Devon and friends just shrugged in what was generally perceived as submissiveness, although their intent was more of an enigmatic gesture.

The top secret night maneuvers proved the catapult to be strong and reliable, able to hurl a heavy water-filled balloon a hundred yards time after time, but a mite lacking in accuracy. No amount of adjusting could improve the reliability to less than twenty yards of an intended target. The provocations by the freshmen were becoming too blatant to be tolerable, and the end of spring quarter was drawing close enough that the secret combination of catapultists agreed that it was time to act. Sunday, May 17, was chosen.

Garven broke his resolution and helped the others dismantle the machine, carry it up to the roof of Stern Hall, and to reassemble it behind a row of sewage ventilator pipes for camouflage on Saturday night. He was there in the night to see the first launching from that location and confirmed that the balloon had landed within ten feet of the near wall of Wilbur Hall. There was one curiosity—the balloon did not break. The conspirators logged that occurrence off as a fluke and pronounced the dress rehearsal trial a success. The machine and its masters were ready for an artillery fusillade on the freshmen sunbathers, who were expected to break the Sabbath the following day. They laid in large stores of water-filled balloons covered with a utilitarian and innocent-appearing tarpaulin.

CHAPTER
Eighteen

Garven had missed a lecture, so he looked for one of the girls in his chem class that Sunday morning. They were not as difficult and competitive as the men and did not seem so threatened or inconvenienced by the request to copy notes. He returned from Florence Moore Hall, studied the notes, did the assigned problems, and was ready for the real action of the day before noon.

It was going to be a hot one. The sun blazed out of a cloudless azure sky, unmitigated by any breeze. The sun worshippers were congregating in small, friendly groups, strictly segregated by class—freshmen near the friendly walls of Wilbur Hall and upperclassmen by Stern. Women had joined their class friends for a day of society and picnics. The lawns were becoming littered with bathing suited bodies, women all in one-piece suits because none of them were brave enough to sport the new two-piece or certainly the bikini style.

Devon was excited, exhilarated, and his enthusiasm was catching. He had Garven, Grantland, Frosty, and David all laughing and pointing as if they had already scored soaking hits on the unsuspecting freshmen; the collective insanity of their mental images was vivid enough that it would have been better if they had left it at that. Garven realized that fact before the five of them ever ascended the stairs to the top floor and the attic ladder to the roof. Still, the anticipation was as compelling as the expectation of Santa Claus. Garven was powerless against the siren song of this new Lorelei.

Devon selected the fullest balloon for the first sally. It was stretched thin by the distention of its contained water. Frosty and David gently fitted it onto the propelling lever arm while Grantland and Garven gradually stretched the rubber bands tightly over the wooden hook attached to the release lever. Devon slid the machine slightly to the left, calculating the trajectory of the swollen projectile as best he could so it would land in the middle of a group of students heavily populated with females.

The sophomores surrounding the catapult were laughing and joking in nervous expectation.

"Y'all twang it, Devon," urged Grantland, unable to be patient any longer. "It's your privilege."

Devon twanged it. He flipped the release lever, producing a satisfying sharp, vibrating note from the overstretched rubber bands. The bag of water hurtled out into the noontime sky with a high, lofting trajectory, so high and fast that it was difficult to follow visually until it began its mischief-laden descent. The sophomores held their breath. The accuracy of the targeting was beyond their fondest expectations. The turgid balloon struck the earth in the dead center of a large, mixed-gender collection of freshmen with the velocity and sound of a bomb. The somnolent students were flung from their daydreams by an instantaneous and complete icy soaking that drenched their magazines, lunches, towels, and new hairdos. Besides the consummate joy of seeing the accuracy of the missile landing and its eminently soul-satisfying results, the conspirators, through their binoculars, could appreciate the consternation on the faces of their victims that betrayed their total ignorance of the source of the attack.

The freshmen down on the ground ran about, gesticulating like ants whose anthill had been stepped on, laughing and swearing. A few of the cooler heads had already started to run back to their Wilbur Hall rooms for their supply of water balloons, intent on serious retaliation for this unprovoked act of war.

Devon and his men loaded and lobed balloon after balloon, raining them down on the hapless freshmen, the west wall of Wilbur Hall, harmlessly on unoccupied patches of grass, and harmfully through one of Wilbur Hall's second-story windows. The freshmen and their female cohorts now realized the puniness of the weapons at their command. They threw a few hundred water balloons on the upperclassmen sunning by Stern Hall, who seemed as surprised as the freshmen over this sudden outburst of a water war. The upperclassmen ran for their own supply of water balloons, but both sides realized that there had been an escalation of hostilities and an introduction of new weapons heretofore not conceived in their limited minds.

The freshmen were too intent on retaliating and dodging the huge water missiles and the upperclassmen were too engrossed in their scramble to escape the onslaught of the freshmen hordes to take the time to identify the source of the skyborne bombs as yet. The freshmen, like the Red Army, concentrated their full attention on offense. Four of the more aggressive and attack-minded young men entered the emergency closet in the Wilbur hallway and ran out with one of the building's fire hoses. One fellow got the water blasting full force. At first, the four sturdies were unprepared for the whiplash force of the fire hose, and they were knocked about like rag dolls in Keystone Comedy slapstick. They sprayed their own freshmen, then they all laughed so hard that they dropped the end of the fire hose, which erratically sprayed in a serpentine, writhing pattern that blasted friend and foe indiscriminately.

The rooftop assaulters kept up a steady barrage, taking turns resting from the considerable exertions required. Sweat poured off the young men's faces and bodies. Water leaked out of some of the balloons, making the roof treacherously slippery. Some of the balloons were either under-filled or over-strong because they failed to break on impact. One such caved in the hallway door of Wilbur, and another took out the legs of a particularly spindly girl who did not get up.

By now, two score outstretched arms with index fingers extended were pointing at the rooftop where the conspirators were working at a fever pitch to unload all of their swollen missiles before the inevitable discovery was made and counterattack could be mounted. Then, as if by prearranged signal, all eyes, including those on the roof, swiveled in the direction of the parking lot driveway. Three carloads of campus police wheeled into view, klaxons blaring. They were followed by two black coupes containing dark-suited, gray-haired, official-looking men.

"Cops!" yelled ninety percent of the voices in the roiling crowd of aroused students.

Now, under ordinary circumstances, this predominately God-fearing, law-abiding, career-protective, Republican, obedient student body would have ceased and desisted from their rowdiness forthwith. Taken individually, that was almost certainly how they would have behaved. But this was a mob, and it was about to become a riot. As an anonymous aggregate, the rapscallion mentality of the collected rabble responded to the legitimate orders by the minions of the law with complete disregard, utter scofflaw. Not in the Stanford way. The freshmen got control of their fire hose and wheeled it around in good order to fire upon the constabulary. The force of the blasting water swept most of the twelve campus cops off their feet.

The sophomores and older students also immediately recognized their true allegiances and began to pelt a storm of common water balloons on those commissioned to protect and to serve. The three administrators, now easily recognizable as Ivan the Terrible, Dean Howard Taft Winslow himself, and even Dallin T. Cheevers PhD, president of Stanford University, were not spared.

Frosty remarked, "Doesn't old Winkler have any kind of life of his own? Who would think he would be skulking around on a spring Sunday to get in his licks on us misbehaving students?"

Just then, one of the more solid water missiles clipped a freshman boy across the side of the head and coldcocked him. He did not get up, either. Garven winced. Seeing the folly of their ways, the five boys on the roof, acting in full accord with an unspoken command, laboriously reoriented the catapult and pointed it in the direction of the intruding body of officialdom. Shortly, a fusillade of water balloons sallied out in the general direction of the cops and administrators. The first shots were long and wide, some caving in the roofs and windows of cop cars and a few students' vehicles. After some adjustment, the catapult was hoisting and hurling its missiles with acceptable accuracy, depending on one's perspective.

From the perspective of the venerable university's administrators, the accuracy was viewed with complete negativity. They took special notice when the nice president, Dr. Cheevers, was hit broadside by an unbreakable balloon and was knocked to the pavement, breaking his arm. One of the cops caught one in the head, which threw him back into his police unit, denting the passenger side door. Fortunately, the balloon hit him in the head so no real harm was done. He went for his gun, but the cooler head of the campus police chief, who had lately arrived on the scene of the civil disorder, prevailed, and the gun was re-holstered. Garven could hear the blasphemous invectives and scurrilous epithets directed at his position on the roof even from that considerable distance.

Ivan Winkler was soaked; President Cheevers was still on the ground, having his arm attended to by a pair of water-logged cops who could not think of anything else to do; and the cops and the dean of students were milling about in chaos. That was to say, things seemed to be going great so far as Garven, Devon, Frosty, Grantland, and David could tell.

"I am thinking it is time for us to make like geese and get the flock out of here," said Grantland with a note of growing urgency in his voice.

"Me, too," said Garven, still laughing about the last pelting Ivan the Terrible had gotten from a band of junior class commandos who had scored a close-in coup.

"Me, three," echoed David. He turned and started walking briskly for the attic ladder exit.

By some sort of convenient telepathy, the mob below now took it upon themselves to create a diversion to aid in the five sophomore conspirators to escape almost as if on cue as part of a well-laid plan. They pivoted like an unwieldy army and began advancing on the innocent girls' dorms, Branner and Cruthers.

Although the purpose of the mob action at this point was nebulous, Dean Winslow could be heard shouting above the din, "Halt! Stop where you are! We will not tolerate a panty raid! You all face expulsion or worse! Halt in the name of the law!"

A voice in the crowd yelled back, "Don't be a nattering nabob of negativity, Dean! Come and get some undies for yourself!"

Whether or not the rioting students had clearly defined the goal of their movements as a panty raid before Dr. Winslow had made the suggestion was now conjecture. However, as if of one mind, the excited and sex-crazed students began to run pell-mell for the girls' dorms with a clear-cut purpose—every man was to have at least one article of feminine underclothing before the day was out.

Garven and company gratefully accepted the respite the diversion had provided and abandoned their war machine and the remaining ammunition, and hurriedly slipped down the ladder and into the stairwells to exit the building. They hated to miss the panty raid but recognized that they could not have everything and were content to bask in the unsung glory of their caper. They were wiser than they had been in the streaker affair, and did not try to play the innocents by sitting primly in their rooms.

Instead, this time, they played the innocents by running up to the downed university administrators and making a show of being annoyingly helpful, of getting in the way, along with a small group of brownnosers who had beaten them to the scene. The cops took their names before shooing them off, thereby ensuring them of an alibi. Garven was proud of that touch since it had been his daring and not universally accepted proposal.

The last two weeks of spring quarter demanded that Garven focus fully on his studies. Up to that point, he was pretty sure that he had aced everything except trigonometry, and he was a hopeless case in there. He came to understand that there had originally been four classes of twenty-five students each at the beginning of the quarter. He had survived the two critical cuts by the hair of his chinny-chin-chin and had the honor to be one of twenty-four remaining students in the now amalgamated class. The injustice of it all was that those twenty-four would all be graded on the bell curve as if the dropouts had never been there. Garven rankled every time he considered that notion.

Biochemistry was proving to be much easier than he had expected; he could even see the applicability of some of the stuff to medical school, to doctoring, and to life, for that matter. The course had thus far covered carbohydrates with all the complexities of stereoisomers versus structural isomers, sugar reactions such as condensation polymerization (loss of water) and hydrolysis (gain of water), and the functions and structure of mono and disaccharides, and of cellulose and starch—the polysaccharides. They had covered lipids like fats, waxes, and the relatively new field of steroids that included the hormones. The steroids, like cholesterol, were incompletely understood, partly because their structures were so different from the other lipids—four interlinked carbon rings plus additional and substituted groups. Garven's term paper for the course was on the properties and functions of the adrenal hormones, with emphasis on cortisone.

The final weeks were to be spent on proteins.

"Amino acids and the proteins they form are the building blocks of all active tissue. Eat peanut butter, cheddar cheese, and milk, and nothing else, and you have them all," said the chemistry instructor, a graduate student whose name Garven could never seem to remember—probably Dr. Staff. "Of course, you also get a world-class case of constipation and die of culinary boredom.

"They are the most complex and numerous organic compounds in living beings; they are at once structural and chemically functional because they act as both building blocks and as controlling substances—enzymes—for complex chemical reactions."

He wrote on the board:

"The amino group is nothing more than $-NH_2$. Add a carboxyl group, $-COOH$, and you have an amino acid. String amino acids together by condensation polymerization reactions to form peptide bonds, shed a water and get a peptide, and hook the peptides up in a myriad of ways until you have ten or more together and you have a polypeptide, and with a hundred or more, you get a protein."

"Simple, no?"

"*Probably not,*" thought Garven. "*There must be something wrong; I seem to be understanding this.*"

He had understood the material so far that quarter, and his grades reflected that understanding, whereas the A's in his other science classes were more a demonstration of what can be accomplished by sheer determination and hard work than by any real enlightenment.

"During our last week, we will concentrate on the energy aspects of bio-chemical reactions and the role of proteinaceous catalytic enzymes. Not to worry about this material for the final, except we will include maybe one general question on energies of activation or enzyme bonding. While we are on the subject of the final, let me reassure you about the last lecture. None of it will be included in the final. The lecture is on the nucleic acids and will be a guest presentation by either of two people who are making real progress in a field that is in its infancy. Either a Dr. Watson or a Dr. Crick will give the lecture. Come and pay attention even if you won't be tested on the material. That goes for the premed students as well, maybe especially. It wouldn't hurt you guys to learn something along the way."

The grad student smiled at his insight into the character of his pupils. Garven knew the man was right on target.

The quarterly dead week was considered a real deprivation to most of the Stanford students—nothing to do but study and get caught up on due and past due papers, and to get the postponed lab experiments written up. Garven, like his competitors for medical school seats, welcomed the socially blank week, in part because it was the first and only time each quarter when he felt as if he was on top of the whole huge mass of his academic require-ments, and because it meant that the quarter would be over in two weeks. He could then settle into that nirvana longed for by industrious students, the blessed, blessed oblivion extolled by the beatniks—the interterm. Stanford did not have a spring break like many of the other universities, but instead rewarded its students by letting them out early for summer vacation. Garven, for one, could hardly wait.

Garven was ready for finals and knew he had done well on them, although he kept a somber expression for his competitors as they did for him. It was considered ungentlemanly even to hint that you might have passed a test, especially a final, let alone to appear to be boastful that you actually had the material covered or to go to the unthinkable extreme to gloat that you thought that you were going to get a high grade. Nonetheless, Garven was confident that he would get A's in German, philosophy, psychology, biochemistry, and creative writing. Prior to the final in trigonometry, he had entertained the wishful delusion that he might even eke out a gentlemanly B in the class by some miracle. The final was a reality check.

There were eight questions—problems, actually—and one true question. Garven could do nothing whatever on the problems to his horror. He filled three blue books answering the ninth question so he could at least make some kind of showing. The test questions were:

1. The angle of depression of Piper Cub tethered to the tarmac from a point on a beacon light 140 feet above the surface of the water is 5°. Compute the distance from the base of the beacon tower to the plane.

2. The range d of a projectile shot at an angle of elevation Ø and with an initial velocity v is expressed by: $d(Ø) = v2/g$ sin 2Ø where g is the acceleration of gravity (32 ft/sec) and v can be assumed to be 85 ft/sec. At what angle should the projectile be aimed in order to hit a target that is 200 feet downrange?

3. In baseball, the four bases are required to form a square with sides 90 feet long. The front corner of the mat upon which the pitcher stands must be 60 feet from the front edge of home plate. Find the distance from the front corner of the pitcher's mat to first base.

...4., 5., 6., 7., 8.,

9. If I have asked only questions you cannot answer, use the space provided in the blue books to tell me anything and everything you know about trigonometry.

Garven took five minutes to determine that the first eight problems were in a language comparable to speaking Swahili to a pig. They made no more sense to him and were no more solvable by him than the senior nerd math tutor's facetious problem about the 888-ton locomotive going up the 8 percent grade. He wasted another three minutes in a silent string of condemning invectives against arithmetic, mathematics, algebra, trigonometry, calculus, and physics (because it used mathematics), and against all present, past, and yet-to-live mathematicians. When he felt better, Garven spent a feverish and concentrated fifty-two minutes in filling the blue books with everything from the Pythagorean theorem to the law of cosines to Heron's formula that he had learned by rote. It was a prodigious lot, and Garven did not understand one word, symbol, or number of what he wrote, but he knew it was all correct.

The grad student who taught the class and did all of the work, and who politely conceded the credit to the professor of mathematics under whom he worked on his doctorate, wrote the following note on the inside cover of Garven's final exam blue book: *"I admire the remarkable amount of trigonometry you have memorized, and even more the fact that everything you wrote is 100 percent correct. That bit of effort is A work. I suggest you find a field other than mathematics for your career goals. Your class grade is C-."*

Under the circumstances, Garven was relieved to get even a C-, his first grade less than an A in his Stanford student career, or from Burton-Cagle, for that matter. He guessed his GPA could stand one bad grade. He could not recall ever being so relieved as he was at this moment, knowing that he would never have to take another class in mathematics again for the rest of his life.

CHAPTER
Nineteen

The young premed student who lived and died for his grades lost all sense of relief, of joy and pleasure of life, and of personal security when he encountered his grade on the final examination in psychology. The raw grades were posted by student number in the long hallway outside the department office. Contrary to his usual small feeling that he should take umbrage at being nothing more than a number to the megalithic university, on this occasion, Garven was glad for the anonymity. Next to his student number was the incomprehensible but starkly clear single letter: "C."

It was impossible, of course, a mistake. Presumably, a clerical mistake. Secretary Elizabeth was not perfect, after all. Nevertheless, Garven knew he would be a nerveless pulp until he could get the correct grade—definitely an A—substituted into its proper place in the official records. He went directly in Elizabeth's office. She was not there, and he even dared to knock on Dr. Simpkins's inner office door; it was locked. At four o'clock in the afternoon, everyone was gone. Somehow, Garven did not think it was a coincidence, the chickens.

Summer vacation was a reality, and Garven had a job lined up in Phoenix. Lyle Durche had gotten the job for him; they would both work for the Union Pacific Railroad freight lines, a trucking subdivision. He was due to start in exactly one week. That meant he could leave no later than three days from now, two if he wanted to see his mother and dad before he got started. He presumed that Lyle had them someplace to live, a grim prospect in view of

Garven's memory of Lyle's place in Cipher, but better than the alternative of having to find a place at the last minute.

Garven had to get the psych grade settled before he left. He would stalk Elizabeth until he could get the clerical error corrected. He had nothing better to do other than to enjoy the sun, the beach, the local girls, the enticements of San Francisco, and half a dozen other pleasant things he could think of. That thought and the memory of his C- in trig produced a morose mood that he knew would persist until he had achieved his purpose.

Elizabeth was not in her throne room the next day, either. Garven's mood darkened. He waited for more than an hour in the mid-morning and again in the afternoon. The day after that, he made a dozen or so spot checks. No Elizabeth. In fact, the building was virtually deserted. Garven concluded that the academicians all took their vacations in the first week of the summer season to avoid having to talk to upset students.

It was late afternoon when he started to trudge back across the courtyard at the rear of the psych building. He cast a doleful look back at the building, at the fourth floor, where Dr. Simpkins had his office. A man walked along the narrow balcony corridor, keeping close to the brick building wall either to keep in the shade of the overhang on that hot day or to avoid getting too near the ornate, low, wrought-iron railing that provided the only protection, flimsy at that, from falling over the side. Garven was not sure, but the figure looked enough like Professor Simpkins to warrant a longer scrutiny. He even put on his glasses. The distant figure set down his briefcase and papers, fumbled with a key, and opened the outside door to the office Garven had calculated as belonging to the chief of psychology.

What to do? It was certainly worth the effort to go back up the fourth floor to see the man if it was really Dr. Simpkins. It was even worth incurring the man's wrath by surprising him during his self-designated vacation period. It occurred to Garven that the professor might well not answer a knock on his office door; in fact, that seemed very probable, and there was not enough time to wait for another day. The best calculated risk for encountering the department head was to meet him on the narrow balcony way so he would have to talk to him, like it or not.

Garven hurried up the building's side stairs to the fourth floor then caught his breath. He did not want to be puffing and sweaty, to appear overanxious when he met the professor face-to-face. He need not have concerned himself. The late afternoon became early evening and the dim light of dusk settled over him as Garven waited on the balcony. The light came on in the office, the only active office in the whole building.

"The red-hot," Garven muttered as he settled into a squat and finally into a comfortable sitting position on the deck.

It was quite dark when the rear office door finally opened. Garven was startled out of a semi-sleep by the shaft of light that accompanied the door opening. It was Dr. Simpkins; at least his wait had not been a complete fool's errand. It remained to be seen what would come of the confrontation.

In order not to startle the professor and to cause him to be any more cheerless with the interference with his privacy, than he was rightfully expected to be, Garven cleared his throat several times while still ten feet away.

Professor Dr. Simpkins jumped. Not quite out of his skin, but close. "Who is it? Who's there?!" he demanded once his heart settled down.

"One of your students," Garven hastened to communicate in order to allay the older man's fears of a potential mugger.

"I see my graduate students on Thursdays. This is woefully inappropriate, Mister… Mister…"It was unthinkable that such a lowly creature as an undergraduate would interrupt the professor, and he never gave that possibility a thought.

"Wilsonhulme, Sir. Garven Wilsonhulme."

"You have the better of me. I don't believe you are one of mine, are you? Have you seen your major professor?"

"I'm not a grad student, Dr. Simpkins. I was in your introductory psych class."

"Psychology, young man, with due respect to the discipline." The professor's voice clearly and intentionally demonstrated his annoyance. "I am busy and occupied. Is there something I can help you with—something brief—something critical?"

The words were hard and delivered with a decided edge and the intent to dispense with him promptly was well evident to the student. "I will get directly to the point."

"Do."

"I found a 'C' after my student number on your spring quarter lists."

"Undoubtedly the deserved credit. You should have worked more diligently, young man."

Garven had just about had his fill of being "young man."He said, "There is a mistake. Hear me out. I promise not to interrupt you; please give me the same courtesy."

The professor was about to launch into a corrective lecture about courtesy, but figured it would only prolong things, so he waited in the semi-darkness for the young man to get through his untimely rendition of his sad tale.

"I did 'A' work on everything all quarter, for all three quarters. I wrote an excellent final; I know I did. So there's some mistake. Probably Elizabeth, she made a clerical mistake. I just want to get the mistake cleared."

"I presume you are referring to my fine secretary, Miss Thorton-Mulberry?"Dr. Simpkins let Garven know that he took umbrage at any undue familiarity and was determined to make this as difficult as possible.

"Yes, Sir. I guess that is her last name. Anyway, I have to leave right away, and I would really appreciate it if you would take a very few minutes and check the error before it gets set into stone by next quarter. Please."He was pleading, and Garven hated that quaver in his voice.

"Will you get out of my hair if I go to the bother of looking at your file, young man?"

Garven would even accept a few more "young mans" if he could get the obstreperous old man to look at the file. Then, for all his stubbornness, Dr. Simpkins would have to acknowledge his mistake, and they could both get on with more important things.

He followed the professor back into his office. The older man took a moment to figure out Miss Thorton-Mulberry's filing system and, finding it most efficient, was able to produce the manila folder entitled "Garven Wilsonhulme" from the accordion file designated 100-103, 1950-51. He looked at the contents then walked to the rear door before showing Garven the pertinent information, presumably to be able to hurry the boy out the door as soon as the damaging information was presented.

"There has been no mistake, young man,"

There was that "young man" business again.

"You were given a C. And a C was recorded. And a C is what you will live with on your record."

He hissed out each "C."

Dr. Simpkins was gloating. "Any further questions?"

"Lots."Garven was angry now. He tried to hide it. "I can see my blue book for the final in the folder. What did I get on it?"

Dr. Simpkins gave an exasperated sigh, and returned his attention to the folder. Garven saw a large "98" in the upper right-hand corner with a red line through it. Below was a "C" and the comment: *"Inadequate answers, skimpy scientific information to support your views."*

The pink haze of mounting anger tainted Garven's vision. He clenched his fists and ground his teeth to control his outburst.

"That doesn't jibe with the 98, does it, Sir? The real reason is all too clear to me. I made you mad by demanding the money you owe me for the hypnosis lab work."

A light blinked on in the professor's head. He knew that he had encountered this obnoxious young man before. Despite himself, he smiled; sort of a small, triumphant smile.

"That is right, isn't it?" pressed Garven. His temper was gaining the upper hand.

"Of course not, young man."

Garven's patience with that appellation came to an end.

"Don't be childish. When I record your C in my official roll tomorrow..." he gestured with the indicated deep-maroon binder with the black back reinforcement, "...it will be perfectly objective."

Garven was looking into the folder. He reached discourteously into the middle of the pile and produced a letter, his letter to President Cheevers, complaining about the injustice of his failure to be paid by the psychology department.

"How objective is this?" he demanded.

Dr. Simpkins felt that he was losing a little of his secure upper hand.

"Don't be impertinent and churlish, young man!" was the best he could manage at the moment.

Garven knew he had stepped over the line of propriety and wondered what it might cost him. He acted impulsively and grabbed at the official roll book in the professor's hand. The professor overreacted, as if he had been physically assaulted. He backpedaled out of his office and onto the balcony, maintaining his grasp on the roll book but dropping out the contents of the manila folder. Garven was beyond rational thought. He followed Dr. Simpkins out the door. The professor looked frightened, defensive. He continued to back up rapidly from the perceived danger from his "attacker." Garven held onto the roll book in a minor tug-of-war.

"Relax, I'm not trying to hurt you," Garven said, the thought that the professor might even report him to the campus police or something flashing into his mind.

Then, it happened. The back of Prof. Simpkins's knees encountered the low wrought-iron railing, and he lost his balance. Garven felt the sudden lurch backwards and lunged to grab hold of the alarmed man. His right hand came up with the roll book, and his left brushed the front of the heavy cotton broadcloth shirt without getting a purchase on the cloth or on Dr. Simpkins's body. Neither man made a sound. They were locked in a frantic, lethally awkward dance to pull the older man back from the brink.

Garven felt that he was going to pitch headlong over the rail. His legs locked against the railing to stop himself. But it was too late to stay the professor's momentum. For an instant, the two dancers in the *pas à mort* fixed their eyes on each other, then the older of the two did a horrifying backward somersault over the rail and down through four stories of air before contacting the brick floor of the courtyard with a sound entirely as would be expected if a watermelon had been thrown over the railing. The only other sound had been a mortal decrescendo groan.

Garven did not even dare to look over the side. It was too dark anyway. He was afraid that he would see something he could never forget. He sagged to his knees and shuddered against the railing. His mind lurched and ricocheted, raced, scrambled, and cried out. For a few minutes, Garven was all but psychotic, unable to make his mind work for him, almost unable to breathe. He threw himself back from the railing and scooted on his buttocks across the balcony and into the lighted office. He sat there, trying to collect his wits, to get himself back into action, but he seemed to be in a trance, a sort of mental paralysis.

The physical confrontation had taken less than four seconds; the entire encounter between the two men had begun no more than ten minutes before. Garven sat there in his stupor for twice that long before he began to be able to think, to assess his situation, and then to decide what to do. In all that thinking, it never occurred to him to rush to the professor's aid; that seemed the ultimate of futility. It also did not occur to him in any serious form to call the police. Instead, he began to think very objectively and pragmatically about what to do to extricate himself.

He added up the elements of the event. It was dark, the two of them had been alone, and so far as he could tell, no one had seen them together. There was no reason to suspect that this unfortunate accident was anything but that, an accident. There also did not seem to be any good reason for his part in it to be known. That would not help anybody, Garven reasoned. He was grateful that he had not voiced his problems with Simpkins or the psychology department to anyone but in that stupid letter to the university president, which no one had paid attention to. He decided to get out of there, just to get out and away.

He got to his feet and surveyed the scattered papers, papers with his name all over them. He looked around furtively; there was still no one there but himself, not that he had really expected to see anyone else. He was still holding onto the roll book. It occurred to him then that the accident did not have to have a completely bad ending for everyone. He flipped the pages to the proper section listing the reportable grades for the spring quarter, 1951, and found, to his profound relief, that the grades, while recorded, were written in pencil. It was a simple matter to erase the C and to substitute an A.

For a moment, he felt like a criminal, maybe even a murderer.

The feeling passed. He knew that it had been a primal response, sort of kill or be killed.

Garven gathered up the papers and returned them to the folder with his name on it. He gave it a second thought and extracted the letter from him to the university president, and crumpled the document up and stuffed it into the pocket of his Levis. He erased the condemnatory writing on his blue test booklet, leaving only the 98. The area of the erasure was slightly lighter that the rest of the book cover, but it was not very noticeable. He was sweating—a cold sweat—and he was pale. At times, he felt like he might faint. He replaced the folder in the filing cabinet, a task made simple by Miss Thorton-Mulberry's fine efficiency.

He debated about what to do with the roll book. It would seem natural for the book to be in the professor's briefcase, so he put it there. He laid the case near the railing. He debated whether or not to turn off the light and close the outside door, and finally decided to do just that. When someone found the professor, they would be more likely to presume that he had fallen in the dark if he put the briefcase outside. It even passed his mind to call in the report of the fall himself, so the body could be found in the dark and even the campus cops could put two and two together—the two and two that Garven construed.

Garven's thinking was back to normal, as clear as his furtive and crafty coyote alter-ego eluding its nighttime predators. He recognized the folly of making any kind of report, of taking any further chance of being involved or implicated. He was satisfied that all traces of his having been there were gone. He switched off the light and closed the door, which was self-locking, to Garven's relief. He slipped quietly along the balcony and down the fire escape to avoid any kind of chance encounter in the stairwells.

It was 10:30 p.m. on June 3 when he made his way via the back stairs of Stern Hall to his room. His friends had all left for the summer and had presumed that he, too, was long gone. He had already packed most of his things; now he hurriedly took the boxes and suitcases down to his car. He was feeling very tired, but his mind was now electrified with adrenaline; there would be no chance of sleeping tonight. He got in his car and left the campus, careful not to break any speed limits or to miss any stop signs. He was in the middle of the Mojave Desert by mid-afternoon the next day and pulled into Phoenix late on the day after that—June 5—having driven straight through.

Whatever else laid ahead, he knew he was through at Stanford. His brain swirled in indecision about what he could do next.

-The End of Book Two -

Excerpt From Saga of a Neurosurgeon Book Three

Heaven and Hell

It was Prof. Newly's announced opinion and intention that no student ever deserved a 100% score on one of his tests, and Garven Wilsonhulme made it one of his lifetime goals to achieve a perfect paper as much for the sporting aspect of it as anything. He had done very well, demonstrating a real aptitude for the advanced zoology subjects. On the mid-term, Garven found the test to be a combination of old test questions which he had meticulously written out and memorized in advance. He was delighted at the opportunity to excel, and painstakingly recreated his mental notes about the previously answered questions. The material was as clear in his mind as if he had held an open book in front of him; and when the time was up in the test, Garven knew that he had handed in a perfect test, blue books full of detailed and accurate argument and description.

Dr. Newly was correct about his tests, even on this one. Garven read his score on the written segment - 99%. At first he was angry; the old man was just being contrary and arbitrary. Then he read the red pencil note explaining why he had lost a point on his perfect paper:

"Your answer was too long."

Garven burst out laughing and caught Dr. Newly's eye. The professor had been watching him to see his reaction. There was a brief bond between teacher and student; Garven stifled his protest.

Synopsis of Book Three: *Heaven and Hell*

HEAVEN AND HELL is a novel of a man's driven life, one of overarching ambition. Here, Garven Wilsonhulme, would-be neurosurgeon, enters medical school and learns about the grim realities of competing for his place in a class where 50% of the students will be gone by the time of graduation. He makes life-long friends and enemies and faces for the first time what it is to be a student of the human condition and what life as a physician will hold for him. He learned a mnemonic ditty for the bones of the wrist: "Never Lower Tillie's Pants, Grandmother Might Come Home" and how to save a boy dying from meningitis. In *HEAVEN AND HELL*, Garven is first introduced to the gripping world of neurosurgery by the man who becomes his mentor. That meeting proves to be life changing.

AUTHOR CARL DOUGLASS, a former neurosurgeon turned fulltime author, writes with gripping realism because in all his novels he has been  there and done that in some measure. He well remembers leaving the small town of his childhood and entering the intellectually gratifying and incredibly competitive world of a major university. He had to grow up and to expand his horizons at lightning speed and with an intensity that he could scarcely have imagined during his boyhood. He loved being a general surgeon during the Viet Nam War era and as a neurosurgeon in the navy, being involved in academic medicine, and having a successful private practice. The long hours of work, the harsh life-and-death realities of the daily life in a complex surgical specialty, and the grim reality of jousting with malpractice attorneys provided the background for his novels. When it became time to retire and to gain family time, it was a transition to a calmer life which his wife of fifty years especially enjoys. Recounting his stories in his novels has become a fulfilling passion. *ANYTHING GOES* is part of that passion.

HONORS, AWARDS, AND MEMBERSHIPS
Phi Kappa Phi University Honor Society
Alpha Omega Alpha Medical Honor Society
BS (Medical Biology) degree—magna cum laude
MD—magna cum laude
CDR/MC/USN

American Medical Association
American Association of Neurosurgeons
Congress of Neurological Surgeons
Fellow of the American College of Surgeons
The Association of Military Surgeons of the United States
Life Member of the Medical Society of Vienna
Diplomate of the American Board of Neurological Surgery

Past President, Our Community Foundation, Wasatch County, Utah
Past Medical Liaison Officer, Deseret International Foundation
Past Chief of Surgery,
Antelope Valley Regional Medical Center, Lancaster, California
Past Member-at-Large, Central Medical Committee,
Utah Valley Regional Medical Center, Provo, Utah
Past Member, Utah State Foster Care Review Committee

www.ingramcontent.com/pod-product-compliance
Lightning Source LLC
Chambersburg PA
CBHW051654260626
47170CB00004B/1491